TARGET CLINTON

by

David Selves

First Published in the U.K. by:
New Author Publications Ltd.
Haltgate House, Hullbridge Road,
South Woodham Ferrers, Essex CM3 5NH.
Tel./Fax: 0245 320462.

November 1993.

ISBN 1 897780 11 7.

Copyright © David Selves. Licenced to publisher for three years. David wishes to retain his moral rights.

Typeset: Statim Services, Billericay, Essex. Tel: 0277 623004.

Print: Redwood Books, Trowbridge, Wilts. Tel: 0225 769979.

Copyright is retianed and no copying or utilisation of all or part of the text of this book may take place without the express permission in writing of the Publisher. All rights reserved.

The text of this book is as a result of the creativity and imagination of the Author and does not intend to relate to any person alive or dead except those persons known to be alive and who are specifically mentioned therein.

U.K. Price £4.99
U.S.A. Price $8.50
Australia Price A$10.95

22nd November 1963...12.22 pm...Dallas, Texas

On any other occasion the faulty air conditioning would not have unduly troubled them especially at that time of year. But for an hour the three of them had been closeted uncomfortably together in the impersonal motel room, each afraid to admit the mental anguish all were secretly harbouring.

They were silent, motionless, waiting for the next eight minutes to pass. And even then there would be none of the euphoria usually associated with a successful mission. There would be no commendations or citations for a task well done. As their file closed so hundreds of others around the world would open.

But these would stay open.

They had foreseen the need for Operation Saviour as early as 1954, conceived it, planned and nursed it. But above all they had concealed it, activating it when the need arose. They had accepted their responsibility as soon as the potential danger was perceived — it was their duty. That, they told each other in their rare moments of doubt, was what they were really paid for: to protect the American people, whether the threat was from within or without.

However, the idea had been planted in their minds and controlled by others without their knowledge.

That Saviour would be successfully completed within the next eight minutes was not in doubt. That the American nation would be saved from humiliation and the world a safer place was not in doubt. What was in doubt was whether or not the nine years of preparation would prove adequate when the inevitable world wide obsession for the truth began. They believed it would, knew it would — but still they perspired.

As the moment approached, Mike Garson glanced at his Rolex and looked impassively at Carl Hankin and George Gillespi. Neither moved as Garson rose to turn on the television and they saw the pictures from Dealey Plaza, Dallas that stunned the world at twelve thirty on 22nd November 1963. They watched in silence for ten minutes before Garson turned off the television.

Hundreds of people had been involved in Operation Saviour over the years, but, as far as they were aware, until four days earlier only the three of them had known the objective. Another two days, and only they would know that they had conspired to assassinate the President of the United States. The man to be apprehended, Lee Harvey Oswald, would be dead. The actual assassin, a stateless mercenary known as Haywood, would also be dead.

Neither Oswald nor Haywood have ever known who any of the three really were. There would be no loose ends. They had nothing to fear.

The three CIA men had identified Oswald in 1955 as capable of being used either for the task of removing the President, should it prove necessary, or for taking the rap. Since then he had been carefully and delicately controlled by suggestion, at times with the help of the KGB. The professionals in the Intelligence Services on both sides of the Iron Curtain had always had a more practical working relationship than their political masters. Oswald had been groomed for the job if a President looked likely to seriously embarrass America. But he was never aware of the fact. His behaviour had been odd, but Garson, Hankin and Gillespi had turned it to advantage; they knew just how confusing the outcome of an investigation into Oswald's history would be. It had been planned that way. They even falsified his performance on the firing range for the better. He thought he could shoot. More importantly, his record showed he could shoot.

The KGB would eliminate Haywood on 24th November when he landed in Italy and set off for his mountain retreat near Ortler. His body would never be discovered. He would never be reported missing.

Garson rose lethargically from his chair to turn off the television. The mood was not celebratory. 'America is safe for some years, but the danger is always there.' His deep Texan drawl reverberated around the tiny room. There was no emotion in his voice at all. He was acting as a functionary, completely impersonal. 'We must plan.'

'But how?' asked Gillespi, the smooth New Yorker from the East side of town. 'It could be as much as twenty years away, even I'll be retired by then.'

'We plan now and in time you'll have to enlist support,' replied Garson, slamming a can of cheap beer in front of each man as he spoke. 'Again, just three men, three patsies, never more,' he emphasised, 'and replace the items every ten years.'

'Okay, but we'll have to use a different angle. We'll come out of this clean, but the finger will be pointed at us and others. Questions will be asked: Why didn't people do their job as they should have done?'

'So you find another angle. Carl and I both retire inside three years. America will then look to you,' said Garson, fixing Gillespi with a cold stare from deep set, impassive eyes. 'God Bless America!' he bellowed, holding his can high.

'God Bless America,' responded Gillespi with equal enthusiasm.

Hankin, the oldest of the three at sixty four, drank but remained silent. He died of a massive heart attack the following day.

22nd November 1963…2.17 pm…Baltimore City Hospital

Rebecca waited patiently in the small anteroom adjoining the labour ward. She had sat there for several hours, alone except for her Father's occasional visits to update her, looking blankly at the plain white walls.

The moment he re-entered the room for the last time, the pain on her father's face told her that the son her parents had so desperately wanted was not to be. 'It was still born,' was all he managed to say.

It *had* been a boy and her mother was now critically ill.

Rebecca Tourle was consumed with hatred for Kennedy and wondered how her father could continue to support him and remain a leading member of the Democratic Party. For her part, she held the Party as responsible as Kennedy himself. Despite denials she believed that the CIA had persuaded Kennedy, who had initially been against the idea, to involve American Marines in the Bay of Pigs invasion of Cuba. However, according to her brother, he had refused to give them the air cover the CIA had said was essential and the marines had perished. On 17th April 1962 her older brother, Simon, had died in the ill fated fiasco. The CIA had hushed up the use of American Forces, the twenty four men all been reported as lost at sea on an exercise. Simon's last letter said otherwise. Neither of her parents knew she had seen it.

It took Rebecca's mother almost a year to recover from the trauma of the ill fated birth, but against medical advice she again fell pregnant in 1967, seeking the son to replace Simon. In May 1968 Rebecca, by then almost twenty five, had a baby sister, Angie.

22nd November 1963...Noon...Dallas, Texas

Lee Harvey Oswald waited alone in the deserted warehouse for the Presidential motorcade. Fools, he thought, all fools. There was no way that he was going to assassinate the President of the United States. He knew he didn't have the ability. He was simply not a good enough shot, although he had fooled those jerks at the Marine training school. He had cheated on the firing range and the most feared and sophisticated intelligence service in the world hadn't even noticed.

He had first suspected that someone was trying to use him in the summer of 1955, during his early days attending meetings of the Civil Air Patrol at Lakefront Airport. That was when he first decided to attach himself to David Ferrie, the homosexual, rabidly anti-communist commander of his training group.

Between mid 1955 and joining the Marines in October 1956 Oswald embarked on a series of actions which confused even him. The most bizarre was openly promoting communism and distributing communist propaganda, which he continued to do even in the Marines. In time he was to defect to the Soviet Bloc, marry a Russian wife and defect back again; all of which he thought would confuse those trying to use him for their own purposes. Whatever they were.

And then he had found out what they were. He was frightened, but who could he turn to? Who would believe him? He considered killing himself, but concluded that would be no use since an operation of this magnitude, and planned for so long, would not fail because of the death of one man.

He had one sole option. One chance to save the President's life and expose the murderous corruption of the CIA. Go through with it, fail, get caught and reveal all in open Court.

22nd November 1963…11.23 pm…New York

George Gillespi was just four weeks and three days off his forty seventh birthday. His term in the US Marines had saved him from an almost certain life of crime. Raised in East New York he had seized the opportunity the service had given him and risen through the ranks at Langley with alarming speed through hard work and dedication. But he did sometimes wonder if someone had been grooming *him*, positioning him to use him for their own special purpose, as they had done with Oswald. He usually dismissed such thoughts.

Tall, still slim and athletic, with jet black hair cut Elvis Presley style, the only pandering he had ever allowed himself was the reshaping of his teeth. Gone was the bent, crooked buck set, with three missing from teenage fights, to be replaced by pearl white dentures. A smooth, all-American smile. Even that, he recalled as he turned the events of the years over in his mind at the end of that most significant day, had been Langley's idea. 'Agents should not have memorable features. If you look like everybody else, you become everybody else. And therefore you become a nobody. Which is how we like you,' Jeff Etam had told him at his third annual review. The implication was clear enough, the unissued instruction noted and acted on.

His mother, who he visited whenever possible, still lived in the slum where he had grown up. She refused to let him buy her a decent house, despite his father being knifed to death on the front steps of their basement flat for cheating the numbers racketeer he worked for. She longed for him to marry and present her with grandchildren, but had now come to accept that he never would. Her son was a loner, a travelling salesman who plied his trade around the great Country as a free spirit.

Gillespi lay sleepless in his bed that night. He knew they were right to have done it. So much had started to go wrong in the Oval Office and, if it had all come to light, America would be the laughing stock of the world. He recalled conversation after conversation, but the two most critical were missing from his mechanically efficient mind. He could not remember who had first suggested the idea of putting some patsies into place back in 1955. It was certainly Garson who had assumed control, but had he actually instigated the activation Operation Saviour?

'It looks as if we have a job to do,' Mike had said when the three of them met routinely in Washington that August.

'Anything in particular?' he had asked.

'Saviour?' enquired Hankin quietly. In Gillespi's eyes he had always been quiet, always seemed troubled by their actions.

'Why d'you think now?' he asked.

'Many people are worried by the way Kennedy is going. People — people who know far more than us about the indiscretions we're covering up — are becoming increasingly concerned.'

'Do people really care about womanising?' asked Hankin in his soft, weak tone that always seemed foreign to his grotesque, physical characteristics.

'The public expect a lot of the President. Washington was exemplary. He set the tone and others are expected to follow,' continued Garson.

'But this is the nineteen sixties,' Gillespi interrupted, 'standards are changing, attitudes are changing.'

'Not where the President is concerned.' Garson was emphatic. 'Washington established an unwritten but binding contract with the people. The President must display dignity, integrity — corporate, national *and* personal integrity — resoluteness, strength of will, self mastery, and be seen to be upholding the highest virtues and values, in public and in private.

Gillespi remembered the words well. His mind had been trained by his father from the earliest day to retain and recall all relevant or potentially significant detail. He also remembered thinking then that they were not the words of the man who had spoken them, who he had known for almost ten years. Someone else had implanted those words: someone else had activated Saviour.

'So a President should give a perfect example for all Americans at all times?' asked Hankin dryly.

'In one,' beamed Garson. 'And Kennedy does not. He's arrogant and irresponsible, he has broken that contract with the people and just about flaunts the fact. He demeans himself and his office by the covert way in which he acts and then expects us to cover up his actions.'

Had they really assassinated a President for that? Or was it the fear that he would be re-elected and that there had been transgressions other than moral? Were they right? And more importantly was he right to do as Garson had said, continue the operation to ensure that the Secret Service was always able to take out a President conceived by them as dangerous to the American way of life or world peace?

Who had been right? Who had really given the order this time?

22nd November 1963...11.42 pm...Chicago

The news of the President's death shocked the entire world. Throughout America events and functions were cancelled as, contrary to the view promoted by Garson in August, the Nation went into mourning for a President of charisma, inspiration, wit and courage.

One event that was not cancelled, however, was the High School dance at Park Ridge in Chicago. Three of the four girls who had organised it were far too determined to allow the small matter of the assassination of the President to interfere with their months of planning or their night of expectation.

The night was a great success, not only as a fund raising and social function for the school, but also for three of the girls personally. Each of them had their heart and eyes set on a different young man and not one of them was to be disappointed. The band paid, the chairs stacked away and the gym again looking like a place for physical exercise, the three couples ran hand in hand through the rain to the cosy cover of Charlie Baxter's hay barn. The fourth girl went home to study.

The three boys, Ron, Mike and Al, had all experienced sex before, as had Emily, but the other two girls were still virgins.

It was Emily's enthusiasm that had coerced the other girls into helping with the dance. But there was only one objective really in mind: a late night visit to Charlie Baxter's barn. Emily had worn no knickers that night and, before the others had even started to embrace, she had Ron on his back in the hay, his trousers down, on top of him, riding him like a bucking bronco and issuing wails of delight.

In Mike's experienced hands Rachel was soon succumbing but Al, whose knowledge was actually limited to two quickies with Emily in the last couple of weeks, found the going harder with the third member of the trio. However, once they overcame their nervousness it was her who made the running.

'Um,' she sighed taking his swollen and throbbing penis into her hands and gently but nervously licking it. 'I want to remember tonight for more than the death of the President.'

She guided his right hand from her breasts to between her legs where he fumbled busily for several minutes before mounting her.

'Yes, yes,' she screamed, setting aside the pain and relishing the sheer pleasure that flowed through her body as he pounded brutally in and out of her. Al was never to become an experienced or delicate lover, but he was to become a force within the Mob. And he would have her again.

It was Emily who suggested changing partners after half an hour. There was something about the rough basic animal approach of the inexperienced Al that aroused her. She hoped then that it would never change, but years later was to regret that it didn't.

The third member of the trio was not the most attractive young lady in the school, but she certainly had one of the sharpest minds and was quick to grasp and develop new concepts, as she proved that night with Mike. She most certainly would never forget the night that Kennedy was assassinated.

23rd November 1963…8.38 am…Lubyanka, Moscow

Lubyanka was the centre of the Soviet Unioln's clandestine activities: home to the KGB and numerous other secret service departments. An austere building, where the real thrust lay inside among the interview rooms which retained within their depths the sinister secrets of three quarters of a century. Access could be denied to the most powerful and senior politicians, even members of the Politburo. It was generally accepted that the most powerful man in the Soviet Union was the General Secretary of the Communist Party, but there were those in Lubyanka who disagreed. General Sergei Zapadny was one who had good reason to disagree that day: the politicians would never have sanctioned this latest operation. They didn't have the stomach for it.

'I didn't think the Americans would really go through with it, Comrade,' he said to Golius as they sat and listened to the news of Kennedy's assassination, 'did you?'

'Oh yes, Comrade General, I never doubted it for one moment,' replied Golius with conviction.

Zapadny looked pensively at the young man sitting opposite him. He had risen fast — perhaps too fast, as some thought — but without doubt this operation was a coup. However, when Golius had first approached him three months ago, Zapadny had not taken him seriously and, if he were honest, his doubts had remained until yesterday, when the assassination had actually happened.

'I know, but what made you so sure, Comrade?' asked the General.

'I learnt during my years in America how powerful their national pride is. They hate to be thought of as vulnerable, not leading the world. They are afraid of being seen to fail. If the President fails, every American fails — it reflects on them all.'

'It is hard to understand, Comrade, but would the CIA really assassinate their own President for that alone?'

'I believe they would, Comrade General, yes. But in this case it is more. They considered him a threat to national security.'

'Did the women we were to use as infiltrators know what they were doing? Did the CIA suspect them?'

'That, Comrade, is hard to say. There is no reliable intelligence on the matter. Certainly they had identified the possibility and, after our success with Profumo in Britain, they would have become increasingly suspicious.'

'As would I, Comrade, as would I,' said Zapadny with enthusiasm, rising from his seat to pour two large glasses of *Stolichnaya*. 'I take it our part of the operation will go as smoothly?'

'Most certainly, Comrade General. It will be completed in Italy as arranged, a routine matter as far as the operative is concerned.'

'And he knows nothing of the truth or significance of the operation?'

'Nothing, Comrade General.'

'So he will be spared?'

'That is the intention. But do you think otherwise, Comrade General?'

'It might be best, perhaps an accident.'

'Very good, Comrade General, I will see to it.'

'And the patriotic gentleman of the CIA?'

'One of them has suffered a heart attack....'

'Really, Comrade?' said Zapadny interrupting with mischief in his eyes as well as his voice.

'A genuine heart attack, Comrade,' replied Golius, taking mock offence at Zapadny's implication. 'As for the others, we do not see them as a threat, indeed they could be useful to us at a later date.'

'It is your operation, Comrade, I will leave it to you.'

'Now another vodka before you leave?'

'Thank you, but there is another related matter that I wish to discuss with you before I leave, Comrade General.'

'Another ambitious operation, Comrade?' asked Zapadny refilling the glasses.

'Yes, Comrade General, of long term significance.'

Zapadny considered the young man for a moment. He had done well but perhaps he too should have an accident. He was beginning to sound over-ambitious and that was dangerous. Dangerous to him, and Zapadny did not like that.

'In what way, Comrade?'

'We were lucky in England to be able to take advantage of the promiscuity of weak men at short notice. We were lucky in America that their Secret Service felt that the President was a danger and sought to remove him. We will not always be so lucky, Comrade General.'

'What have you in mind?' asked Zapadny intrigued.

'We have wasted nearly twenty years since the last war. Our long term planning has ignored western sexual behaviour, which is becoming more promiscuous.'

'But we play on that, do we not, Comrade? We employ the vice women to compromise those we wish to use.'

'I was thinking of something a little deeper. Recruiting

idealistic young women in the Universities of the west who will later marry men who will rise to positions of power and influence. In that way, in twenty or thirty years we could have an agent in Downing Street, the White House, the Champs Elysees, General Motors or the Imperial Chemical Company — we will have them by the balls, as the Americans would say!'

'An ambitious idea, Comrade,' said Zapadny excited by the simplicity of it and now quite certain that Golius was going to have an accident. Whoever controlled such an operation would command unrivalled power and authority. Only forty seven himself, Zapadny had to be wary of Golius' progress.

'I see serious practical problems, but the idea is nonetheless not without possibilities. What sort of young woman would you target?'

'What they call the middle and working classes. Those attending University who are from poorer backgrounds, whose parents are not wealthy. They are idealistic, they want to be lawyers, teachers and doctors, They want to redistribute wealth, to see everyone equal. It is called having a "Social Conscience".'

'As I say, Comrade, it has possibilities. Please prepare a paper for me to consider in the same way you did for the Kennedy operation. One hand written copy to be handed to me personally.'

'Yes, Comrade General,' replied Golius knowing that as with the Kennedy operation, he would have to retain a copy in case of need. Watching his own back was the most serious part of his job.

22nd November 1963...9.14 pm...Hope, Arkansas

Roger Clinton sat bleary eyed and stared at the evening newsreels showing yet again those fatal seconds at twelve thirty that day.

'Bring me another crate of beer, will you?' he yelled, a

command rather than a request to no-one in particular. There was no response.

'Jesus, what does a man have to do in this house to get a drink,' he shouted, staggering to his feet and swaying towards the kitchen door. 'The damn President gets shot but I can't even get another beer. What's this damn world coming to?' he continued pushing past his younger son Roger and opening the cupboard door. 'And no damn beer left!'

'Mum's gone for some, Bill's gone with her. They shouldn't be long.'

'Better not be,' he slurred. 'So who's drunk all the damn beer? You?' He pointed an unsteady finger at Roger, who did not reply.

'That Billy boy then, was it? That little toad who shits on me to the law about attacking his mother. I've told him I'll mash his face in if he gives me grief, so help me I will and him drinking my beer does give me grief.' His words trailed off weakly as he slumped over the kitchen table to begin the uneasy sleep of an alcoholic.

Virginia Blythe had been widowed shortly before her son William was born, when her husband, William Jefferson Blythe 3rd, a heavy equipment salesman, had been killed in a freak motor accident. She had then left the young boy to live with his grandparents at their grocery store in Hope while she went off to study at nursing school. When young William was four she returned and married Roger Clinton with whom she shared a stormy relationship, at one point divorcing him because of his drinking and violence, only to remarry him shortly afterwards at which point young William, then fourteen, changed his name from Blythe to Clinton.

During the first marriage Roger and Virginia had given birth to a son of their own, Roger junior. However, William's relationship with his stepfather, who had legally adopted him, continued to be stormy, and there was no respect or love between them. The relationship between the boys waxed and waned but, despite the hardships which the family suffered and the turmoil they lived through, there was always a strange and undefined family bond between them all that even stretched to William and his stepfather.

This bond was to continue throughout their lives, but when William was twenty-one his stepfather died and the relationship with his mother blossomed even more. William was already embarked on a career that would influence more than the affairs of just his family. there was still one important influence to enter his life, but that of his mother would remain with him and prove to be of great significance as the years rolled by.

3rd December 1963...2.00 pm...Santa Monica, California

The pomp and solemnity of Kennedy's funeral was not present at the small private service in Santa Monica for Carl Hankin. He had no family and very few friends. Despite the time of year, it was a bright day and the late morning sun reflected from the highly polished funeral cars as they made their sombre way through the rows of neat graves to Carl Hankin's final resting place.

'Always on the cards,' said Garson as the coffin was positioned for lowering into the ground in the bright Californian sunlight.

Gillespi was uneasy. He had realised in the last few days that, apart from working in different sections of the CIA, the only things the three of them had in common was having little or no family. And "Saviour". He had begun to wonder if Garson was a sub-ordinate of another more powerful and influential group. 'Lucky to live this long you mean?' he replied, mixing the tone of statement and question.

Garson looked at him hard with those sharp eyes set deep into his worn face. 'Which means?' he asked.

'Not sure really, Mike,' replied Gillespi. 'The last couple of weeks have taken their toll on us all, you must have felt it.'

'No,' he replied. 'I've just been doing my job, serving my country as I've done all my life. To me one task is much the same as....'

Never again would George Gillespi complain about a cold. His sneeze at that moment meant that the bullet destined for him whistled past his left ear and buried itself in the sacred ground beyond. Mike Garson fell to the ground, dead before he reached it, a high velocity rifle bullet having entered his head between his eyes and exited via the back of his skull.

The minister stood, his mouth falling open as Gillespi jumped into the safety of the grave, smashing open the plywood coffin as it crashed against the bottom with the full impact of Gillespi's weight forcing it down, The pallbearers fell aside, the lowering ropes jarred from their grasp, and the few other mourners scattered in panic. Garson had been a part of a higher authority, it was clear that he formed no part of their future planning.

There were no more shots. They were professionals who would not risk getting caught, or worse still hit by Gillespi returning their fire, although they were likely to be well out of his hand gun range. They would have another chance.

CHAPTER ONE

There was something about young William that his mother, Virginia, had always known was special. At first she thought her feelings were natural, enhanced by the fact that her husband had been killed before Bill's birth. By the time he went to Georgetown University in Washington, she knew it was something more.

She looked at him as he stood there with the all important envelope in his hand. 'Open it, Bill,' she said rather timidly. 'Come on, open it.'

'Okay,' he said as he started to tear the seal.

Since the age of sixteen he had shown a growing interest in politics, inspired by Kennedy. She knew that his time in Washington had only increased his desire to run for office. What would the future hold for him? She smiled as he stood there, now twenty two years old, towering above her.

'Well?' she asked anxiously.

A smile began to form on his fresh and innocent face. 'Your eldest son,' he began slowly and calmly, 'has a degree in International Affairs!' he finished with a characteristic wild burst of enthusiasm.

'Bill,' she gasped hugging him, 'I *am* so proud of you. Your father would be proud of you! It's a long way from selling heavy equipment to a degree. Roger would also be proud of you,' she added, with rather less ebullience, but with no less sincerity. Roger had died while Bill was at Georgetown.

'And what now?' she asked, fearing the answer, knowing she was about to lose her eldest son. True, he would never desert his mother, he would always be there when she needed him, but now he really would fly the nest, he would be truly independent.

'England. Oxford,' he replied quietly. She had noticed many times during his formative years that his brashness, almost arrogance (some would say typical Leo behaviour) never showed when they were alone together. To her he was always modest, considerate and kind. He had protected her against the worst of Roger's excesses, despite some of the threats the man had made against him.

She was silent. Shocked, almost disbelieving, at length she managed to whimper, 'Oxford University?'

'Sure thing, Ma. Oxford University, England,' he repeated with pride. 'I'm going to be a Rhodes Scholar at University College.'

She would miss him. He would not be home as often as he had been from Washington and that was rare enough. Arkansas was hillbilly country — melon country he called it — he would never settle there again. 'How long for?' she asked, unable to hide her fears or feelings.

'Two years,' he replied kindly, understanding her concern, 'but I'll be home for vacations. It'll be little different from Washington, you'll see.'

She didn't reply. She knew he meant it. Bill Clinton had a big heart, just like his father, and it beat faster for no-one than his mother.

The ancient English City of Oxford was to be his home for two years. There he would pursue his main interests in life with a vengeance — music, politics and women, but not necessarily in that order.

Almost as quickly as he hit the bottom of Hankin's grave, George Gillespi surveyed the immediate surroundings for signs of the gunmen. There were none. Too many places to hide. Cemeteries had always been security nightmares. You needed a chopper to do the job properly.

In seconds he concluded that they had fled. He knew he must do likewise but the problem was where to. No safe house was safe and he was too far from his own backyard for comfort. He had no cover, no bolt holes, no friends in California. His first objective was to lose himself and think. Then probably Mexico to calculate and plan.

'Tell the police I'll be in touch,' he yelled to the minister as he sped across the well-kept graves towards his car. 'And tell them the dead man is CA, his papers will be on him.'

'But what...' began the reply that Gillepsi never heard as he changed direction from his own car to the hearse. At the last moment — if he was still being watched, they'd expect him to make directly for the hearse in case his own car was booby trapped. That would be their line of view. Thankfully the keys were in the ignition and before anyone could move or speak again he was gone. He waited at the cemetery gate for several minutes, his eyes meticulously recording every detail, every movement either in the street or behind him. It would be several minutes before either the undertakers or the minister could reach a phone to call the police. He did not hurry.

Certain in his own mind that no threat existed, he pulled quietly and inconspicuously away. He made immediately for the funeral parlour, the last place he would be expected to go, parked the hearse and caught a bus to the main shopping centre where he lost himself in the crowd.

As he walked among the thronging crowd Gillespi recalled the events leading up to the shooting. He had seen nothing, suspected nothing and obviously neither had Garson. He was certain the cortege had not been followed; he had checked. Whoever they were, they had lain in wait. How did they know who would stand where, which side of the grave? Had it mattered? Would the shots have come from behind if they had stood the other side of Hankin's final resting place? Suppose the line of fire had been obscured?

Surely one of them would have noticed a marksman moving among the gravestones. He thought he had been alert, but he had seen nothing.

He was confused. The shot that had taken out Mike Garson was perfect. There was no reason to believe the rifle trained on him was in the hands of anyone less expert. They had fired simultaneously. He would have been hit despite sneezing. Not cleanly, not with the precision that had killed Garson, but he would have been hit and in all probability killed. They had meant to miss him. Why?

'Whatever you may say, Rebecca, he was a fine President and a fine man, even if the rumours of his failings are true. I'll not have you speak like that in my house about anyone, let alone the leader of our proud nation who has been so callously slain in cold blood, said her father, appearing to suppress the worst of his assumed anger as they watched the Kennedy Funeral on television. His inner feelings were not quite so patriotic, but they were not for publication, even to his daughter. He had given his word. He was a man who kept his word.

'No, father, he was not a fine man. He was a cowardly, womanising, self centred, conceited bastard who sent my brother to his death.'

William Tourle looked slowly up from the television, his face aged beyond his forty nine years. The photograph above the television of him with his son, taken on Simon's twenty third birthday just over twenty months ago in early April 1962, was of a man who looked many, many years younger. His pale blue eyes were sharp and alert, his skin still soft with a radiant, infectious smile. A powerful, friendly head on a powerful, friendly man so proud of his son in the Marine's uniform. A far cry from the lifeless face that blinked slowly at his only daughter, now his only child.

She was young and vivacious, but he could see in those warm passionate blue eyes, so like her mother's a hatred he had never seen in one so young before. He knew what Simon's death had done to him, but until that moment he had no idea how it had affected her. Her venom surprised him. Did she know about Simon's letter? Surely not, she couldn't possibly.

He waited before he spoke again, stunned not so much by her words but by that look of hatred; it frightened him. He was ageing, his life more than half over while hers was just beginning. A pretty girl of five feet seven, with the same long legs and beautiful flowing blonde hair that her mother had at that age, when they first met. People had often said that Simon looked like him at the same age; he could never see it, but she was her mother's daughter, there was no mistaking it. And how long would it be before Barbara's true smile returned, if ever? It had been a long harrowing twenty months for all of them which had taken its terrible toll. He was only just realising how terrible.

'You cannot blame the Commander in Chief personally when an exercise goes wrong, be it a training exercise or active combat,' he said kindly.

'You can when he takes it upon himself to send men to their certain death for his ego and ignores the advice of the professionals to protect them.' She was curt, unyielding to his change of tone.

He fixed her in his glare. 'What do you mean?' he asked slowly and deliberately, showing no feeling.

'You know,' she said sternly, hating himself for the antagonism she was feeling towards her father, whom she loved dearly.

'Do I?' he asked with suspicion, dreading a confrontation with her. Why should he not tell her about Simon's letter? She obviously knew about it. Had Simon written to her? That thought had never occurred to him — or the White House. Why was he holding back? Who was he trying to protect, a dead President? The furrows deepened in his forehead and he felt his eyes tighten in their sockets. His neck and shoulders began to stiffen, his stomach tensed and he clasped his hands in an ever tighter grip as he looked at her, longing to hold her, longing to cry. Barbara had wept for days and at night cried occasionally for several nights after the news of Simon's death. He had yet to cry. Until this moment he had thought that he had carried the burden of that terrible knowledge alone. But if Rebecca knew about Simon's letter, did Barbara know also?

'Yes, you do,' she replied slowly with awesome purpose. 'Why pretend. Why protect the man who sent my brother, your son, to an early and unnecessary death?' Her tone and manner were uncompromising.

It was the word, "unnecessary" that really struck home.

Yes, he thought, why indeed? 'How did you find out?' he asked rather lamely, suddenly feeling relief at sharing the burden.

She paused, aware more than ever how much her father had aged of late, especially since the baby's death. Her hatred for Kennedy and all he stood for consumed her, but that could not, should not and must not extend to her father, even if he still supported and defended the man she blamed for her brother's death. She owed him more than that. She owed him her love, her compassion and her understanding.

Rising from the chair she moved towards him on the sofa. 'I saw Simon's letter,' she replied gently as she clasped his trembling hands. The tears, the pent up, frustrated tears of over twenty months, had started to flow. They were to continue on and off for several weeks, and probably saved him from a complete nervous breakdown. He had known for months how close he was to it, but would not seek help. He had always been a proud man.

'How?' he asked in a whisper, holding her to him.

'The phone rang one day as I was passing your study and I stopped to answer it. It was you,' she said looking deeply into his troubled eyes and smiling at him, 'and you asked me to take a message. As I rummaged for a pen I saw the letter, but took no notice of it then. It was only after I'd taken down the number to give Mom and started to leave the room that I thought it must have been one of his last letters. I'd never had a letter from him, and went back to read it.'

'You poor girl,' he said slowly. 'It must have been awful for you.'

'It was, but to be honest it numbed me at the time, it didn't seem real, I knew from your call that you weren't coming home that night, and when I couldn't sleep I slipped downstairs and read it again. I felt guilty at first, but as I read it again and again my anger just grew.'

'Did you say anything to your mother?'

'No,' she replied more curtly than she had intended and continued, softening her tone, 'I probed a little the following morning and decided she didn't know.'

'Did you say *anything* to her?' he asked again. His tone was anxious.

She shook her head, 'No.'

'Thank God.'

'So she doesn't know?'

'No. I didn't want either of you to know. Didn't see what good it would do. It wasn't as if Simon had died in action for the sake of America. I was called to the White House, you know.'

She was shaken, 'You were?'

'Yes. Before the officer who broke the news left me he asked me if we had heard from Simon before the exercise. I told him yes, immediately before.

' "Immediately?" he asked — his voice was sharp — "and was your wife aware of the contact?"

' "No."

'His parting words were, "The President may wish to speak to you himself," not that I took them seriously at the time, but later that evening I received a phone call and next day I visited the White House, all expenses paid. The situation was explained to me in detail — I think I was one of four similar visitors. They denied Simon's story but were afraid that, in view of the tension the invasion had caused because of the help we'd given the exiles, if his letter became public knowledge it could actually provoke war.

'At first I thought they were being dramatic, over-reacting. But the President was a worried man, a very worried man.'

'And what did you do?'

'Agreed never to speak of it and came home and burnt the letter. I think that's what's troubled me most all this time. I burnt Simon's last letter.' He struggled to speak the final words, they hurt so deeply, but the relief was immeasurable.

'My poor, poor Pop,' she said as they held each other and wept together.

So why was he more important than Garson? Was Hankin's death really natural causes or was his overworked heart given a little encouragement to call it a day? Hankin had never said much in all the years they had worked together on Saviour, but he always seemed to know more than Gillespi about the planning. Had Hankin been orchestrating Garson all this time? It had been done before. Put someone in front of you without them knowing it, place yourself with them on equal or even inferior terms in a group and observe. A very successful way to control an agent.

Was it possible that Hankin's death was from natural causes? But that broke the link to Garson, and because he might suspect foul play, he had to be taken out. Surely not. Would it have mattered anyway?

It still did not answer why they deliberately missed him. What did they expect him to do next? Where would they expect him to go? Who would they expect him to contact? And more importantly, perhaps vitally for his survival, what would they *not* expect him to do?

Would they try to contact him? Why not deal with Garson quietly in a less obvious manner? What was his special value? Was it a warning to him, play it our way or else? If that was the case, an advertisement would appear in the Washington Post in the next few days. The question was what to do if it did. After all, it was only an assumption on his part that they had missed him deliberately, if he was wrong on that and responded to any contact he really would be in trouble.

It was just two days later, two days of sleeping rough and using all his experience in the field, when the first advert appeared. The Agency were calling him in, signalling that they, at least, were not looking to take him out. They would have found the three false passports he kept in the glove compartment of his car, but not realised that they were expert forgeries. Langley would have accepted them at face value, they knew he had them. There would be an all ports notice on him in his own name, but it was unlikely to extend to his aliases as they thought they had his false passports. He decided to wait a few days more, to read the paper and digest the coded messages. He was still uneasy.

A week had passed since Garson's death and the messages were still giving him the all clear. It was time to decide. If he went back in there was an element of risk. 'Shit,' he said aloud as he lay on the old iron bedstead in his lodgings, 'if they can organise the killing of the President, why not lie a little to me before sending me to join him.'

He needed a contact, someone to trust on the inside, but it was impossible. Anyone he trusted would believe it was safe for him to go in. They would not know what plots were being hatched elsewhere. He would read the message that morning and decide. He had the three genuine false passports. He still had two thousand dollars and he could cable Switzerland for more. He was certain even Langley had no knowledge of that account.

Mario's coffee bar was always busy at seven in the morning, a mixture of those who had slept out looking for breakfast, those who were staggering home, those who had been working for hours cleaning the beaches and walkways and those who simply enjoyed the early morning.

'Hi,' said his host as he entered the little coffee shop. 'Black, no sugar?'

'You got it, thanks.'

'Thanks,' they each said as the coffee and money passed opposite ways across the counter.

Gillespi noticed something different about Mario's manner that morning. He was not so relaxed as usual. Gillespi said nothing and sat down at the back table close to the exit to the toilets and the service road. He read his paper, sipped the coffee, barely tasting it. There was no message.

He started to lower the paper, considering the possibilities. He saw him at once. The man had obviously never had an annual review meeting with Jeff Etam; hare lips could be operated on. Gently, carefully he raised the paper again. There were about thirty people in the bar but only four of them between him and the hare lip. One at the bar, a couple of stools away from the agent, two at a table on his left and slightly behind the agent and the last at a table on her own directly between him and the hare lip. Which was the second agent? Or was he outside?

The man on the stool wore sandals and bermuda shorts. He had a heavy ginger beard, a huge beer belly, and was deeply suntanned. Unlikely.

The two sat at the table to his left were possible candidates, just ordinary looking people. But that would make three agents and whenever possible they worked in pairs always keeping each other in sight. Again unlikely.

The woman was about thirty, attractive, no jewellery, tanned but not, like the man on the stool, from living in the sun. A leisure tan, not a working tan. Dressed for the sun, either on the beach or in the town, she would be one of the crowd, were it not for her handbag. The black leather bag resting on the table, just to the right of her right hand and slightly open towards her, was the only place in that outfit where she could hide her gun.

Were there more outside, back and front? Mario had been uneasy. This was not a chance sighting. They had expected him and had not wasted the few dollars the advert would have cost that morning. He could handle those inside, the woman first, a clean shot through the paper, and then the hare lip. Agents were trained not to shoot when there was a hostage, and then often told at the start of an operation to ignore that part of their training. This would be such an operation, but none of them would know why he was wanted or perhaps even who he was. The probability was that there would be at least four back and front. It was going to be a bloody mess, but as long as it was not his blood it troubled him little. Killing was something he had become accustomed to long ago. Death was the foil of life; without the other, neither could exist.

'Mario,' he called just as he had done on previous mornings, but this time only lowering the paper enough to get a sighting on the agents. 'Another coffee when you're ready, please.'

'Coming over,' replied Mario with his usual enthusiasm. He could have no idea that the previous mornings had simply been a rehearsal, or that this was to be the first and last performance.

In the split second it took Mario to cross between him and the woman, Gillespi dropped the paper and drew his gun. The first shot hit the woman between the eyes, killing her instantly. The second, fired over Mario's left shoulder, the burly man a trembling shield, was equally effective with the hare lip. 'No-one move,' he said more calmly and authoritatively than in any movie.'CIA' he continued flashing his badge, not that anyone inspected it.

'There are others outside and we don't want any more deaths than are necessary. Do exactly as I tell you.'

They simply nodded but Mario seemed confused. Did he know the others were CIA agents?

'Now I want you to open that door,' he said to the beer belly, 'and take a seat out and sit on the porch. Leave the door propped securely open.'

The man did as he was told; neither he nor anyone else spoke. 'Right,' called Gillespi, 'you're my eyes, I want you to tell me what you see.'

The man gulped and slowly began to speak. 'Two parked cars, a Ford convertible and Buick.' His voice was strained, uneasy.

'Louder. Keep going,' yelled Gillespi, 'every single thing you can see. Repeat it and describe how it changes. Keep talking, don't wait for me to reply.' Again there was control and complete authority in his voice.

After several minutes the man stopped. 'I said keep going,' yelled Gillespi, who had now opened the rear access door to the toilets. Swiftly, silently, he moved backwards so that even those in the coffee shop did not realise he had left. He had checked earlier and, as on every other morning, the back door was open with Mario's pickup truck backed hard against it. They would be waiting across the street, at an angle of forty five degrees with their guns trained on the canvas cover for any sign of movement. He had decided against sacrificing Mario, or one of the others, as a distraction. Perhaps he *was* going soft in his old age. Flat on his belly, he slid unheard and unseen out of the doorway and under the pickup behind its double rear wheels.

He could see three of them.

There was no time to find the fourth, if there was a fourth. He eyed the two to the right, aimed and fired. Before the second hit the ground Gillespi was rolling out from under the pickup. He was in through the driver's door with the ignition started before the first shot was returned, tearing into the canvas cover. Another deliberate miss or just bad shooting. From five feet away? No-one missed at that distance.

He gunned the engine to life and swung the pickup hard to the right, driving over one of the dead men as he screeched towards the crossroad and swung left away from the main street. It was then that he saw the fourth man stationed at the rear. He was lying flat in the back of another pickup parked in the side street, his head and the grenade launcher just visible, side by side over the raised tailgate.

He swore as he swerved right in an abortive attempt to change direction. Mounting the far pavement he demolished a fire hydrant and crashed the pickup into the opposite wall, but was out and running before the grenade tore into the truck, setting it instantly ablaze.

The pickup was his only immediate means of escape. Three blocks away he had stashed a rented motorbike and had memorised a route out of the City impossible to follow in four wheels. As he ran he glanced over his shoulder in time to see the pickup explode but still there was no-one in pursuit. Where were they?

His heart pounding, his legs moving swiftly and mechanically and his mind more puzzled than ever, he raced on. There were no shots and the street where the motorbike was garaged was quiet as he turned into it. He froze as he undid the padlock and opened the lock-up door.

'Okay, George, you can stop running now. I need to talk to you.' Carl Hankin was sitting in the shadows, calmly awaiting his visit. His voice was as quiet and unassuming as ever.

'But....'

'It had to be, I'm afraid. But don't worry, you're in no danger, I promise you.'

Hearing footsteps outside, Gillespi moved deeper into the garage so that Hankin, who appeared unarmed, was between him and the doorway, his gun trained directly on Hankin's heart. 'Okay, cut the shit and tell me what the hell is going on.'

'All in good time, George, but this is neither the time or the place.'

'Now. Here and now or you'll never walk out of this garage.'

'Then nor would you,' replied Hankin, his usual soft tone giving no sign of emotion or fear.

'I'll take my chance. I have so far.'

'They're running out. So far you've been protected, protected by me, George. But,' he continued even more slowly than usual, 'if I am not here to protect you....'

'Who are you? What are you? Who are those people outside?'

'As I said George, all in good time. Now we'll walk out together, me in front if you like, you behind, gun in my back. I mean you no harm, George, believe me.'

'Why the hell should I?'

'You really have no choice, we can't stay here for ever. If nothing else, you'll want the john and get hungry.'

'What about Mike? Was that you? Is he *really* dead?'

'Yes, he's dead. I'm afraid I was responsible, but you were never to be hit, although it nearly went wrong when you sneezed!'

He'd never known Hankin smile before.

'Think, George. If I wanted to kill you I could have done

it at the Cemetery or once we found you again. I could have killed you when you waited at the Cemetery gates or when you opened that door. I do not want you dead.' His words were emphatic, convincing.

The logic was there, that he could not deny. He also realised he had been under observation more than he had been aware. But he was at a loss to understand where they had been at the Cemetery gates, unless they were concealed in the hearse. That was it, it had to be. He had no cards and no way out. Although he had no idea how many men were outside, it was a reasonable bet that he would never be able to shoot his way out of it. His only hope was to leave with Hankin as he had suggested, but he had one last try to call the tune.

'Okay, we go, but on the bike, you in front.'

'I'm afraid it won't start, George. No rotor arm.'

'Liar, I checked it this morning,' said Gillespi with false venom. He knew he was beaten. He would have to go along with Hankin, for the moment at least.

'Check it again. We removed it after your visit this morning.'

'Okay, you win, so we go. Where to?' said Gillespi giving all the right body language. However, he remained alert. He was still looking for a way out and equally importantly a way to assume command over Hankin. Freedom would never mean safety unless he knew what the hell was going on.

'Difficult, that one, George. I'm happy for you to choose but we have to get there. You won't get in any car I provide and we can't walk through the streets with you holding the gun to my back.'

'I'll buy it, Carl. You haven't got me here to kill me. Not yet. For the moment I have a value. I don't know what it is and I'll be watching carefully to see if it suddenly goes out of date. If I reckon it has, then you really will be in that coffin.'

'That won't happen, George, trust me.'

'Do I have any choice?'

'No, but I've lost four good people to get you alive. Why would I do that if I wasn't on the straight.

There was no reply to that.

While Gillespi had been hiding out in California, Lech Zielinski had been partying to celebrate the death of John F Kennedy, who he saw as a pro-communist, wet liberal. Born in the slums of Warsaw in 1936, Zielinski knew what it was like to live in a country occupied by an oppressive power. He was smuggled out of Poland in 1947 by his grandfather, his parents having been killed during the Second World War, and he spent his adolescent years with another Polish family in New Orleans. His grandfather had died two days after reaching his old friends in America.

He had first met Lee Harvey Oswald when Oswald joined the eighth grade at Beauregard Junior High School, and it was Oswald who had introduced him to David Ferrie. Zielinski hated queers, but there was one thing he hated more: Communists.

Having left school Zielinski had joined Harvey's International Drug Company as a junior. It was a small concern, but by the age of twenty one he had become its top salesman. He had drifted away from Ferrie and the Civil Air Patrol by then, but kept up contacts with those older, potentially more influential members of the group. It was to serve him well.

In 1961, with his employer in serious financial trouble, Zielinski had taken over the assets and customer base of Harvey's without the liabilities for the modest sum of $25,000, which he had borrowed from Nat Peters, a confirmed homosexual and a wealthy former disciple of Ferrie. Peters' family, all American and the source of his wealth, knew nothing of his sexual learning, and loans totalling a further $100,000 were to be forthcoming as Zielinski built a formidable business to take on the international giants.

George Gillespi listened intently for over an hour. 'You really expect me to buy that bullshit?' he asked when Hankin finally finished.

'It's the truth, George, every word of it, believe me.'

There was something about Hankin's gentle manner that made it difficult not to believe him. He was near nineteen stone and had a soft kindly face. A less likely looking CIA agent Gillespi had never met, but his record was first class.

'So where do we go from here? What if I refuse to accept what you say?'

'If you are not prepared to continue,' he emphasised the word "continue", 'to exercise your duty for the good of the American nation, then I will have to consider what further use you have, if any.'

The gentleness of the words meant they almost lost their meaning. They were not spoken in a threatening manner.

'You mean you'll get rid of me, just like Mike?'

'Yes.'

'Then I have no choice?'

'No, but don't think you can cheat me. Don't think you can walk out of here and double cross me. I may be dead but I still have influence,' he finished with an evil smile.

'And what when you really *are* dead, what then?'

'You'll find out when that time comes. Those who pay the bills know all about you. Do your job, do it well and you'll have nothing to fear. Screw up and the Haywoods of this world are two a penny, especially for unimportant hits.'

'Okay, I'm happy. So can I leave?' asked Gillespi, 'I need a hot shower and a steak.' He was far from happy, but the only way out was to agree. Perhaps he'd take a holiday and simply disappear.

'No problem, George, but don't think you can cheat me. It'll be no good agreeing now and then changing your mind. Wherever you go, whatever you do, the paymasters will find you and deal with you.' It seemed Hankin was reading Gillespi's mind.

'I understand, but do I get to meet the paymasters? Do you ever meet them?'

'No, but I can contact them and if anything — natural or otherwise — should ever happen to me, they'll contact you.'

It was early evening when Gillespi checked into a small hotel for the night. Although he had an important decision to make, that could wait. First he needed a shower, then some food, then a good woman. Or two.

'Can you trust him?' asked the disguised voice on the phone.

'Yes, I think so,' replied Hankin, 'but as I told you before, he was totally committed to the task until you insisted on removing Garson.'

'That, I'm afraid was essential.'

'Maybe, but I would be uneasy if I were him.'

'So you watch him and if he looks likely to cause any trouble you deal with him. As before, just apply for an allocation of men as needed using the same authorisation. There will never be any problem. However, if he doesn't cause any trouble and doesn't look likely to, leave him be. He might even be useful one day.

The following morning Gillespi felt better, much better. It was time to think.

He had been instrumental in the assassination of an American President and, for almost ten years, in ensuring that the capability to assassinate a President existed, to be used when necessary. But what made it necessary? Who had decided it was necessary? Why had they faked Hankin's death? And, perhaps most significant of all, why had Garson been killed? What did he know? Was it better, safer, not to know?

Never one to dither, he would make his decision over breakfast.

CHAPTER TWO

For a man of such wealth and influence, Harry Powers had a modest life style. His home was simple but tasteful, but his office was blandly decorated and sparsely furnished. The man himself was unassuming to look at. In his middle fifties, a neat, tidy little man of just over eleven stones, there was nothing memorable or striking about him physically. His uninspiring feature concealed as sharp a mind as existed anywhere. Once he spoke, his authority was total. He was all-commanding.

The other five men gathered in his office in Detroit that Tuesday morning knew of each other but had never met before. They were amongst the most powerful and influential businessmen in the United States. In the world. Lech Zielinski was the only one to decline the invitation.

'Gentlemen,' he began, having poured and passed round the coffee in farmhouse mugs, 'firstly I thank you all for coming at such short notice and on such scant information.

'I will not beat about the bush, such is not my way,' he continued in his direct manner, not even allowing himself an inward smile at the deliberate pun his audience were unaware of. 'In 1992, this Country of ours will go to the Polls to elect a President for the next four years. Those four years will later be seen in history to have been the most significant ever, not only for the peace and prosperity of the world, but for the prosperity of the American economy, which means in effect our businesses.

'Events in the Soviet Union pose a frightening prospect militarily, but at the same time they present the largest, most exciting corporate opportunity the world has ever seen or will ever see. There will never be anything like it again, believe me.'

He did not need to spell it out any further; they all nodded in complete agreement. 'Largely due to the politicians, the Japs were allowed to steal the march on us after 1945. If we leave it to the politicians they will do it again in

Eastern Europe. We must prevent it. We represent the heart of the free market American business. It is our corporations who win the orders that create the jobs that make America prosperous, enabling Governments to spend billions of dollars policing the world. Not that I'm against that, or ensuring that American interests are upheld and protected.

'George Bush is a powerful world figure and is good for American interests abroad. But while he plays the world stage, affairs at home are neglected. We all know that the world is in recession, but on top of that we have the additional problem of the amount of US debt that the Japs own. There are now collated figures but my guess is that they own over half of all American medium to long term corporate and Government debt. In corporation speak, they have a "controlling interest".

'The Gulf War was a great success, a great ad for America, but the euphoria will not last. Bush's ratings are so high they frighten me, and when the pride dies away the people will be looking to their pockets and there will be a backlash against Bush. He is not the best President from our standpoint, but he is acceptable. However, my fear is that, having become unsustainably popular, the pendulum will swing the other way and the Democrats will beat him with a dead cat. It will be a vote for change. Change for the sake of change, nothing more.

'Any Democrat is bad news for us and for business generally, you do not need me to tell you that or to spell out why. But it's worse than that. The two leading candidates are Clinton — the Arkansas Governor who can't say no and never keeps a promise — and Paul Tsongas who, whatever the pollsters and others say now, simply can't win. When it comes right down to the bottom dollar, people won't vote to pay more taxes, even if they should.

'Clinton talks of things in his past that he remembers like yesterday, but he forgets anything that will embarrass him. Let me give you an example. He once called an Attorney and the police because his stepfather, a heavy drinker, was physically threatening his mother. The guy had actually fired shots on an earlier occasion when Clinton was younger, and he filed a sworn deposition about the incident at the Garland Chancery Court. He now maintains there was never such an incident.

'Tsongas is not so bad, but he's not relevant. Whatever the pollsters say, Clinton will win the nomination. But I wouldn't leave either them in charge of an empty trashcan, let alone the most powerful nation in the world. I'm sure you feel the same.' There were nods of agreement around the room.

'Clinton, like Bush in my view, has no fixed ideological abode and, although they are both ready to assume any outfit that fits if they think it will appeal to the electorate, Bush does have some honour. In my view Clinton will say or do literally anything to get elected and then just forget it.

'Clinton doesn't miss tricks, and that James Carville guy running his PR is brilliant. We've not yet seen how good Carville is, in my book, and although Clinton only polled 25% I think he set his band rolling when he dubbed himself the "Comeback Kid" on the night of the New Hampshire Primary.'

No-one spoke but they listened intently. Powers knew they would be with him on this one. Once they saw the advantages.

'Despite dodging the Vietnam draft and his apparent womanising, my analysis so far indicates that Clinton is likely to win the Democratic nomination and, if my reading of Bush's future fortune is right, we'll end up with Clinton as the next President. That, gentlemen, will be a disaster for America in every respect, for not only do I see him as weak, not only do I see him as unable to stand up to all the the liberal pressure groups, but he has a powerful and influential wife who publicly supports many of the liberal organisations some of us don't even think should be allowed to exist. The true extent of her influence is still to be calculated, but from what we've seen in Arkansas it's considerable. I'm certain she'd be active in Government and have more than his ear.

'Now if a man wants to enjoy the pleasures and company of attractive young ladies, who are we to criticise? I doubt that anyone in this room has always resisted such temptations himself. That is not the point. My research suggests that this man is an out-and-out philanderer whose wife stands by him because she is pushing him relentlessly towards the White House, where she will pull the strings.

'I am told that in the next Arkansas State elections his opponent will lay bare the details of five recent affairs. Apart from his other shortcomings, a President like that would be a national liability. We cannot permit it. Kennedy barely got away with it and there was far more secrecy about such things thirty years ago. For the sake of the American people we have a duty to prevent it, and any Democrat — especially Clinton — ever becoming President.'

He looked around the room but no-one spoke, no-one reacted, they were too experienced. 'More coffee?' he asked removing the jug from the hot stand.

'Are you suggesting that he is dealt with, that his wife is dealt with or that we embark on a campaign to totally discredit him?' asked John Edwards, a tobacco man.

'None of those, although all have their merit. What would we achieve? My hypothesis starts from the fact that Bush will have become too unpopular to win. We have to assume there is nothing we can do to help him. We therefore have to ensure that a Democrat does not win.'

He paused, not so much to gauge their reactions — he knew they'd give nothing away — but for effect.

'We must present our own Independent candidate, finance him and install him in the White House.'

'Does instal mean control?' came the immediate question in a tone of heavy concern. It was from a traditionally loyal Republican supporter who, Powers knew, shared his views.

'Oh, no,' he replied emphatically. 'It is not our job to run the Country any more than it is the job of the wife of the President to run the Country. I am suggesting that it is our job to ensure that the man who is running the show is capable and qualified to do so.'

The meeting only lasted a further twenty minutes, by

which time each man had committed two million dollars to the launch fund and agreed to underwrite the cost of finding and promoting an Independent candidate for the Presidential Election of 1992.

Harry Powers felt a great sense of relief. He was a patriot who loved his Country dearly and could not bear the thought of seeing it humiliated on the world stage, impoverished at home and outsold in the emerging markets of the old Soviet Bloc. It was not so much personal satisfaction he felt as they all left but that feeling of excitement that the Pilgrim Fathers must have experienced when they first landed in America. Indirectly, Powers already had some experience of America being humiliated. His older brother, Frank, had been at Pearl Harbour and, even after all the years of visiting him in the Naval home every week, his injuries still shocked him.

He looked at the pictures of his father and grandfather on the plain cream office wall, the only personal objects in the room. They would approve, he thought.

Golius' report had been both comprehensive and persuasive. At first, Zapadny's instinct had been to eliminate Golius and control the operation secretly himself, but that view mellowed as he re-read the paper. Perhaps, he thought, it had been de-signed to change his mind. If that was the case, then the man was dangerous but also extremely perceptive. And useful.

The most crucial point to Zapadny personally was the long lead in time; twenty to forty years. The operation would therefore run well beyond his time in service. After a few days' thought he had decided not only to accept the proposal as presented but also to put Golius in sole charge of it. If it were ever to produce a major triumph he would receive the credit, but as he reviewed the proposals again he became increasingly aware that it was likely to be a posthumous credit.

As he cleared his personal effects from his official residence on the eve of his retirement in 1983, Zapadny reflected on the fact that, although Golius had risen to prominence in the KGB, he still remained in sole personal charge of Operation Redskin. Although it had yet to deliver any outstanding individual successes, the list of people in places of influence, and married to people in or approaching places of influence, as impressive.

Zapadny would miss the luxury to which he had become accustomed when in Moscow, but his retirement dacha would suit his needs. He had never married, had few friends and had therefore invited Golius to share with him that final evening in his official apartment.

'You choose your targets well, Comrade,' said Zapadny passing over his files. 'There are some very promising possibilities.'

'We have had some wastage, Comrade, but there are some well- placed ladies sympathetic too us in all the western countries and we even have a handful in Australia. They include the wives of two US State Governors, the wives of a permanent under secretary and a junior minister in Britain, a middle ranking civil servant in Germany with lesbian inclinations and the wife of a minister. In France the pattern is different. We have three well-placed sleepers, but that is exactly what they are — mistresses. It seems normal in France.'

'How can you be sure that they will do what we want if the need arises?'

'We keep in touch. Those who have been on the programme over fifteen years have shaken off their doubts. They know why they are there.'

'So we are very close to them. They know our motives?'

'Where I think it appropriate.'

'Good. I congratulate you, Comrade. A first class operation.'

During the years leading up to the breakup of the Soviet Bloc, Operation Redskin achieved numerous minor successes, mainly in the field of industrial rather than political espionage. After Yeltsin's rise to power the KGB found its wings severely clipped, but Golius continued almost single-handedly to maintain Operation Redskin, increasingly confident that before much longer he would have a major coup. His only worry was, would the Kremlin now welcome it?

Harry Powers was not amused as he read the morning papers. He did not like Ross Perot, he had never liked Ross Perot and now, just as the dossier on Clinton was looking as if it could prove highly destructive to the Governor of Arkansas, Perot announced that he was running for the White House as an Independent. They were days away from choosing their own candidate, who would be either Al Denton, the self made multi-millionaire banker, or Ted Canon, a member of one of America's oldest and most successful industrial families.

'Damn that man!' bellowed Powers as he threw the paper across the room.

The telephone rang.

'Yes,' he replied, 'I've seen it. It couldn't be worse. We can't run our man as well and Perot will never win. People won't take his seriously, John.'

'So we must meet immediately. Shall I arrange it?'

'Please, John. And,' he hesitated, 'we must consider the possibility of having a traitor in our midst. Another week at the most and we would have named our man.'

It was almost midnight when the six men met in Powers' office.

'There is absolutely nothing we can do to stop Perot,' began Powers, 'but what concerns me most is the fact that he's announced his decision to run when he has. It might be pure coincidence, but that seems most unlikely.'

'I agree,' said Matt Andrews, an oil man from Texas, 'but that's the way of it. Better turn our guns on Clinton. There's nothing else we can do.'

Andrews was a striking figure who always wore large, loudly checked sports jackets with brightly coloured shirts and cream trousers. Under protest he would sport a tie, but any accidental gesture towards colour co-ordination between his shirt and jacket was usually abandoned. His clothes matched his character; warm and friendly, but there was a streak of iron in this lankly, smiling, broad-shouldered Texan. A mass of red hair topped off a man who was genuinely larger than life.

John Edwards could not have been more different; a quiet, dapper man who resembled a London stockbroker from the 1950s rather than an influential, well-established and very powerful member of the tobacco industry. His mind was clear and sharp, but unlike Powers, he did have a sense of humour. He owed his position to birth. Always neatly and soberly, even casually, dressed, he looked considerably older than his thirty nine years despite the early morning fitness routines which kept his body in perfect condition. Like so many successful executives, including Powers but certainly not Andrews, his blue eyes had that cold, steely look whenever anyone looked into them. Matt Andrews by contrast had warm, friendly green eyes, but he would raise a fist with little provocation to resolve a dispute and had done so many times.

Ross Perot, the billionaire businessman from Texas, had let slip on the King show in February that if there was enough public support for him he might be prepared to run for the Presidency. And enter the race he did. Not once but twice. Each time self-destructing, but not before he had ripped the election wide open by dislodging loyal supporters in both camps. But primarily in the Republican camp.

Perot's first sortie aroused public anger to such a pitch, against both Bush and Clinton, that he began to outstrip them both in the polls. Never, since opinion polling began, had an Independent candidate achieved this.

Perot's intervention had killed any chance of Powers realising his dream of installing a President in the White House, but it never for one moment damped Clinton's resolve or determination.

By the time Clinton reached the Democratic Convention in Madison Square Garden, New York, in mid July, he was on a roll. Unopposed and with Al Gore his running mate already announced, the Democrats believed it was the power of Clinton at that convention which started to pull droves of Perot supporters into his camp, actually causing the Texan to withdraw.

'Step aside, Mr. Bush.' began Mario Cuomo, New York's Governor, as he introduced Bill Clinton that night. 'It's time for a change, someone smart enough to know, strong enough to do, sure enough to lead. The Comeback Kid. A new voice for a new America.'

Clinton had somehow succeeded in uniting the warring factions of his party. Even Jesse Jackson, the veteran liberal campaigner and scourge of many past nominees, was forced to admit that it was a "convention of almost unnatural harmony". He was, however, to make a passing comment later that night of telling significance to the future of Bill Clinton. "Politicians should adopt policies not because they are popular or would win votes but because they are right."

The atmosphere at the Convention was like a group of reunited friends at a carnival. One evening in the Sheraton Manhattan Hotel the crowds chanted louder and louder for the newly-remarried Teddy Kennedy to strip. The point was reached where he could not resist and off came the jacket. The shirt and tie soon followed.

The three and a half thousand delegates had come to party and party they did. 'I'm just glad I left the wife behind,' said a delegate from Washington as he caroused in Central Park. It was wild stuff for those from the backwoods, and although the experienced old hands had seen it all before, it had an extra sparkle this time. 'New York looked like a scene out of a Roman Orgy,' the New York Post reported, and the talk of the week was the nudity.

It was not that the Senator from Massachusetts had gone all the way, but that New York had just legalised topless bathing and it had unleashed a wave of uninhibited skin-baring all week. No doubt inspired by the bikini-clad young women cruising around Madison Square Garden in an open truck.

CHAPTER THREE

Despite wishing to vomit and being barely able to breathe he lay silent and still for over three hours in the mass of bodies soaked in their own blood and excrement. He'd no idea how many there were, he'd not counted them when they'd been herded from the school hall. Slowly he hauled his frail body from the mass grave in the shallow ravine and crawled into the surrounding glade, thankful that the bastards had not bulldozed it over like some of the other graves.

Hamdi Dimic's only crime was to be a Muslim.

But he was alive. He would fight back. He would avenge the murder of his family. Slowly he stood and stared into the ravine from which he had just dragged himself. The ravine full of twisted, skeletal bodies, which just hours earlier had somehow still managed to breathe life, despite their desolate state. There was little for even the vultures to pick at. If there had been any food in his stomach he would have vomited again, but it was three days since he had eaten. His weight was down to a little over six stones, a far cry from the fit young man who, almost twenty five years earlier, had rowed for Oxford while a Rhodes Scholar at University College.

He took one last look at the final resting place of his family and so many of his friends before turning to make a fresh start in life. He now had a mission.

Every step was a hardship, his bones brittle, his skin sore and dry. Worse still, this was Serb territory now. They had taken the village and only Serbs would be left. He knew that not all Serbs approved of "ethnic cleansing", but they were too scared to speak out or to help even their friends. There was only one person he could turn to, his grandmother's old friend Zena Mladic. So, slowly, painfully, he made his way towards her house.

'Quick, quick,' said the old lady as she saw the haunted figure at her door. 'Quick, quick, before you are seen.'

His ragged clothes were heavily stained, the smell was appalling.

'How?' The one word conveyed the horror of what she saw; there wasn't much this eighty four year old widow had not seen in her lifetime. She had buried two husbands and four sons from war.

He could barely speak, 'All dead,' he began as she gave him a cup of water.

'Serb soldiers did this?' she asked, shamed.

'Yes,' he nodded.

'You must stay here, they will not look for you here. I have food, not a lot but enough. I am old, I eat very little.'

'No, I must go as soon as I'm cleaned up. I cannot risk being found here.' He spoke the words slowly and painfully. She appreciated them but could not desert him by allowing him to leave. If he was found with her they would shoot her as well. But at her age, what was there to live for in her country now anyway? This was her friend's grandson, she must help him, but in truth she would have helped anyone in that state, Serb, Croat, Muslim, Jew, it mattered not. To her they were simply people.

She fed him a little gruel — he was physically unable to feed himself — cut his ribboned clothes from him, bathed his sores and then he slept.

For almost a week she fed and nursed him night and day. He slept for most of the time, slowly moving from gruel to bread, and life invaded the corpse again.

'I can never thank you enough,' he said on the ninth day as she brought him his food.

'There's nothing to thank me for,' she replied. 'I am ashamed. Ashamed that my people could do to anyone what they did to you and others. Did we learn nothing from Hitler? Must we live it all again?'

He did not know what to say, he was too tired to think. He ate his bread and gruel and slept again.

By the fourteenth day he was able to get up and walk unaided. He sat in her tiny stone cottage on the edge of the village of Sipovo and felt betrayed. Betrayed by his own people. Zena was the exception. This civil war had turned neighbour against neighbour. He remembered the last time he had felt so betrayed by friends, at Oxford. He had been arrested and charged with possessing cannabis. There were dozens of people at the party, and he never knew who had planted the drugs in his coat when the house was raided. He had always had his suspicions — it had come down to just two people. But he had been shocked last year when, during the American Election it had emerged that Bill Clinton had smoked cannabis while at Oxford. He had not thought of him in that light before.

'Zena, I will never be able to thank you,' he said as he busied himself tidying around the room.

'There is no need, it was my pleasure to help an old friend's grandson.'

She paused. Although only a simple country woman she had seen much hardship in her life, learned about passion, human nature and the need to grieve. 'Do you want to talk about it?' she asked quietly.

He smiled. All that learning, all that education. All denied to her and yet she was more perceptive than he would ever be. She understood people; perhaps you couldn't teach that. 'Yes,' he said quietly, relief sweeping through him.

'How did it start?'

'They came into the village firing shots into the air. We were having lunch, Mum and Dad were with us, we've all been eating together to save food.'

'All of you, the children as well?' she asked with horror.

'Yes, all of us.'

'They must have come into the village from the other end or you'd have heard them.' It was hard to believe, looking at him and listening to him then, that Hamdi was an educated, intelligent man who had run a successful law practice before Yugoslavia had torn itself apart with civil war. A shadow of his former self, the confidence and presence had gone. He resembled a tired, dying, little old man struggling to think coherently, string more than a few words together.

'I heard nothing and even my old ears would have heard gunshots.' 'They were wearing masks and combat fatigues. They rounded everybody up into the school hall and started going through our papers. All the Serbs and Croats were ignored but the Muslims were pushed at gunpoint into the playground.'

'Dreadful, terrible,' Zena murmured slowly with anguish.

'I didn't count how many of us there were, it was several hundred. When they'd sorted us out from the others they marched us at gun point to the woods and, although we tried to stay together, they were watching and deliberately split families up.

'We were to be questioned, they said, but we were not allowed to talk and then when we reached a clearing they told us to stop.' His voice was heavy with emotion. 'I could not see the ravine at first, but then, as the rounds of gun fire started, the bodies just toppled forwards into it, and the crowd pushed forwards from the back, driven on at gun point.

'They just fell over the edge like skittles, one by one into their open grave.'

He stopped speaking, emotionally exhausted, but still not crying. She knew he had to cry, for only then would the healing process start. She had experienced it, she led him on. 'Did you see the children die?'

The question shocked him. He had not seen his parents or wife after the school, but he had seen both the children die. They were screaming for him and for their mother. 'Yes,' he answered somehow still holding back the tears, bottling up the pain. 'Yes,' he said again somewhat louder, 'I saw them both die.' This time there was no emotion in his voice at all, he was in deep shock as he vividly recalled the scene. In his mind he could hear the screaming, see the masses of people thrashing about, hear the gunshots, but his memory was dominated by the children's forlorn faces and their screams of 'Mummy! Daddy!'

'And what happened to you? How did you survive?'

At first he didn't reply, she didn't push him.

'I jumped,' he said simply at length.

'I jumped,' he said again after a pause. 'They were lining them up across the top of the ravine and gunning them down line by line, so when the line in front went down I jumped forward with them and simply lay there. Before I knew it the next line had fallen on top of me and their blood was running everywhere.' His voice tailed off. He was exhausted, but still he did not cry. Zena knew he had to.

'Did anyone else jump? Did anyone else survive?'

The thought had never occurred to him. He had never looked. Fool, he thought, who else might have survived, perhaps knocked into the ravine rather than shot. What if it had been one of the children? He began to tremble as the double enormity hit him. Could he have saved his children? Was it is fault they now lay dead in a pile of rotting human bodies? His mind was frozen but he felt his skin tighten as the warm sweat formed on it. It was only then that the aching pain in his eyes was eased as slowly moisture formed in them. The tears began. They continued all night.

For two days and nights she nursed and fed him continuously, during which time he told her how he had lain there just waiting to make sure that the Serbs had left before climbing out of the grave and making his way to her house.

'It was awful, Zena, fighting my way up through those layers of dead bodies. Many of them I recognised even if I did not know them.'

She could only imagine. Not that any civilised person could *really* imagine what it had been like for him.

Lech Zielinski looked out across the city of Kansas from his penthouse office on the sixty-fifth floor of the Harvey's building. He was not a happy man, but then, unlike some of the others in the pharmaceutical industry, he was not a worried man. He'd had problems before and dealt with them. That, he often argued, was what problems were for. The fact that his present difficulties, and those of his industry, were being caused by the First Lady cut no ice.

Three years short of his fiftieth birthday, with his first grandchild expected in a few months, he was not going to allow some jumped-up, egotistical southern liberal lawyer to destroy his life's work. He'd had to fight for what he'd got, and he'd fight to keep it.

Although a ruthless man in business, Lech was soft and gentle at home. He had married Georgina when they were both seventeen. It was her parents who had brought him up after his arrival in America and his grandfather's sudden death. The marriage served merely to formalise what had evolved, but neither of them had ever had eyes for any other and her death from cancer three years earlier resulted in Harvey's having the largest cancer research department in the world. Lech was determined to find the cure. Money was no object, although the commitment had forced him to decline Harry Powers' invitation to join a group of businessmen sponsoring a Presidential candidate. As it turned out, that would only have been a waste of money.

Lech prayed his only child, Samantha, would bear him a grandson, someone to continue the Harvey's business, someone to play baseball with. The man was still fitter than many twenty years his junior, running a half marathon every other weekend and a marathon once a month. Short and broad, there was little fat in his eleven stone. He was a powerful man in every respect. He ran a hand through his still youthful mop of wavy brown hair and scanned the city skyline with his dark brown eyes as he stood at the window thinking, plotting.

His first decision was whether to act alone or with others.

If with others, should it only be with others in the industry or should he try to pull in Harry Powers' syndicate. That would give him greater financial clout, but was that the answer?

Perhaps that first decision could only be taken after the second decision. What exactly was he proposing to do?

The telephone disturbed his thoughts.

'Yes?' he answered, with a discernible touch of his original Polish accent. He kept it that way deliberately.

'Samantha for you, Mr. Zielinski.'

'Thank you, put her through.' There was a click. 'Sammy, darling. Good to hear you, how are you?' He felt more excited about the birth of his grandchild than he had been about Sam's own birth.

She spoke in short sharp breaths. 'Not very well. The ambulance is on its way.'

'What's wrong?'

'Complications. The doctor isn't sure.'

'Is Michael with you?' he said.

'No, he's going straight to the hospital. I've just rung him. He was about to go into Court, but he's giving it to someone else. He'll be there before me.'

'So will I. You'll be fine, my darling, we'll get you and the baby the best, the very best.'

Lech immediately left for the hospital, which was about ten minutes' drive in the city traffic. He had never been there before as Georgina had stayed in a private clinic, but he was immediately impressed with the setup. It was a modern building, no more than seven or eight years old at the most, but more importantly it was apparent even from the reception area that the equipment was start-of-the-art. It felt right. He was happy, for the moment, that his daughter and grandchild would be in good hands. His instincts, his initial unproven reactions were rarely wrong.

'Is she here yet?' he asked anxiously as he entered the hospital lobby where his son-in-law was waiting.

Michael smiled nervously. 'No, Pops. I've spoken to Millie. They left twenty minutes ago, so it's too soon.'

'Did she give you any idea what's wrong?'

'No, none. You?'

'She didn't know, but more worrying, said the doctor didn't know either, which is why they're bringing her here.'

'I doubt the doctor would tell her anyway, Pops. He's a wise old bird. If there was anything to worry him, even the slightest thing, he'd send her straight in here. He wouldn't want you on his back if anything went wrong!'

It was another fifteen minutes before the ambulance arrived and half an hour after that when a subdued looking young doctor approached them both.

'I am afraid,' he began hesitantly, 'that we have a serious problem on our hands. I understand from Doctor Hine that Mrs. Comart's mother died of cancer.'

'Yes, that's right,' interrupted Lech impatiently, 'but what goddam relevance has that to Sammy's pregnancy?'

'Mr. Zielinski, this is going to be particularly painful for you because of your business and all that you do for cancer research.'

The words chilled him. Lech Zielinski suddenly felt helpless and afraid, his usual bravado out of reach. He knew money, power, influence, all that he had built was powerless to help him save everything that mattered to him. All too vividly he recalled the surgeon explaining Georgina's cancer. He had felt ashamed then by his helplessness. He had failed her and how he was to fail his daughter and his unborn grandchild.

'Go on,' he said slowly and quietly.

'Doctor Hine tells me that your wife's cancer started with leukaemia.'

Michael had never met Georgina and anxiously interrupted, 'But leukaemia can be cured now, can't it?'

'Possibly, especially in children. But it is a cancer of the blood and the infected blood can infect the body's cells if it is not redressed early enough. That I suspect is what happened to Mrs. Zielinski and I am afraid,' he paused as he looked at the two shaken men before him, 'I am afraid,' he repeated, 'that it has also happened to Mrs. Comart. There's no way of telling how long she's been infected, but personally I simply can't believe that she's had it for twenty seven years. The connection with her mother's illness can only be co-incidental, despite the relatively small number of such cases of this particular nature that we see.'

'The car crash,' said Lech almost inaudibly.

'I'm sorry, the what?'

Michael had no idea what he was talking about either. He had only met Samantha three years ago and Georgina had been dead for five. 'The car crash, she was seventeen. A juggernaut hit them and Sammy lost a lot of blood. The paramedics saved her life in the ambulance by giving her blood direct from Georgina. She'd have died before they reached the hospital otherwise.'

'Did your daughter not have a blood test when your wife was diagnosed?' asked the doctor, unable to hide his surprise at this revelation.

'Yes. They gave her the all-clear. We never thought about it again.'

'What about the baby?' asked Michael.

'It has to be infected.'

'Can we save it, can we cure it?'

'Maybe, maybe not, we really don't know. We have to decide whether to leave Mrs. Comart carrying the child in the knowledge — and I'm afraid this will hurt — that she will die before the child is born, or whether to deliver the child by section now and hope that we can save it and cure the leukaemia.'

The words were flowing over Lech. He was hearing them but not absorbing them. He already had the message.

'We must try to save the baby,' said Michael, 'Sammy will want us to ...'

'She has already said so, Mr. Comart. Why don't you both go in and see her? She needs to talk to you.'

Harry Powers, John Edwards and Matt Andrews had tried hard to put their sincere concerns at Clinton's election behind them, but they had failed. They were not mavericks, they were patriots. The other three had fallen by the wayside after Perot's re-entry, but in reality had lost interest once Perot announced his candidacy in the first place.

'My bet will always be that Jim Peters was Perot's man and

told him all our moves from the start. He might have even got the idea from us, but we'll never prove it and what good would it do us anyway?' said Edwards as the three gathered before dinner in the bar of the Washington Hilton.

'It's all history. The result is we're in the shit as a nation and it's getting worse, ' said Andrews, a few drinks ahead of the field, as they moved away from the bar to a small corner table.

'The worst of it,' said Powers, 'is Hillary. You know I saw a sticker in the back of several cars on the way over here from the airport that said "Honk if you hate Hillary". The woman's a menace.'

'On that we all agree. But what does the poster mean by Honk?' asked Andrews with a chuckle. 'I know what an oil man means when he says honk and he's not talking about sounding his horn!'

Powers did not respond. His business and his country were serious matters to him. 'As we have all been gathering information on the woman I have taken the liberty of bringing a secretary with me. I assure you she is totally trustworthy and have arranged for us to eat in a private room. Ali will record our findings to date and then collate them into a report.

'Then what?' roared Matt Andrews with a laugh as he drowned his scotch. 'We know the woman is a goddam menace. What good does writing it down do?'

'We look for the points where we can apply pressure,' replied Edwards, 'and hope that we come up with something powerful enough to influence the situation.'

'Hm,' said Andrews getting up from the table and moving towards the bar. 'I'd take a horse whip to her or, better still, have her taken out at dawn and shot! Another drink?'

'No, we won't thank you, Matt. There is wine with the meal and I think we should make a start,' replied Powers, showing, not for the first time, some concern at the way Andrews drank.

'Then I'll just take one in with me,' replied Andrews picking up another large scotch.

For the first half hour they talked over the problems of the Presidency generally. 'I think we should concentrate on our main objective tonight, Hillary,' said Powers as they started the main course.

'I was at a dinner party here in Washington last week,' said Edwards, 'when a well-connected Democrat floored them with a joke that summed up the whole situation.'

'I'm not sure jokes are relevant, John,' said Powers.

'Let's hear it anyway,' chipped in Andrews, starting on his second bottle of claret. 'A fine vintage. I congratulate you, Harry.'

'Okay, okay,' responded Powers impatiently, wishing they had met in his office with only coffee to drink.

'Have you heard that Clinton wants six more Secret Service Agents assigned to Hillary? After all, if anything happened to her, he would have to become President.'

Matt Andrews laughed but Powers remained impassive. 'As you say,' he said, 'it does sum up the position.'

'Have you heard about the time their car broke down after the Election?' asked Andrews still laughing at the joke.

Powers' irritation was beginning to show, but Andrews appeared to be becoming increasingly drunk, either not noticing or not taking any notice. 'No, Matt, we have not and don't want to.'

Andrews continued anyway, 'After the mechanic had fixed it, Bill asked how much he owed him. "Oh, that's alright, have it on me," he said giving Hillary a hug and a kiss. "Who the hell was that?" asked Bill as the mechanic drove off. "An old boyfriend," replied Hillary. "Just think," said Bill, "if you'd married him, you'd be the wife of a garage mechanic." "No," said Hillary firmly, "if I'd married him, he'd be the President elect".'

'Thank you, Matt. Again pertinent, but we are not here to deal in jokes, however apt or illustrative. We are here to deal in fact.' Powers spat the words out, no longer hiding his distaste as Andrews started his third bottle of wine.

'Where do we start with her?' asked Edwards.

'We know that, at school in Park Ridge, she was study mad. An A Plus student at Eugene Field Grammar School and at Wellesley College.'

'She became the goddam President of the College,' interrupted Andrews, 'and now she's as good as President of this goddam country.'

Powers controlled his anger. Even in his drunken state Andrews showed he had not only researched his subject but remembered it. 'That's right, Matt ...'

'And what's more,' continued Andrews, totally ignoring Powers, 'according to a guy called Ernest Rickets who was one of her classmates, she didn't smoke or go out with boys.' His sarcasm was heavy. 'All the woman ever did was work, and their former senior campaign adviser, James Carville, said,' Andrews paused to take another glass of wine, 'if I remember the words correctly, "If you throw in an IQ of a zillion and a character of steel, this is a person of considerable influence",' Andrews smiled at them both as he filled his glass yet again. He'd done his research better than either of them. But why was he bothering? They both bored him, neither of them had any imagination or knew what excitement was. Why was he running with them?

'So she's not got much in common with Bill then!' said Edwards. 'By all accounts his college life, especially at Oxford, was one long round of booze, women and drugs. He's admitted to smoking pot but says he didn't inhale it! It makes you wonder if that joke about the mechanic has some truth. America is not ready for a woman President even now, and twenty years ago, when she married Clinton, it would have been unthinkable. Margaret Thatcher wasn't even leading the Conservatives in Britain until seventy-six.'

Conversations like this annoyed Harry Powers. He was not a man to trivialise. He hated stopping off at all the points along a road to look around and consider the scenery, however interesting or relevant. He drove straight down the highway to his destination, eyes fixed on the horizon. 'That's as maybe,' he said, 'and no doubt we will look at all of that in detail later, but now we're concentrating on Hillary.' Edwards decided not to make an issue of it. He knew Harry Powers' mind well enough, had done for twenty odd years. Andrews decided to order another bottle of claret.

'She's also into the church ...' began Edwards.

'And what's more ,' said Andrews drowning out John Edwards, 'she got every damn Girl Scout badge when she was a kid, honours galore at school and organised everything and everybody the whole time. None of the mothers in the district could get their sons to do anything, but Hillary could, she had them all running round like headless chickens. But if we believe what we're told she didn't like them and she wasn't giving them any personal favours .... Sorry, John,' he continued again with heavy sarcasm as the claret arrived, 'I cut you off.'

'That's okay,' said Edwards, as impressed as Powers by Andrews' ability to accurately recall information despite the volume of alcohol he had drunk, but not as concerned by the drinking. 'She was impressed, some say mesmerised, by a Youth Minister.'

'Donald Jones, First United Methodist Church,' interrupted Andrews, knowing exactly what he was doing and saying.

'Yes, thanks, Matt,' said Edwards holding back his smile while Powers remained expressionless and said nothing. 'Jones was obviously a serious influence in her life; she tells people she is deeply religious and murmurs a prayer to herself continually.' Edwards paused, waiting to see if Matt Andrews would come in with the words. He simply poured himself another glass.

" 'Dear Lord be good to me"...'

" 'The sea is so wide and my boat is so small," ' said Andrews smiling. He might be very different from Harry Powers in many ways, but in one respect he was no different — he did things his way, on his terms, in his own time. Not when someone set up an opening for him to make them look clever.

'Are her parents religious? They were Republicans, weren't they?' asked Powers, knowing the answer but trying to lead the conversation.

'But she changed all that,' boomed Andrews. 'Campaigned for Barry Goldwater and then, when she was at Wellesley College in the mid sixties, she became excited by the student activity. It changed her completely. She became an anti-militarist, a convinced liberal.'

'Was it a cover?' asked Powers with striking force.

'A cover?' Edwards was confused by the question.

'You know,' said Andrews, 'you want to change from A to C but not admit it. So you change to B to distance yourself from your old stance and campaign enthusiastically, while all the time working away quietly for C.

'No,' continued Andrews firmly. 'This woman's got balls, she's a woman of conviction and, like the rest of her career-minded liberal cronies, she has a crusading zeal. They're a lacklustre group, mostly lawyers, but they stick together socially as well as in business. Not that it's easy to decide when they're socialising.

'She's clever enough to use them all,' said Powers wanting to push his point until it was dead.

'Not if you listen to Auberon Waugh!' laughed Andrews tossing in another well-researched throwaway line which he doubted either of them would understand. As usual, he was not as drunk as he appeared. Damn you both, he thought, I'll show you who's done his homework properly.

Again Powers was impressed. If only the man didn't drink, but at least the rate of consumption was slowing at last.

'I've not heard,' said Edwards.

'He was very direct, as usual. "My own suspicion is that if Mrs. Clinton were really clever, she would hide the fact that she thinks herself cleverer than her partner." '

They all thought on that for several minutes while the coffee was poured. It was Powers who inevitably brought them back to the task in hand. 'So she's an individual, she's a crusader from an upper middle class, serious minded, devoutly

Methodist family, but is she running the White House? Is she a threat to our country in any way? Is she a security risk? When Martin Luther King was assassinated, she marched with a black armband.'

'Ah,' said Andrews. 'so did hundreds, thousands of students, don't read too much into that particular issue; rebellion, nothing more. As for being a risk,' he said slowly, suddenly sounding completely sober, 'you first have to define what you mean by a risk. I'm sure she's a capable administrator and whether you agree with what she did or not, you need look no further than the way she sorted out the education system in Arkansas. She reformed it single handed.

'Here she oversees over five hundred political staff who will tell you that her instructions are clear, concise, direct. Brother, is she direct. You know, she's got more senior level political aides than Al Gore. But,' he paused to make sure they were both totally attentive, 'is she as clever at assessing people, their worth, their character? I say not and I say that *is* dangerous, especially from one with so many feminist, liberal friends. She wants exactly the same number of blacks, whites, men, women and doesn't give a shit about the ability of the people or their general suitability. Look at the cock-up over Zoe Baird's illegal nanny. No-one in their right mind would have considered her for the job, but Hillary insisted it be a woman. That was the most critical factor, not the points we would all take into account.

'Yes,' he said with purpose as he lit up a large cigar, 'that makes her a risk because her influence is immense and her judgement is poor. Thank God we're not standing over nuclear buttons the way we used to.'

'Bush would have won if we were,' said Edwards quietly. Neither of them argued with him.

'She denies it, of course,' continued Andrews, 'but it's plain for all to see. At least you know where you are with Hillary. Bill is so slippery you never know what he really thinks. Defining his beliefs is like trying to pin a custard pie to the wall — not so Hillary.

'She's left and she's committed to getting Bill to see it all her way on everything, but never more than on social issues. Just look at all that tosh on the gays in the military. Bill, for all his faults, had worked out that the best thing to do was to be a little conciliatory and work out a quiet arrangement to defuse the situation. Oh, no! Public display of force, complete cock- up, all down to Hillary.

'She's a leftie alright, but what really worries me is that the staff in the White House now are afraid to talk to anyone, ask any lobbyist. They're terrified of her, of losing their job if she finds out they've so much as said hello to anyone from the press.

'Risk, you ask. She's a damn great liability in my book, but what the hell can we do about it. Like most feminists she should have been strangled at birth. Now, I want a large brandy and then I think we call it a night.'

'There is still much work to do,' said Powers anxiously.

'Then you do it without me tonight, buddy. It's been a long hard day. I suggest we resume for breakfast, six o'clock or earlier if you like. They say Hillary rises before dawn and I leave you with something Jerry Brown said — "She's not the Virgin Mary, is she?".'

For Lech and Michael the wait at the hospital passed desperately slowly. The baby, a boy, Lech Michael, was born by Ceasarian section later that day and lived for just twelve hours. The leukaemia had taken full hold and he had serious breathing difficulties. He was simply too premature to survive. The funeral was a private affair, the three of them and Michael's parents.

It was barely three weeks later when Lech went through the ordeal of another funeral.

'Stop by at the house for a drink, Michael?'

'Thanks, Pops, I'd like that.'

'And I think it's time to call me Lech. I was too old, Michael, too set in my ways to marry again, but you're not.

There's no knowing what tomorrow holds for any of us. I just hope it will bring you more happiness than the last month.'

'Thanks, Lech, I appreciate it. I'll just run Mom and Dad home and be back in about an hour, okay?'

'Fine, we'll have supper as well. Stay over if you like.'

'Maybe, we'll see.'

It was almost six thirty when Michael arrived back in Kansas, having decided he would stay the night.

'I want to show you something,' said Lech as he handed Michael his spritzer. 'It's nearly thirty years old and is likely to cause something of a shock, so sit down first.'

Michael was bemused, but sat as asked.

'On 13th January 1954 when I was at Junior High School, a new boy joined the class. His name meant nothing to anyone then, but it does now — Lee Harvey Oswald.'

Michael looked at him hard. He was surprised. Not surprised by the fact that Lech had been at school with Oswald, after all everybody went to school with someone somewhere, but surprised that Lech had never spoken about it before.

'Go on,' he said.

'We got on quite well and he took me along to meetings at the Civil Air Patrol. In fact, that's where I met the man who lent me the money to buy and expand Harvey's in the first place. The operation was run by a queer called Ferrie, David Ferrie, but apart from being queer, which was regarded differently thirty years ago, he was obsessed with fighting communism. As you can imagine, I hated communism. I think I hated communism more than the Nazis — the Russians were supposed to have liberated us. Anyway, I went along for a while but got bored. I was more interested in working than playing soldiers.

'I never saw Oswald again but the day he died I received this.' Lech handed an ageing brown envelope to Michael. 'Go on, open it. Read it aloud.'

' "22nd November 1963

' "Dear Lech,

' "I know how much you must have suffered in Poland

from the Communist Party and what you will hear about me between when we last met and now might mean you don't want to read this, but please do.

'"Many years ago I was set up by the CIA. I don't know when. But once I realised it I decided to play along with the game. This seemed fine until a few days ago. Then I discovered that they want me to shoot the President, yes to kill John Kennedy. That is why they have had such an interest in me all these years. I think it probably started in 1955 and what worries me is that because of your background they might have been trying to use you as well.

' "I'm supposed to shoot him at 12.30 today but am going to miss and then get arrested so I can tell all in Court. There is no-one I can turn to for help, no-one will believe me, but I don't want someone else to get caught as I have. I'm afraid I might not get to Court, that they will kill me first somehow. But I'll make sure when I get caught that it will be odd if I'm shot then.

' "I think there are three people running me, one is a man called Mike Garson and another is Carl someone. I don't have a name for the third, but I did set him up once and managed to get this picture of him. It's only a quick snap, but it's something.

' "I'm not wild about Kennedy but people can't just go round shooting the President when they feel like it.

' "I know how much you hate the commies so I'll leave you to do what you think is right. I'm sure if I don't get to tell my story that everything will be so confused and mixed up buy the CIA that no-one will know what to believe so there is no chance of me being believed. Who knows.

' "Yours sincerely

' "Lee"'

Michael sat speechless for several minutes and then spoke softly. 'Firstly, I'd like another drink please, Lech.'

'Sure.'

'You've never shown this to anyone before?'

'No.'

'But why? It explains everything, it answers all the questions.'

'Does it, Michael? Sure it only does that if you believe Oswald and I'm not sure that I do, so why should anyone else?'

'But it's the missing link. It explains why he was there and didn't shoot. Remember there were no powder stains on his hands. It does explain what has never been explained.'

'Maybe, maybe not. But I was happy to see Kennedy dead. I didn't really care who killed him or why, so I left it.'

'You *left* it?' asked Michael in amazement, 'You held the key to one of the world's greatest crime mysteries and you simply ignored it? I can't believe it.'

'The way I looked at it was this. It was trouble. If Oswald was right and I went wading in, then I'd have the CIA looking for me. I had to think of Georgina. We'd been trying for years to have a baby and she was finally pregnant. I couldn't put that in jeopardy. There was the business to consider. If it was the CIA, then they'd taken out a President and the man they'd set up to take the rap. What threat would I pose, a Polish immigrant? I'd just disappear.'

'So you did absolutely nothing?' Michael was incredulous.

'Well, not quite. I did look into the two names Oswald gave me. Wasn't difficult. The second was Carl Hankin, a senior CIA agent who suffered a heart attack the day after the assassination. He was dead before Oswald, before I got the letter.'

'Ominous.'

'I thought so until I learnt that he was sixty four and grossly overweight. When Garson was shot dead at Hankin's funeral, no-one was ever caught for it, I knew it was right to keep out of it, for my family. What use would I be to them dead?'

'I can see that, Lech,' said Michael kindly. 'And what of the third man?'

'I did nothing. I put it all back in that envelope two days after Hankin and Kennedy were buried, and have never touched it again until tonight.'

'Why open it tonight?'

'I've always wanted to know the truth, but was too scared. I don't think they can hurt me now. I don't think they'd hurt you and so they can't hurt my family.

'But why do you tell me?'

'I'm very fond of you Michael. I know how much you loved Sammy and she you. It is possible that you might get caught up in whatever happens and I wouldn't want that. If you'd rather I did nothing, then that's the way it will be.'

'No way, Lech.' Michael was positive. 'You do what you have to do. My job is to find the truth without fear. I'm an attorney. They didn't get Jim Garrison and he wrote a book about his suspicions.;'

'Yes, Michael — suspicions, not evidence.'

'But as you said, Lech, who's to say this is not a pack of lies anyway?' Michael tossed the envelope back to Lech.

'Well, if you're happy, I'd also like you to help me. Quietly. No risks. Just help me with the first part, the difficult part.

'Which is what?'

'To find out who the third man was.'

'Maybe, maybe not. But if we know who he is I want to find him, if he's still alive.'

'That could be another matter and looking at that picture if he is still alive he must be around eighty.'

'Agreed, and the probability is that he's been dead like the other two for almost thirty years.'

'And if he has been what then?'

'We'll see when we know.'

'I'll help, Lech. I start tomorrow.'

'Thank you, Michael,' he said with true gratitude. 'And there is just one other thing I want to tell you.' His tone had become heavy, serious.

'I have decided to set up another trust for research into cancer generally but especially leukaemia.'

'In addition to Georgina's?'

'Yes. Georgina's trust will be insignificant by comparison.'

'But it's millions of dollars.'

'The Samantha and Lech Michael Comart Trust will have everything I own as a capital base.'

Michael was stunned. He had no real idea but at a guess it ran to several billion dollars. 'Everything, including the stock and the house?'

'I'll keep the house and enough to live on, but all the stock will be transferred to the Trust. Every dime that Harvey's makes will go back into research and the Trust will own the rights. When we find the answer Harvey's will make the drug under licence, which will mean even greater profits and it will all go back into medical research.'

'But you invest heavily from profits into research now.'

'But it doesn't *all* go back into research now. True, the reinvestment is substantial, but even when it's total, I doubt that silly bitch in the White House will ever understand why we have to make a profit. If we didn't make the profits we do there wouldn't be any drug development at all. But she's a liberal. Let's not waste our breath on her, not tonight.' Michael was puzzled by the last two words, but decided not to read anything into them that wasn't there.

The following morning Lech appointed two private investigators from England to find out every last thing there was to find out about Mr. and Mrs. William Jefferson Clinton.

CHAPTER FOUR

'Bridget. It's Sally-Anne, how are you, darling?'

'Bored, darling, totally bored. And you?'

'Offended if you must know, grossly offended,' responded Sally-Anne Knight curtly.

'My poor darling. You don't sound over happy, whoever has upset you so much?' The tone mixed mockery and concern. Bridget was not sure which way to jump yet.

'The Clintons,' she blurted out almost in tears.

'Well, darling, you're certainly not the only one, so I shouldn't take it personally. What have they done?' Mockery was getting the upper hand.

'Refused my seventeenth dinner invitation,' replied Sally-Anne indignantly.

'There may be others who have been refused more, you never know,' said Bridget, who was never going to admit that she was one of them. Bridget considered herself to be the most important hostess in Washington, if not the entire country. The daughter of a clerk in a linen factory, she had climbed the social ladder dramatically through three marriages, the last being six years ago to Bradley Harworth, a textile tycoon. Nearing fifty, money kept her reasonably attractive, but most of her exercise was taken naked with more or less anyone who was interested. Her vanity extended to ensuring that all her body hair that was not removed was silver blonde, and the plastic surgeon tidied her face every twelve months and tightened her bust as and when required, usually about every three years. As a young woman she had enjoyed a slender frame, with abnormally long legs which enabled her to look most men directly in the eye. About the only parts of her body that had remained in trim without artificial help were those legs and her small, beautifully formed bottom.

'More than seventeen, impossible!'

Sally-Anne Knight was a few years younger than Bridget

but had slipped down the social ladder, yielded to drink and let herself go physically. The eldest daughter of a former Ambassador, she had first married at nineteen. It had only lasted a little over six months. Her husband, a welder, walked out when he discovered that she did not bring any real money with her and that she, like him, had continued to play the field.

Her second marriage had been to an accountant of whom her parents had both greatly approved. If he had either been better in bed or prepared to let her have some sexual freedom they would probably have remained married. Jeff, however, had swept her off her feet at thirty eight and the arms trade had given her the life style that she had enjoyed as a child.

Despite being slightly overweight, she did not look dumpy and radiated a charm on her sober days. But the toll of drinking was beginning to show around her puffy eyes and in her thickening and increasingly flabby neck. Jeff paid her little attention now and, she confided to Bridget (which she knew at the time was a foolish thing to do) that the physical side of their relationship had ended and that she needed a young stud to give her a reason to get back into trim rather than into the bottle. It was, of course, catch 22 and she knew she was losing.

'They're not like the Kennedys. I remember,' said Bridget, lying with boastful pride, 'that Jackie and Jack were always at our dinner table when I was a girl.'

'It's her you know, it's Hillary,' interrupted Sally-Anne with venom.

'I think you're probably right, darling, but we can dine without them. Who needs them? After all, they're becoming a laughing stock and in time they'll be begging to come to our dinner parties and we'll say no, sorry, we don't want you. Brad is sure they'll be ostracised and he'll not even get nominated again.'

'That is just what Jeff was saying last week. "The comeback kid won't come back from this one." '

'He's right, but life *is* so boring at the moment. We're thinking about going on a cruise for a few months, forget about it all.'

Sally-Anne was instantly enthused at the prospect. 'Really, what a wonderful idea! Perhaps we should get up a party, that would be fun!'

That idea had not occurred to Bridget and she was not sure either that she liked it. Or that Brad would, for that matter. On the other hand, Brad had always had a soft spot for Sally-Anne Knight, so perhaps he would not be averse. Part of Bridget's plotting, however, was to get Brad out of that bimbo Angie Tourle's bed and back into her own, not Sally-Anne's.

'We were thinking of it rather as a second honeymoon and we're not all like that English aristocrat MP!"

'Oh, darling, yes!' exclaimed Sally-Anne excitedly, 'He's rather dishy but I don't think it was true, not like that anyway. Look, darling, why don't we have a dinner party anyway? I'll throw it, a really big one, invite just everybody, but everybody, except the Clintons.'

'Everybody?' exclaimed Bridget wondering what Jeff would say about the cost. Armament manufacture was not as buoyant as it had been in times gone by, but that was not her problem.

'Yes, everybody. Democrats galore but not Al Gore!'

'Have you been drinking already, darling?' asked Bridget wincing at the frailty of Sally-Anne's attempted joke.

'Just a couple of little ones, darling.

'Yes, we'll do it. Hollywood stars, press barons, the elite of the elite but not the Clintons.'

'And if they decide they want to come?' asked a suspicious Bridget.

'They can't. I simply will not have them in my house after they've been so rude.' Sally-Anne sounded as if she meant it.

'Will Jeff agree to that?'

'Jeff will agree to anything for me, darling?

'You'll help me?'

'Yes, I'll help you, darling. When do we start?'

'Lunch today and we'll draw up the list.''

'Ah,' said Bridget, pausing — she had a session with her facial adviser. A very attractive young man. Half an hour last week, two hours this. You couldn't get too much of a good thing. 'Sorry, darling, I can't do that. Tomorrow?'

'Tomorrow it is then. One o'clock at Alfie's.'

'I'll be there.'

'We'll show 'em,' said Sally-Anne replacing the receiver and pouring herself another large gin and tonic. 'We'll show all those trendy liberal lefties they cannot treat the real Democrats like this. They need us.'

Bridget was twenty minutes late for lunch. Her facial adviser had managed to fit her in again that morning for "a quickie at half past twelve."

'I'm so sorry to be late, darling,' she said approaching the table.

'Don't worry, darling, no problem. You look absolutely radiant,' muttered Sally-Anne jealously. She knew she was losing her style, losing her glamour. The drink was only making matters worse.

'My facial adviser, darling. He does the most wonderful things to me!'

'Perhaps I should try him?'

'I'm afraid that's not possible, darling, he just can't take any more clients at the moment. But you'll be the first to know if he can, I promise you.'

'How very kind of you. Thank you, Bridget,' said Sally-Anne, thinking, "You bitch. You're spending Brad's money pretending to have facial advice just so that you can screw some young stud, you horny old bitch."

Over lunch they drew up a list of three hundred and fifty guests and selected a date which, as far as they knew, was socially free.

'The invitations will be printed and posted tomorrow,' said Sally-Anne. 'It is going to be *the* party of the decade and *they* will not be there.'

'Did you say anything to Jeff?' asked Bridget, still suspicious that he'd be unhappy about excluding the Clintons if they wanted to come.

'Yes, he thinks it's a wonderful idea.'

'And if the Clintons should hint that they would like to come?'

'Stuff 'em, he said.'

'Really?' responded Bridget, somewhat surprised, although the previous evening when she had mentioned the idea to Brad, she got just the inkling that the idea was not new to him. Were the men in league and, if so, why? Brad had actually suggested the date they had settled on, 'Nothing going on anywhere that night as far as I know. Might be a good one for it.'

During the three weeks that Hamdi stayed with Zena the situation in Bosnia worsened considerably. The Vance-Owen peace plan, doomed from the start in the eyes of the Muslims, was long since buried and the violence continued to escalate. Atrocity after atrocity was perpetrated by Serbs, Croats and Muslims alike. Although he would be considered biased, Hamdi was in no doubt that the Serbs were the worst offenders.

'You are probably right,' said Zena. 'But why do we have to fight at all? All my life I have seen fighting. It never ends, it never changes anything.'

'I wish I knew, Zena. There are many like us.'

'Then why the fighting? Why do the people not stop the generals, refuse to fight?'

'Life, sadly, is not that simple. Look at the referendum in Serbia. The people don't want the fighting and the bloodshed and yet they reject the peace plan. It's pride. They want to be Serbs, to reject all those years of frustration at having no national identity.'

'But why through fighting, killing? Killing their friends. I don't understand, never did and never will. I am an old lady now.'

'But a very brave old lady,' said Hamdi with kindness. 'Without your help I would have died. I was too weak to live and had no food. I owe you my life.'

She was moved. 'It was nothing.'

For a while they didn't speak, soaking in the silence. It was broken by the distant crack of gunfire echoing through the valley. Zena turned to Hamdi and clutched his hand with a force that shocked him from one so old. 'What will you do?' she asked.

'I will head for the hills. There are safe Muslim camps there, well protected.'

'And if you are caught?'

'I'll take my chance, Zena. We must all take our chance now.'

'Then take these also,' she said handing him some well worn papers. 'You will have to say that you lost the picture, but it might help you avoid capture and torture by my people.'

The papers were those of one of her dead sons. He had been a few years older than Hamdi, but as he looked now it was impossible to tell. 'I don't know what to say.'

'Say your prayers. You will need them. I can let you have some food to help you on your way,' she said, tears welling in her old eyes.

'You have been too kind already. I know you went without food to feed me, I couldn't take any more. I will go tonight and with luck will be safe in the camp before morning.'

'There is an old bike in the outhouse, it might be useful.'

'Thank you, I'm sure it will be.'

He waited until it had been dark for a couple of hours and, with the Serb papers in his right shoe and his own in his left, set off on his journey to the snow covered mountains, high above Novi Travnik. His biggest problem was that he was as likely to meet Croats as he was Serbian soldiers, and neither of his papers would save him then. He'd use his own, he decided, he'd die as himself, not someone he had never met.

By dawn he was crossing the freezing pass feeling relatively safe for the first time since setting out from Zena's old stone cottage. If he met force now, it would be — or should be — Muslims.

And it was.

They questioned him for twenty minutes, passing his papers between them continuously before agreeing to take him to their mountain retreat.

'I saw the anti tank mines on the road outside Travnik, they looked new,' he said.

'Tonight,' was all one of them said in reply.

He had known it would not be easy. Why should they trust him? His false papers were beginning to trouble him. Suppose they searched him? 'There were men in the trees with Kalashnikovs, dressed in fatigues and wearing balaclavas.'

'How many?' asked one of them.

'I only saw six, but I could not be sure if that was all.'

'What else did you see?' asked the man, still wary of him.

'Nothing, why?'

'Last night the Croats burnt out a village further down the valley. We lived side by side with Croats, no problem until two army trucks drove up just after seven and started pushing people out into the street.'

'It happened to me,' said Hamdi, 'but it was the Serbs. They killed my parents, my wife and both my children.' Somehow he controlled his feelings as he spoke.

'Where was this?' The question is curt.

'Sipovo.'

'Then you know. It matters not which gun is pointed at you, they are all the same when they fire.'

'They are all Russian you mean,' said the big man at the back who had not previously spoken at all.

'And the west won't help us. Bastards. Even the food the Americans drop goes to the Serbs.'

Hamdi knew only too well that the US Airforce had not been able to accurately target the Muslims with the food because of the height of the planes. He knew also that Clinton had ordered the drops with firm opposition from other nations, partly because it could make the land relief operation harder and partly because of the logistical problems of delivery. He guessed it was really a PR exercise to deflect attention from other issues and make him look compassionate. He'd read somewhere that when Clinton was at University in Washington he'd delivered food parcels to the poor.

'Thatcher and Bush would not have let it happen, they would have helped us,' said the big man. 'You know in Moscow they distribute leaflets praising the Serb resistance to Muslim and Catholic aggression. They tell you how to become a mercenary fighting for Belgrade.'

'Tell me more,' said Hamdi as they reached the mountain top hideaway. It was nothing more than a few tents and makeshift shelters under outcrops of rocks. Not only must these people not find his false papers but he must never mention that he knew Bill Clinton. The anti western feeling was electric throughout the camp. They felt cheated, rejected, disowned. They felt alone.

'In Moscow they talk about helping our brothers in Slavia under western siege. It is scandalous.'

'How do you know all this?' asked Hamdi, intrigued, by what they claimed. He could well believe it, but how would they know hidden away up here high in the mountains?

'The BBC, we listen to the BBC.'

Hamdi was amazed, not just that they were able to receive the BBC but that they were able to understand it.

'You all speak English?' he asked.

'No, not all, but Moncilo speaks good English. He went to Oxford University. He spends all his time listening to the BBC and does nothing else.'

Hamdi thought he detected a slight resentment. Listening to the radio was obviously perceived as a soft option.

'But he explains to us what we do not understand,' said one of the others.

'I must meet him but tell me more about the Russians, I

did not know this.'

'There are many in the Russian army who think the politicians are wrong to side with the United Nations, they even put a wreath on the Kremlin wall saying the "Eternal alliance of Slavs" with the Russian and Yugoslav flags.'

'That is right,' said Moncilo, eyeing the new arrival suspiciously. 'It is also true that the liberal intelligensia in Russia talk openly about the unfair way that the Serbs are treated. They blame the west, they blame the Americans and they are increasingly using the argument to attack Yeltsin.... But enough, you must be hungry. Come join us in what little we have to eat and drink and tell us all about yourself.'

'Thank you. Your English is good.'

'And yours?'

'Much the same, I went to Oxford as well.'

'Really! To study what?' asked Moncilo appearing to warm to Hamdi a little.

'Law, and you?'

'Law, also.'

'Did you practice?' asked Hamdi.

'Yes, in Belgrade. I was one of the first to feel the change. Come, let us eat and talk.'

Moncilo was a year or two younger than Hamdi and physically much bigger and stronger. His wiry brown hair had started to recede and his brown eyes were set deep into his weathered face. He had a reassuring manner about him that captured Hamdi's trust from the first moment. He would not have been out of place as a solicitor in an English market town.

'Lech, Michael,' he said as soon as the phone was answered. 'The third man was George Woodrow Gillespi. An East New Yorker who served in the Marines and then joined Langley. He went missing after Hankin and Garson died, but there's no death certificate filed in his own name, not that that is conclusive.'

'No, if he didn't buy it immediately and fled, he's hardly

likely to have kept his own name.'

'That's what I thought.'

'Michael, you're a genius. How did you find out so quickly?'

'Don't ask, Lech. I mean don't ask, please.'

'That bad, huh?' Michael did not reply. 'Okay. Can you let me have all you've got on him as soon as possible? I'll put some detective firms onto finding him. We'll soon know one way or another.

'Sure, but there's more.'

'More?'

'Yes, firstly I've got a good, clear 1963 picture and it's in colour.'

Lech was excited, 'Go on.'

'He was involved in a shoot out in Santa Monica before he disappeared. Killed four CIA agents. That's all the computer lists, the fact that he killed them. No indication of what they were doing there or what the connection between them was.'

'Careless, leaving information like that,' said Lech thoughtfully.

'Not really. It turns him into a fugitive and no doubt they thought he would soon be found and then killed during capture. Doesn't really give us anything....'

'Other than somewhere to start,' replied Lech enthusiastically.

'Thirty years ago!'

'There will be people who remember, there always are. Even if they only remember what their Grandpa told them.' Michael could hear the word "Grandpa" paining Lech. He no doubt thought of his own Grandpa as well as young Lech.

The package arrived the next morning by motorbike. Michael had done well in the space of a few days. Lech had deliberately used London firms for his Clinton enquiries and was tempted to do so again. He'd told them he wanted a first report in a month. That was just over three weeks away. Perhaps he should instruct another London firm, to give them three weeks for the preliminary report and then go over there himself.

He had a busy day ahead of him with the tax authorities in connection with the new trust. He would decide tonight.

Harry Powers was worried about Matt Andrews continued involvement. With his drinking seemingly forever on an upward spiral, he could not be relied upon. It wasn't that he would deliberately cross them, the man had more sense than that, but loose talk could be as dangerous as treachery.

The finalised dossier on Hillary Diane Rodham Clinton ran to three hundred and seventeen pages of double spaced print.

'It's all here, Harry,' said Andrews taking his coffee as the three of them met in Powers' office to discuss the real problem, William Jefferson Clinton.

'But *is* he the real problem?' asked Edwards after some discussion of the information they had compiled. 'Did you see her on NBC a few weeks ago? She denied that she had anything to do with the fumbled nomination of Lani Guinier, but she wasn't convincing. Said something about reading in the papers that she was backing people she's never met and had no interest in. I just didn't believe her.'

'Nor me,' said Andrews, 'and even David Gergen said he had an interview privately with her before he was appointed to sort out the PR mess. She's Lady Macbeth alright. The press are right about that at least.'

'That's as maybe,' said Powers, showing his impatience again. His partners were forever drifting off the subject. 'We have discussed her at length already and prepared our dossier. We are now looking at him, so let's stick to the task in hand. Is that asking too much?' The two men grunted acceptance.

'Is Ali going to take notes again?' asked Edwards.

'No, every word in this office is automatically taped. We will prepare the dossier from the meeting, word by word.'

'Always taped?' asked Andrews showing concern.

'Always, Matt.'

'So every word I've said in this office you can prove and quote,' he bellowed in anger.

'Including those, Matt.'

'You bastard. I'm not playing games like that with you. How the hell can we air the subject fully and objectively if you're taping it all and can use it later against us if it suits you?'

'I'm out of this, stuff your concerns, you'll never do anything anyway. This charade has already cost me millions of dollars and what's to show for it? Goddam dossier on a trumped up legal broad who's pulling the strings in the White House. I knew that from Time Magazine!'

Powers was very tempted at that point to let Andrews go but his instinct told him he would be useful later, possibly as the fall guy in the event of any ultimate action. 'Okay, Matt, if it troubles you that much I can get Ali to take notes. Believe me, the tapes are only for efficiency, and once the meeting has been written up they are wiped clean.'

'I'd eat shit before I'd believe you,' spat Andrews.

'That would be your choice, Matt, but it's true. Would you like Ali to join us?'

Powers' calm reassuring manner annoyed Andrews; people like that always annoyed him. Hell, he thought I'm in it now anyway. If he's got the old tapes, he's got the old tapes and there's nothing I can do about it. But no more.

'Okay,' he said belligerently, 'get her to take notes and I'll stay, but not here. I'd never know if the tape was on or off.'

'So you don't trust me,' replied Powers accusingly.

'Too damn right I don't!'

'Look,' said Edwards, trying to calm the situation, 'I can see both points of view and they are both valid. If we are going to carry on, and I think we should, then it makes sense to use a hotel and for Ali to take notes. That way no-one has anything to worry about.'

'Okay, okay,' said Powers, 'but no drinking, we are working.'

'I work better with a drink,' snapped Andrews.

It was almost an hour before they were installed in a conference room in a nearby motel with Ali sitting ready to take notes.

'So where do we start with this bastard, his women or his haircuts?' asked Andrews rolling his large Scotch around provocatively in his hand.

'We start as we mean to go on, with fact and only fact. No hearsay,' replied Powers in bad humour.

'What do we know about his college days?' asked Edwards, again acting as peacemaker.

'Spent his time at Oxford screwing women, drinking, playing the saxophone and smoking dope. How the shit did he ever become President?'

'Matt,' said Powers angrily, 'we are dealing in fact, not rumour, not innuendo.'

'He's admitted all that!'

'Look, if you two really are going to spend the entire day more interested in putting one over on the other than dealing with the task in hand, then I am leaving,' said Edwards with considerable force.

'Okay, okay,' responded Andrews irritably. 'We know the guy grew up in a violent house where his stepfather was usually drunk, and that his mother liked to spend her time at the horses. He hacked it through college, Georgetown University, Oxford University and then to Yale where he met the dreaded Hillary.'

'He was elected Governor of Arkansas in 1979 and made such a mess of it that they kicked him out in 1981. He spent the next two years going around saying he was sorry, he'd made the mistakes of a sincere but inexperienced young man, and he conned the people into re-electing him in 1983 and he's never given a straight answer or kept a promise since.'

'We need to be more precise, Matt, put flesh on the bones. At times you do it and at other times everything is so bland as to be, frankly, quite useless.'

'Cut the bullshit, Harry,' bellowed Andrews. 'What is this, some sort of game? Who the hell cares about dossiers? Who needs them? What the hell are we going to do with them anyway? Please, Mr President, this is what you're like and this is what we think you should be like, would you mind changing? Oh, and while you're at it we'd like you to re-programme your wife as well. Forget it!

'The simple fact is that the man is a chameleon. He's always trying to impress. He tries to please everybody, especially that silly bitch of a wife of his. He bows to pressure from here, there and everywhere, as good as tells the world he's been having an affair and he *is* President of the United States, for God's sake. Now, when we were trying to stop him by beating him at the Poll it made sense, but what on earth are we writing dossiers for?'

'I can see what he's driving at, Harry,' said John Edwards in a voice and tone as calm as Matt Andrews' had been excited and emotive.

'I will tell you then,' said Powers removing his glasses, which he rarely wore, and starting to pace the room. 'But first, Ali, I don't think we will need you to record this. In fact, I think you can probably take the rest of the day off.'

She left without saying a word.

'The fact is that, if we collate everything into one dossier on each of them, I believe they will indisputably look like security risks.'

'Like what!' stormed Andrews.

'Security risks, serious security risks that put in jeopardy not only the United States but the western world.'

'But, we all know that now! You're unreal, you're nuts, you know that?' said Andrews. 'Obsessed with files instead of opening your eyes and simply seeing what everybody else can see.'

'Everybody, indisputably?' asked Powers gently.

'Yes,' snapped Andrews.

'The CIA, the FBI, do they consider them security risks?'

'No, of course not, they look at it differently. A security

risk to them is someone who would deliberately jeopardise the nation. Even I don't think for one moment that either of them is going to pass secrets or whatever. What we mean is that they might do something that will endanger the world, or give some nutter a job just because they are black or a woman or a man or a white or whatever flavour is needed to balance the books this week.'

'That is why we need the dossier, so that the CIA and the FBI see it that way as well. The press might even help us, we'll see.'

'So what do you expect the CIA to do?'

'Don't tell me you don't remember 22nd November 1963?'

'You *are* mad! D'you reckon they knock off another President just because we give them a couple of dossiers?'

'Correctly handled, yes.'

'And if they won't do what you want them to do?'

'Then we do it ourselves.'

Andrews stared at Powers, the blood draining out of his face. 'But,' he stammered then started to shake his head. 'I mean Jesus Christ, man! If the wheels were ever on your trolley they're way off now. Are you seriously saying that we are spending our time researching this asshole who's become President in order to bump him off?'

'Yes. Does that surprise you?'

'Nothing surprises me about you any more, Harry, nothing.'

'Are you averse to the idea?' Powers natural calmness was unruffled.

'If you mean, if someone did away with him would I think it wrong, then,' he paused, 'no, probably not. But don't get the wrong idea. I've thumped a few lads in the bar in my time and will again but I'm not into assassinating Presidents. That's another game, another league.'

'So you want out?' asked Edwards quietly.

'*You* knew?' roared Andrews.

'No, but it seemed to be the only eventual outcome. If it

transpired that the man was bad for America, bad for the world, then we would have to do something about it.'

'Who knows what would be left to protect come 1996, the way he's going.'

'You're mad, both of you. Count me out,' snorted Matt Andrews. He slammed his Scotch on the table, grabbed his stetson and left.

'He may be a problem,' said Edwards.

'I think he'll come round,' said Harry Powers, smiling. 'I have a dossier on him which Ali will have given him by now. It's somewhat thicker than Hillary's and also contains pictures.'

'And what have you on me?'

Powers smiled a perfectly wicked smile. 'Let's get back to the job in hand. We have much to do.'

It was a soiree on a grand scale, the like of which Washington's magnificent Georgian mansions had not seen for over a generation. The society hostesses plotted and planned to ensure that they were seated with the right people, would be seen and photographed in the company of the right people.

Calculating mothers spent days ensuring an invitation for their sons and daughters and made the most meticulous arrangements to ensure that they would casually meet the right sort of potential long term partner. Golius would have been impressed by the attention to detail. The gossip columns ran to yards rather than inches during the preceding week but no contact was made with the Clintons. They were not to be granted the honour.

'Do you really mean to tell me that they deliberately didn't invite the Clintons? That's what I call style!'

'Is it true the Clintons refused the invitation six times? Gee, that's too bad.'

And so the whispering continued all evening and on into the early hours, much to Sally-Anne Knight's amusement. No-one would ever forget this party. The one the President had not refused but the one to which he had not been invited.

'Have you seen Brad, darling?' asked Bridget shortly after eleven thirty, by which time Sally-Anne was moving into a state of highly satisfied oblivion.

'Not for some time, Bridget darling,' she replied with just a hint of scandal in her voice.

'What about that tramp Angie Tourle?' asked Bridget barely disguising her venom. She too had enjoyed a few tipples.

'Oh, I can see her now,' replied Jenny Wilson, as relieved as Bridget to see that Angie had not disappeared with Brad. 'Look, she's dancing with that old senator from the midwest.' The three of them followed her gaze. Jenny had her own designs on Brad Harworth and although now in her late forties she still had the looks and energy of a woman twenty years younger.

'The silly man,' said Bridget despairingly. 'He'll give himself a heart attack behaving like that with the little tramp.' They watched the two of them simulating sex while clasping each other in the centre of the dance floor. 'But that still doesn't answer where Brad is?' Bridget's voice was troubled; little tramps you knew about you could keep an eye on, ones you didn't know about were another matter, although a more difficult problem.

'I've not seen Jeff for a while either, darling. Maybe the boys are all together doing whatever it is boys do when they're alone together,' said Sally-Anne who added with little or no subtlety, 'Which I'm sure is very different from what they do when they're alone with girls!'

'You've got a one track mind, Sally-Anne, and it's disgusting,' said Bridget.

'It's no different from yours, darling, except that I don't have a facial adviser,' she snarled back. 'Perhaps you'll be embarrassed by what Jenny is about to tell me. Maybe you should leave us alone.'

'I rather doubt that,' replied Bridget, eager to consume

even the tiniest morsel. 'Who's the subject?'

'Bill,' said Sally-Anne slyly.

'Bill?' exclaimed Bridget who, like many others she knew, privately had the hots for the youthful-looking President.

'The same,' said Jenny. 'You know I was at Oxford with him?'

'No, I didn't,' Bridget replied, thinking, I didn't know she was *that* old.

'Oh yes,' said Jenny smugly, milking the connection for all it was worth, not admitting that she had never actually met the man. However, she did know people who knew him well, including her best friend Sarah, who had idolised the suave, sensual post graduate. 'Bill and I go back a long way, well before Hillary.'

'Whatever did he see in that woman?' asked Sally-Anne of no-one in particular.

'Power, darling, power,' replied Bridget with a mixture of bitchiness and honesty.

'Well, it certainly wasn't sex appeal like all his other girl friends before and since,' smirked Jenny. 'I hear Larry Nichols says he got proof of five affairs between the last two State Governor elections.'

'Did you ever....' began Sally-Anne, who had lusted after the President ever since she had first met him at a Democratic rally for George McGovern back in 1972. That was before she had started neglecting herself and going to seed.

'You really mustn't ask a girl a question like that, Sally-Anne. How could she possibly answer?' Jenny said impishly.

'No,' said Bridget, 'it's a bit like that nasty little man on New Hampshire TV asking Bill if he'd ever committed adultery. He had to say I wouldn't tell you if I had, didn't he?'

It became increasingly obvious as the conversation developed that what was really irking the three women was not that the Clintons would not come to dinner but that his reputation for sexual exploits was legendary, true or otherwise, and that they wanted him yet could not have him.

'So tell us about Oxford, darling. Was it really all that they said it was, parties and more parties.

'More or less, but I shouldn't talk about it now, even to you. Not now that Bill's President, it could only embarrass him.'

'But how could you embarrass him just talking to us, darling? We're all friends, and, more than that, we're all Democrats. It was us that stuck by him when all those terrible stories were circulating about the women in his life. When all those lies were being made up about Gennifer Flowers, and that nasty little man Larry Nichols was trying to dirt him in Arkansas. We're his friends, darling.

'But what we're talking about now is before all that, before he was even married and I for one feel happier with a President that's seen some life and sown a few wild oats than I would with one that hasn't.' Bridget was desperate for gossip, truth had never concerned her.

'Well, I suppose,' said Jenny, feigning reluctance, 'if you promise not to repeat a word then I could tell you about just one party. But you know what the press are like, if they get to hear about it they'll drag it out again just to try and trash poor Bill, even though they were doing just the same thing at his age and still are!'

'Of course, we won't say anything, darling, will we, Sally-Anne? You can rely on us.'

'No, not a word,' replied Sally-Anne through a thickening alcoholic haze that would make it difficult for her to remember anyway.

'Well in that case, maybe I can tell you about just one evening. Actually it wasn't really an evening or a night it was a day or more of sheer ecstasy, pure physical excitement and titillation.'

'Really,' said Bridget hardly believing the statement and suddenly realising how often Jenny's name had come up in Brad's conversation recently. Was she tracking a bimbo when she should be tracking a trained and experienced tigress? Trained, at least in part if what she thought she was about to hear was true, by the then rampant and all conquering future President.

'I'd gone to the party with my boyfriend, a lovely lad called Hamdi. He was arrested that night for being in possession, but he was about the only person there not on it, as far as I knew. I never saw much of him after that, no-one did. He kept himself to himself. Muslim, I think. I know he said it would bring great shame on his family, although the rest of us just laughed it off.

'Anyway, it started about six one evening with a group of us drinking as we often did in The Turf. One or two people were smoking the weed then, but they banned you if they caught you on it in there, so most people waited until we got to the party. It was quite an affair, hundreds and hundreds of people. There were folk making it everywhere but Bill was playing in the band for part of the time. I just watched him making love to that sax, his rhythm, his movement was mind blowing.

'It was later that we met on the stairs. I'd just been to the john and he was obviously going in that direction and I just lost control of myself. There was no excuse. It just happened.'

Bridget wanted to yawn, but Sally-Anne was now agog just waiting for the next mouth teasing sentence. Silly bitch, thought Bridget who had probably screwed twice as many men as the pair of them put together and no doubt given them considerably greater pleasure.

'So what did you say in this uncontrollable state?' asked Bridget, stifling a fake yawn.

'I asked him if he needed any help with his ablutions!'

'His what?' asked Sally-Anne amazed.

'His ablutions. That's what my father always called them, but he knew what I meant alright.'

' "Well that depends," he said. "On what?" I asked.'

' "On how steady your hand is, for one thing!" '

'Ooh,' said Sally Anne, with a sharp intake of breath.

Bridget shook her head. 'I don't believe a word of it, not

a single word,' she declared after the oohing and aahing had died down. 'I know he tried the weed a few times but Bill Clinton knew then where he was going and *if* he was screwing anywhere, and I'm not saying he wasn't, it wouldn't have been on the stairs at some drugged up party. He was social climbing, attending the smart parties, wooing the debs and making contacts. That guy's never done one thing in his life that wasn't a part of the "promote Bill Clinton" campaign to further his career, and I say that includes marrying Hillary.'

Jenny looked hard at her. How ever did Brad put up with the bitch. No wonder he had to look elsewhere for his pleasures, poor man. 'And that master plan to further his career I suppose includes getting out his tool from time to time to play away from home?'

'*You* don't know that he does.'

'He's as good as admitted it. Your trouble is you're a has been horny bitch that can't get as much as you want now. The young men don't fancy you like they used to and you certainly can't get near the President. Word is that the reason he won't come to your house, despite the dozens of invitations, is that he knows you'll make a beeline for him. And believe me, my dear lady, he would rather lose office than face that again.'

Jenny didn't even see the champagne until it was dripping all over her head. Bridget walked away from then, a smile on her face. She had wanted to do that to the bitch for a very long time. It might have been a good vintage, it might have been a waste, but it was worth it. She clutched her empty glass and searched out that handsome young waiter for a refill.

CHAPTER FIVE

'The girls seem to be having fun, Jeff,' said Brad Harworth sitting in Jeff Knight's opulent study at his Washington home while the party-goers enjoyed themselves all around.

'Yes, Jeff,' agreed Miles Waterford, 'this sure was a great idea. You'll lift the morale of the Washington Democrats with this party, and God knows it needs lifting.' His voice had all the usual buoyancy.

'It was not their morale that prompted me to arrange this gathering, Miles.' Jeff's tone was almost officious and took Miles by surprise.

'It wasn't?' replied Miles.

'Brad knows what I'm thinking about, but I would like to bring you in on my thinking, if you're interested.'

'Interested in what, Jeff? You know there's always room in my wallet for another deal or two!' boomed the giant from Alaska. The big cheerful man was often thought of as Canadian rather than American. In manner and dress he resembled far more a backwoods lumberjack than a wealthy American of independent means. He did work, however, in his way. His love was fishing so he wrote fishing books. Whether they sold was irrelevant. It gave him pleasure just to do it. He had never married and spent most of his time living alone in his cabin on Lliamna Lake. Apart from his obvious physical strength, his most prominent features were a bulbous nose and even larger flappy ears. Everything about Miles Waterford was large, including his sense of humour and his generosity. He was one of America's greatest supporters of good causes.

'This is not exactly a deal, Miles,' replied Brad with an air of solemnness.

'Lighten up guys, this is a party, not a wake!' he boomed.

'How d'you feel about the President, Miles?' asked Jeff getting straight to the point.

'Asshole!'

'That's it?' asked Harworth with surprise.

'It's enough ain't it. It says it all. A man who says "yes" to everything and then forgets what he's even said yes to, is a asshole. You know I read the other day that his mother was talking about the fact that he forgets things and she said, "Bill and I have always been able to do that. I know people are amazed at this, but we would always put away anything unpleasant." What sort of jerk is that?

'One who says, "People expect me to remember things I don't remember all of or to share things I thought I was never meant to share," ' replied Jeff.

'What, like Gennifer Flowers' bed?' roared Waterford knocking back his bourbon.

'Right!' cried Brad, patting Miles' back. 'Right!'

'Mind you,' continued Waterford, 'he sure remembers going to therapy with his brother when Roger was caught in possession of cocaine. Even said he learnt about himself then!'

'I read that, Miles, but what a man for President.' The solemness had returned.

'Tell me about it. I'd given up on us before New Hampshire and even afterwards. Tsongas scared the shit out of people with what his programme would cost and Clinton just plain scared the shit out of people. I reckoned Uncle George had a one way ticket back to Pennsylvania Avenue.'

'We all did, so what changed?' The solemnness was still there.

'You asking me?' said Miles lazily.

They both nodded. Pair of bores, he thought as he looked at them. Sat behind desks all day, no fighting spirit, no sense of adventure, no passion. Both just over fifty, both pretty conservative in their approach to life, except for the women. In fact, he wondered what they were doing in the Democrat Party anyway.

Brad Harworth was actually slightly older than Jeff Knight, but Waterford would not have recognised either of them away from their natural habitat, where, with beautiful younger women, they behaved like adolescents. At times people thought in such situations that they were brothers, slimly built around five feet ten, dark complexions with no special features, they were both just one of the crowd. Even the scar on Jeff's left cheek from Vietnam had faded over the years, but he wouldn't have it removed. To him it was a constant reminder of his youth.

Neither of them replied immediately.

'You asking *me*?' Miles said again.

'Yes, Miles, we are,' replied Knight sitting in the floral two seater sofa. 'What do *you* think changed it?'

'Balls, nerve,' replied Waterford functionally.

'By which you mean what exactly, Miles?'

'Hey, what is this, the third degree?'

'Curiosity, Miles. Things aren't right, that's all,' said Brad trying to lower the tension.

'That's sure true!'

'And we're too close to it here in Washington, that's why we're interested in the way you see it.'

'Well, I can respect that. Must be sheer hell living here in the midst of all the political intrigue and infighting.' Brad and Jeff both missed the heavy sarcasm of Miles' words.

'So what do you mean by balls, Miles?'

'It was also that guy James Carville. Mad as a hatter, but one hell of an organiser who can see an opportunity where others see disaster. Just look at what he did with the Gennifer Flowers cock-up.' Miles paused to smile weakly at his joke and the others obliged him by returning the smirk just as weakly. 'Just as the scandal was blooming,' he continued, smiling again, 'he talked Clinton and the wife woman into going onto television live to talk about their marriage. Hell, it was embarrassing to watch but it worked, didn't it?'

'It worked alright,' said Brad with remorse.

'Hey, Brad, we won! For twelve years we've been shut out. We won, God damn it man. Clinton won it for us. His sheer tenacity, his refusal to quit, like the salesman that just doesn't hear objections, that's what won it. I love those guys.'

'So it was Clinton not Carville?'

'Team effort. Clinton had the brassneck nerve and the stamina but Carville is a ruthless, intuitive strategist. He's aggressive all the time, never lets up, and he pushed Clinton all the way. Mind you, to be fair, Clinton can think on his feet, he sees chances where others see brick walls.'

'So what's wrong in the White House? He doesn't even see brick walls there after he's walked into them!'

'The woman.'

'As simple as that?'

'Yep. I credit Clinton with shutting her up and repackaging her when she started to become a liability. All that crap about vote for us and you get two for one.'

'Clinton not Carville?' asked Brad gently.

'Yep. It might have been Carville's idea, I don't know. But I sure as hell know that, hard bastard though he is, she'd have seen him off if it had come from him. She'd have eaten him. No, it was Clinton put that into place, just as he got her using her married name and out of jeans when he lost in Arkansas. No Carville around then, was there?'

'No,' they were forced to agree.

'So why did she go back to using her maiden name after the Inauguration?'

'Now that I don't know,' replied Waterford thoughtfully as he sat for the first time. He poured himself yet another bourbon.

'Mighty fine drop of spirit you've got here, Jeff.'

'Glad you like it, Miles.'

'Sure beats some of the rough stuff we have back home!'

'Do you think it's because she feels untouchable now?'

'How the hell do I know that? I sure as hell wouldn't touch her, but I'm sure he must!'

'D'you think Carville would sharpen up the act if he was at the White House?' asked Brad.

'Hell, no, the man's a self confessed lunatic. It might be black now in the White House, but it would be far worse with him there. He's for winning elections where you can change your mind and forget you ever did things, not for running a damn country.'

'But isn't that the way the country is being run?'

'Maybe, but Carville himself said, "I wouldn't want to belong to any Government that would have me in it," and I reckon that's a relief to Clinton because it's one payoff he hasn't got to make.'

'Okay,' said Brad thoughtfully, 'so are payoffs the problem?'

Miles felt increasingly uncomfortable and poured himself yet another bourbon. He didn't like big, grand houses at the best of times, especially when they were lavishly furnished. He liked the open, the mud and grass of a river bank or the side of a lake. The fields and mountains, the great outdoors. His favourite spot was near Bethel on the Kanektok River in Alaska. His mind drifted from the luxury of the heavily draped room to Alaska, the last great wilderness, at its heart the Kanektok River where he fought the chinook salmon as it raced off in the fast currents of the main river, testing him to the full. The chinook salmon was his greatest challenge, a fast, hard fighter. In the summer the river was so clear that he could see the fish swimming, streaking beneath the surface water, their attractive red colouring clearly visible. The room looked drab against this memory. Once hooked, the fish reacted with long surging runs, shaking their heads, creating periods of arm aching tension for any angler, even one as strong as him, as they hung broadside in the current. It was hardly surprising that they were known as the king salmon, the rod caught record catch being a mind blowing 97 pounds 12 ounces.

In the summer months Miles would spend days in his boat on the crystal clear Kanektok River chasing the king salmon, rarely showing any interest in the sockeye, chum and humpback salmon or the Dolly Varden char, arctic grayling and rainbow trout that inhabited the river in quantity.

'Look guys, I can see that you want to know what a hillbilly like me thinks, especially as that's what Clinton is really.

They're all hillbillies in Arkansas. I've even heard it said that some of the more rustic characters down there go out pot-shooting at Hell's Angels for sport! But, hillbilly though I might be, this is a party, lighten up!'

Brad stood and walked slowly towards the window. 'I'm sorry you think we're leaning on you, Miles, but what you have to tell us is really important. We've been given a special task to perform, not for the Party but for the Country and your input is vital. We need to know how you see it and maybe, just maybe, you will also have a role to play in saving this Country if it comes to it.'

'What sort of melodramatic bullshit is that?' Miles sneered.

'It isn't bullshit.'

'Then who's given you this task?'

'You wouldn't believe us even if we could tell you,' said Brad, filling Miles' glass again.

'I think we'd best terminate the conversation before we say too much, don't you, Jeff?' continued Brad in a low key, retaking his seat.

'I fear so,' replied Jeff, 'we'll drink up and rejoin the party.'

'Thanks anyway for sharing your opinions, Miles. It does help, believe me.'

When he came to look back on it Miles Waterford would not believe how easy it had been for the two professional manipulators to sway him. He later recalled the words, which sounded almost childish, but he also recalled the conviction with which they were delivered. It was the drama that had made him stay.

'Well you just hold on there a second or two. I've not said I won't help. It's just that I'm not into all this heavy analysis. I like to keep life simple. That way I get to keep control of it, understand it. Now if you guys want to talk about the President and his shortcomings, why, that's fine with me.'

The other two hid their relief, but did not like what followed.

'I don't get into Washington too often, thank the Lord, and I rarely get to parties like this. Let's not spoil it. I want to go down there out into the garden and enjoy the party some more.'

'Sure, Miles, we can talk later,' said Jeff.

'You bet we can. You two fellas come on up to my cabin on Lliamna Lake and we'll jaw away all day and night for bit. I feel comfortable there, I can think there, can't do that properly down here.'

'Well….'

'I'll not have another word said. You've shown me hospitality tonight, I'll return it. Not as grand but every bit as good, you'll see.'

'Yes,' said Brad positively, realising it was the only way to pursue the matter but also immediately laying a contingency plan in his mind. 'We'll do that, in fact I think we could both enjoy a spot of fishing.'

'That we would, Miles, thank you,' said Jeff picking up Brad's lead.

'Now we've got one or two things to sort out, Miles, so if you're happy why don't you get right back to the party and we'll join you in a bit?'

'That's mighty hospitable of you. I'll do just that,' said Miles cheerfully drowning his bourbon and leaving the room. He'd bought some time to think. Besides, he had been taught to get a fight onto his land, onto his terms, when he had no idea what it was about. What the hell were they driving at?

'Is he spoofing us?' asked Jeff as the door close.

'I don't think so,' replied Brad thoughtfully.

'You don't think he caught on quicker than we wanted?'

'No, but I'm going to get Angie to give him a night or even a few days he won't forget, just as insurance.'

'The bugged apartment?'

'Yes, I changed the videos before I left last time. They'll run for eight hours, we can change them again if we need to.'

'I'm sure eight hours will provide enough!'

'That depends how long he sleeps. Did you see what he drank in here? And he never turned a hair.'

'Michael,' said Lech the instant the phone was answered. 'I'm going to London for a few weeks. With any luck when I come back I will know all about the Kennedy assassination and we might even be able to go public with the truth.' Lech felt guilty about the deception, he liked Michael, but it was too soon to burden him with his intentions and indeed it might never be right to do so. Michael was a promising young lawyer, Lech had lived his life, what right would he have to jeopardise that future for his own revenge and recriminations?

'That *is* fantastic,' replied Michael barely able to conceal his excitement and wondering why he was trying. If Lech really could solve the mystery of the Kennedy assassination it would be the making of his already promising legal career.

'Have you found Gillespi?'

'Yes, he's still alive and has been living down in Mexico. But he won't come back here under any circumstances or for any amount of money. I'm not even sure he's going to turn up in London, but he said he will and from the way he sounded on the phone I think he's straight.

'What did you say when you rang him?'

'I told him the truth. I am an old friend of Lee Harvey Oswald and I read him the letter. I don't think he believed me at first, but I copied him the letter and the photos, that made him think!'

'Wasn't he worried that you were the firm and had finally found him?'

'Yeah, but I told him if that was the case I wouldn't be ringing and sending him pictures, I'd be sending the undertakers.'

'And he accepted it?'

'More or less.'

'But how did you find him? Surely if it was that easy for you and it's not taken long, then the CIA would have found him?'

'The thought occurred to me and I don't know the answer yet. I hope to learn a lot in London.'

'When are you back?'

'Not sure yet, a few weeks is my guess.'

'I'll see you then.'

'Sure, I'll be in touch, maybe even ring you from London.'

'I'll look forward to it.'

As Lech replaced the receiver he felt even more guilty. In business he was and always had been a hard bastard who often operated with no regard for any rules at all. To his family he was considerate and loyal. Michael was family and Sammy's death didn't change that. The question he could not bring himself to even ask was, would he involve Michael if Sammy were still alive? In the end he avoided it by telling himself that if Sammy were still alive he would not be embarked on his present course. That is what he had told Michael and it *was* true.

Lech was looking forward to London, it was three years since his last visit. He decided not to use a big hotel but to stay in a small privately owned club he had joined twenty years ago, the Fox House Club in Clarges Street. He knew several Americans who used it and had been introduced to it himself by Bob Lang, the Detroit steel magnate.

When he made his reservation and asked after the owner, Stanley Bricusse, he was told that Stanley had retired the previous February. The only difference to the Club was that the ground floor had been refurbished and the menu extended. Some people, the smart set mainly, would have considered the Club a little tatty previously, but Lech hoped it had not lost its old London feel and charm by being refurbished; he was not to be too disappointed.

Gillespi was living in Mexico under a false name but all he had told Lech was that he would travel under another identity and did not wish to be met at Heathrow. Lech had cabled $10,000 to cover Gillespi's expenses, which had been collected from the bank immediately it arrived.

Gillespi was uneasy, but he was an old man and for years he had longed to tell the truth. Maybe this was the best way, to tell a friend of Oswald's and let it all come out after his death. He was not relishing the journey and, as he left the small but comfortable bungalow that had been his home for the last seven years, he seriously wondered if he would ever see it again. The firm no longer worried him at seventy seven death was no longer an issue to worry about. It was to be a long journey, that worried him.

'Adios,' he called to his neighbour Maria as he slammed the door shut behind him, his small holdall giving no hint of the time he would be away.

'Adios,' she replied with an infectious smile.

'I shall be away several weeks, Maria,' he said, not wanting her to worry. She was a kind soul with seven children and no husband. He had slipped out one day two years ago and simply not come back. No-one knew why.

Gillespi's route took him south to Brazil and from Rio de Janerio he flew to Frankfurt, Frankfurt to Paris and from there by train to Calais and Hovercraft to Dover. He had spent just one night in Rio and another in Frankfurt, but arrived in London the night before Zielinski. He was still fit. He had kept himself that way as a matter of principle.

Although Lech offered to make arrangements for him to stay at the Fox House Club, George had declined. He had lunch at the Royal Overseas League in Park Place and then spent an hour in the men's cloakroom closeted in a cubicle with a mirror and the contents of his holdall.

He emerged with his still rich black hair now grey ginger and looking a few years younger than previously. He was sure the Pole would have an up to date photo. Then, having visited Simpsons in Piccadilly and Austin Reed in Regent Street to buy clothes, Ted Somerfield checked into the Fox House Club at ten past six on the Tuesday, saying almost nothing and retired immediately to his room where he watched television all evening. Lech had told Gillespi about the Fox House Club when he had offered to book him in. Stanley Bricusse's retirement had made it even easier to book in on a fictitious recommendation.

After a hearty English breakfast the sprightly old man took a stroll around Green Park and watched the tourists outside Buckingham Palace. The Royal Standard was flying, but he never saw the Queen enter or leave in the hour or more he sat there. He decided not to visit.

He lunched in the Fox House Club, abandoning his intention to be an Australian the moment he saw the six foot six Australian barman. Immediately he was Canadian, not what he wanted, but it would have to do.

'How long you here for, sir?' asked the amiable barman, David.

'Not sure yet. Just looking around the old haunts, spent some time here during the war.'

'Not been back since?' asked Ann the redheaded young grandmother who managed the bar, restaurant and reservations.

'No, not at all,' he replied with a soft smile. 'Often thought about it but never got around to it. I said to myself recently, if you don't do it now, Ted, you never will.'

'Well you just enjoy it, love, and if there's anything we can do to help just let me know. If you need a restaurant or cab or whatever just let me or Karl, the butler, know.' And was a genuinely warm eastender.

'That's very kind of you.'

'No trouble. We get a lot of people like you coming here to stay. Many of them old seafaring friends of the last owner, he only retired early this year. In fact we've got an American gentleman coming to stay tonight for a bit who was asking after Stanley when he booked up.

'Really? I'll look forward to meeting him. It's amazing how often us Canadians get mistaken for Americans!' said George with a smile. 'Now can I get you good people a drink?'

'Oh I didn't,' began Ann concerned that she had upset

Mr Somerfield by calling him an American. She knew how touchy some people could be about that sort of thing.

'My dear young lady, I am not in the slightest offended and I would like you both to have a drink with me. I simply make the point for clarity, nothing more,' he said, delighted to have found it so easy to establish the fact that he was not an American.

'Thank you, Mr Somerfield, I'd like a white wine and David usually has a lager. Actually I'm not sure that he is an American, he sounded like one but his name sounds Polish.'

'I'm sure we'll see when he gets here. I'm not as young as I was so I think I'll just catch a little sleep. Could you wake me at six and perhaps arrange a restaurant for about eight o'clock and a taxi if it's far.'

'Leave it with me, Mr Somerfield. Any special type of cooking you'd like?'

'Surprise me, my dear. I eat everything.'

The administration was very informal in the small club and Gillespi noticed that his name had simply been ticked across the diary on the hall table after he had booked in. When he arose from his afternoon sleep and returned to the bar, Zielinski's name had also been ticked.

'Mr Somerfield,' said Ann as he entered the bar. 'Good sleep?'

'Yes, thank you and I'll have a Scotch and water please, no ice.'

'I've booked you a table at The Greenhouse in Hays Mews and the taxi will pick you up at five to eight. You might just see Mr Zielinski before you go, he booked in while you were asleep and asked to be woken at seven thirty.'

Lech had also asked Ann to arrange an evening meal for him. She thought it would be a bit pointed, perhaps even rude to book them both into the same restaurant when they didn't know each other and so he was going to Langans in Stratton Street, but not until nine o'clock and as he had mentioned Gerry's Club would no doubt be going on whereas Mr Somerfield, she reasoned, would simply want to come back to bed.

'I'm expecting someone to phone me, Ann,' said Lech as he left the lobby to walk to Langans, 'probably not until tomorrow, but I've not got his name! Friend of a friend. We agreed to meet up as we were both going to be in London this week. If I'm not here could you arrange a time for him to come here or I'll meet him wherever, I'm free all day Thursday and Friday.'

'Certainly, Mr Zielinski, no problem. You just leave that to me.'

Steve Waite hated his turns on the Network Shift, known as "Ns". They were boring and, on the few occasions that he'd received any calls, they'd been non-events.

The CIA had a network of informers, sympathisers, sleepers, spies and ex-agents around the entire world. Although they each had different contact numbers the calls were all routed through to the one place — The Network Room. A small clinical room on the first floor at Langley with two consoles, each housing a computerised switch board, which were permanently manned. When a call came in the dialled number appeared on the screen with details of the caller and his identity codes.

It was Steve's third night on the shift, only two more and that would be the end of his "Ns" for another six months. Thirty two years old, the football mad agent had joined the CIA when his promising professional career with the Dallas Cowboys had been cut short by a serious shoulder injury eight years ago. He still kept himself fit by regular exercise and a sensible diet, which never included alcohol and smoking was something he abhorred.

Women had always played a significant part in his life and he was fast approaching the age at which he thought it would be right to settle down — but what sane woman would marry a CIA agent?

His physique gave him his choice of women. Standing

several inches taller than most men, with sharp angular features, broad square shoulder and black curly hair, the fashion and film world had been a serious alternative to Langley when he was forced to change his vocation. But they held no appeal to him. They were synthetic, shallow with simulated excitement. Steve needed his adrenalin to run for real.

His screen flickered into life as the phone rang.

'Hello, Langley Motors, how can I help you?'

'11-17-26-81, Northern Bear.'

'When does the sun rise?'

'After the morning call.'

'Everyday?'

'Except Sundays.'

'18-96-47'

'21-09-83'

'Hi, I'm Steve, what can I do for you?'

'I'd like to meet.'

'Why?' They were always reluctant to arrange meetings without any knowledge of the subject, apart from the risk of exposing an agent.

'Is this line secure?'

'Yes.'

'I believe I have some information that could save the President's life.'

Steve pushed the loudspeaker button, all calls were taped automatically and then pushed a second button that put the call onto the loudspeaker on the Duty Officer's desk. The details of the caller then appeared automatically on his screen as well.

'Say again, please.'

'I believe I have some information that could save the President's life.'

'Can you be more explicit?'

'Not on the phone.'

Steve's earpiece came to life. 'Arrange a meeting,' said the Duty Officer. This sympathiser was not considered to be a time waster.

'Are you happy to travel?'

'Yes,' came the answer in the ear piece.

'You say where and when.'

'Point 39, seven thirty tomorrow evening.'

'Agree,' came the instruction.

'Agreed.'

The line went dead and Steve's earpiece summoned him to the Duty Officer.

'We've known this man for twenty years. He's sound,' said the Duty Officer scrolling the information on the caller across his screen. 'Not the type to hype a situation.'

'What are all these Points?'

'His idea according to the computer. An agreed rendezvous in every major city identified by a Point Number.

'Here,' continued the Duty Officer passing Steve a computer print out. 'A bar JFK airport.'

'Do I go alone?'

'No, I'll assign Scott Pulsat to you.'

'Fine.'

'I'll have you covered in half an hour for the "N", speak to Scott and leave you both to get on your way.'

'Right.'

John Edwards had moved to Los Angeles because his wife was attracted by the glamour of the movie set. Most of the WASPs who lived in Orange County were similarly attracted. But they had begun to live in fear of the violence and crime which gripped the city centre. The beating up of Rodney King by four white policemen and their original acquittal had not caused a problem but merely highlighted it. After film making, crime was probably the biggest industry in the city. In some sections of the City, the criminal classes were a law unto themselves.

It was against that backdrop that Richard Riordan, a white multi millionaire estimated to be worth $100 million, was elected the first Republican Mayor for over thirty years in June 1993. Tom Bradley, the black Democratic Mayor had held office for twenty years had retired and not sought re-election, but even so the previously unknown Riordan's victory over City Councilman Michael Woo, a liberal Democrat, by fifty four percent to forty six percent came as a major shock.

It was not such a shock to John Edwards. He had voted for Riordan, who spent over $4 million on his campaign, purely because he believed he would do something about the crime explosion. Time would tell but the combination of local unrest and disappointment in the first months of the Clinton Presidency had lead to a lot of staunch Democrats to support Riordan.

A week after the election Harry Powers came to stay for a few days.

'I know you've got local problems here, John, but when a Republican get's elected in Los Angeles then the situation *is* serious, really serious, and we must act.'

'I agree, Harry, but I wanted to talk to you without Matt and to introduce you to someone here who just might help us with our task. I'm not sure Matt is ready to accept the responsibility yet.'

'What had you in mind?'

'Well it was Waco and that jerk David Koresh that gave me the idea.'

'Just another of the President's little mishaps. Whatever possessed him to go in like that?'

'To be fair we don't know that he did and Janet Reno did say she had taken the decision without him knowing.'

'Maybe, but its hard to believe he wasn't aware of what was going on, especially after his experience with those Cuban refugees at Fort Chaffee when he was Governor of Arkansas. They went on an arson spree and burnt down a barracks, forty injured and Clinton had the National Guard put on alert.'

'I didn't know about that,' said Edwards. He was relying on the other two to research the situation. He always relied on others to research situations, but would never shirk from taking decisions based on what he was told. It also gave him a cop out when things went wrong. He was only acting on the available information.

Although the two dossiers never left Powers' side, he no longer referred to them during every conversation. He could almost recite them work perfectly, robotically.

'Yes, hell of a problem and Frank White capitalised on it when he beat him in 1980. Mind you, he had so much to trade on then, including the rises in gasoline and automobile taxes which made Clinton so unpopular, that it would have taken a miracle to save him and he actually only lost by forty eight percent to fifty two percent.'

'I knew nothing about that, Harry, but certainly Waco was a monumental balls-up. Why didn't he just carry on waiting?'

'We'll never know. Maybe there was a real danger that Koresh was going to ignite the place on God's orders anyway. You can never tell with those people.'

'I know someone who says otherwise and I want you to meet him, that's why I asked you down.'

'Some people call him a kidnapper, but I'd call him a snatcher back. There are so many of these fanatical religious groups around now that are brainwashing people into joining them that a whole new industry has grown up snatching back juveniles who've been coerced into joining them.'

'Only juveniles?' asked Powers. 'What about husbands or wives who get sucked in?'

'That's a problem because if they're adults then they are responsible for themselves. People have brought charges against the snatchers for getting them out against their will when they've been hired to do so by friends or family.'

'So they go in and snatch them back. What interest is that to us?'

'They actually do far more than that because having snatched the kids back they have to be de-programmed. If you just left them they'd go right on back into the sect. They have been brainwashed. You must remember the Jonestown massacre when hundreds of people killed themselves, not one of them can have been in control of their mind.'

'Okay, but why does it interest us?'

'Most of these groups are professional and highly ethical people who work in small teams and charge in the region of $30,000 plus expenses for a job, so they don't earn that much each. But I have come across one member of a group based here in Los Angeles who is totally professional but not quite so ethical.'

'And he can be bought?' asked Powers now appreciating the significance of what Edwards was building up to.

'Yes. He can be bought, but it is better than that.'

'Then tell me for God's sake and stop going all round the houses, John,' said Powers irritably.

'He's got Aids, and he reckons he caught it at a Democratic Convention nine years ago.'

'So he's motivated. But a guy like that must have spent years screwing all sorts of women around Los Angeles and the chances of catching Aids must be greater here than in Madison Square Garden at a Democratic Convention.'

'True, but what matters to us is that he thinks he caught it there. What do we care if it's true or not?'

'Agreed, so when do we meet him?'

'Tonight, nine o'clock.'

'What do we know about him? Can he be belied upon and most importantly is he able to do what we require?' asked Powers with all his usual lack of charm.

'He comes very well recommended and I have no doubt that he can do what we require of him. I assume we have decided then?'

'Do you see any alternative?' asked Powers menacingly.

'No,' replied Edwards after a short pause and with some exasperation.

'Good,' responded Powers with purpose. 'And what of this recommendation, can we rely on it?'

'Yes, it's from a friend of mine.'

Powers was somewhat taken aback. He had not previously considered assassination to be something that either

Edwards or any of his friends would have had experience of, any more than he had himself. 'Tell me more.'

'One of my friends discovered that his daughter had been sucked into one of those off beat religious groups.'

'Like Koresh?'

'Similar, but smaller, yes.

'Anyway, he hired this man Friggli to get her back.'

'Which he did?'

'Yes.'

'But how does that qualify him for our task?' asked Powers giving every indication of becoming irritated again.

'If you would only shut up and listen for a moment instead of behaving in such an objectionable way you might learn,' barked Edwards, as surprised as Powers by his tone.

The two men were silent for several minutes. 'Okay,' said Powers at length, realising that he would have to accept the story the way it was to be told. If Edwards did have the assassin, then half his problem was solved. 'I'm sorry, please carry on.'

'Initially Friggli asked if my friends simply wanted their daughter back or whether or not they wanted the cult leaders taken out altogether.'

'And?' said Powers totally unable to control his natural manner.

'At that stage all they wanted was their daughter back. They didn't really care for anything beyond that.'

'But?'

Edwards decided to hold his temper this time. It was no good, Harry Powers was Harry Powers and would behave as Harry Powers always did, whatever anyone did or said.

'When she was safely back home and had been deprogrammed they changed their minds and he killed them all, very clinically, very efficiently and didn't even charge any extra fees. You'd have approved,' added Edwards cynically.

Powers ignored the last sentence. 'Which suggests that he enjoyed it. That *is* good.'

'Yes, there were seven of them and he dealt with them slowly over three months in order to avoid a big publicity clash. In fact I heard that the police were so pleased to be rid of the cult leaders that they took no notice of the last couple of deaths, which were barely reported, and they have closed their file.'

'Good, good,' said Powers thoughtfully, 'but what changed the parents minds? Did that influence Friggli?'

'I don't know. But I can't see him having any compassion for a draft dodger. As for what changed their minds, I'd rather not talk about it. I find it too upsetting.'

'Nonsense,' shouted Powers, 'Friggli knew, so I must know before I meet him.'

'If you must,' began Edwards nervously.

'Yes, I must,' insisted Powers.

'She had drifted towards the cult the way most kids do, by being slowly worked on in a coffee bar until she was ready to be enticed to their "temple". However, when she did visit them she decided it was a mistake and wanted to leave....'

'But they wouldn't let her.' It was a statement not a question.

'That's right. They suggested she sit and talk it over for a while, presumably thinking that she was indoctrinated enough for them to persuade her to stay. She can't remember how long it was, but it was several hours later when she still insisted that she wanted to leave. They kept trying to get her to have a drink, but she refused.'

'Drugged?'

'That was her guess as well. Anyway, when finally she said she had made up her mind up and wanted to go, they made to release her but then effectively kidnapped her.'

'What did they do?'

'Is this all really necessary?'

'Yes.'

'Well, they bound her hands in front of her, bound her feet, blindfolded her and left her sitting on an upright chair for several hours while they played music interlaced with hypnotic suggestion.'

'But for suggestion to work I thought you needed a willing subject. Surely the ability to remind herself of pain by pulling on the bindings would have enabled her to resist the suggestion.'

'I've no idea,' replied Edwards, 'but it didn't work and the following morning they offered her food but she wouldn't take it. They undid the blindfold and lowered her into a coffin, which meant she was lying on her back staring at the ceiling in which psychedelic lights gyrated for hours and hours.'

'What about nature?' asked Powers troubled by the small detail of the story.

'What?' replied a puzzled Edwards.

'A crap.'

'Oh, I've no idea. If she told her parents they certainly omitted it from the story when they told me.'

'Okay, carry on.'

'I was trying to,' said Edwards with no real conviction in his words. 'After several hours, during which she tried to keep her eyes shut though the power of the lights wouldn't let her, they again offered her food and tried to talk to her. She refused food and wouldn't talk.

'They kept this up for at least twenty four hours and then she did accept water, she simply had to, poor girl.

'Again they tried to talk to her but all she would say was that she wanted to leave and that was when they nailed the lid on the coffin. It was uncomfortable but she decided the only thing to do was to try to sleep. It worked for a while but then they started playing the music with the suggestion again and that is when it started to work.

'She lay there helpless, nailed into a coffin, cold, hungry and afraid with her back now hurting. Then suddenly the music stopped. That, she said, was the worst point. There was absolute silence and all she could see was darkness.'

'The air holes must have been in the bottom.'

'I've no idea,' replied Edwards, 'I haven't given it any thought.

Powers had. 'Go on,' he said.

'She can't remember how long it was. She had lost all grasp of normality. All that she remembers is the darkness, the cold and the silence. She thought she was going to die. She started to see apparitions, ghostly and shadowy figures in front of her which she wanted to brush away with her hand, but couldn't.

'And then suddenly there was the music again with the suggestion and she started to answer the questions. Slowly she started to repeat what she was told to repeat. The lid was removed and she stared into the pyschedelic lights again and responded to the suggestions.

'She can't remember how long that went on for but, as she became more and more responsive they released the bindings, she began to eat and drink and was absorbed into the cult community.'

'So to what extent was Friggli motivated to kill by what he heard of her story?'

'Not at all. His job is to snatch back kids like that and he asked at the outset if the parents wanted the leaders taken out or just their daughter returned.'

'Yes, but he's not new to the job. He has some idea of what they get up to, even if she had been totally willing and not required a little persuasion to finally join them, it would have made little or no difference to him.'

'I think what scared my friends most the first time that they met Friggli, was the fact that he was so willing to kill, that he talked about it so calmly. Like you or me asking them out to dinner or what colour they wanted the kitchen painted.'

'Okay, so we think the man has killed before….'

'We know the man has killed before,' interrupted Edwards with unusual force.

'Okay, we know the man has killed before but he could think of himself of a saviour. There are many who would argue he was not a murderer but a distributor of justice, if a little rough and unorthodox. What makes you so sure that he could kill for the sake of killing? He must have seen some horrific sights in his business.'

'What my friends said about him — and don't forget how he feels about Democrats.'

'No,' replied Powers thinking. 'If we have a problem perhaps we should tell him that Major General Harold Campbell was reprimanded, fined and forced to retire, if he doesn't know. That should wind him up if he was a regular and I suspect he was.

'Who's he?'

'A former fighter pilot and Vietnam vet, now an airforce general, who said at a military banquet for maintenance workers at some airbase in Holland, that Clinton was a, "pot smoking, skirt chasing, gay-loving draft dodger." '

Enzo Friggli was waiting for them in the downtown bar as arranged. He'd been there since eight o'clock, but only sipping a cold coffee while he watched for signs of anything suspicious. He was a professional, he'd been trained to be a professional. Thirty five, dark, lean and tall with a ramrod straight back, he looked like a military man. His dark blue eyes concealed all emotion. They rarely seemed to move but never missed anything. As dispassionate a man as even Powers or Edwards had ever met, his slightly olive coloured skin was evidence of his Italian ancestry, just a generation back, on his father's side.

He made no attempt to move as the two older men approached him. 'Hello,' said Edwards as they reached the table. Friggli nodded. 'May we join you?'

He nodded again. The atmosphere was tense, uncomfortable; both Edwards and Powers looked out of place, knew it and felt it.

'Tell me about yourself?' said Powers bluntly.

Friggli stroked his stubbly chin gently before taking out a cigarette. He lit it and blew the smoke into Powers' face.

'No, buddy, you tell me about you,' he replied equally bluntly but more menacingly.

'I am just an employer who is looking to fund a job that

needs doing. That's all you need to know.'

'No, buddy,' repeated Friggli seeing that it irked Powers considerably to be spoken to like that, 'you want a job done by me, then I ask the questions, not the other way about.'

It was inevitable, Powers decided in those few moments, that the right man for the job was going to be a man like this. Powers had never worried about liking people he did business with and some of it had been pretty shady, but he had never done business with a man like this.

'Okay, what d'you want to know?'

'What sort of job is it? Is it a snatch back?'

'No, it's not a snatch back, it's more permanent than that,' replied Powers as they eyeballed each other with impassive stares. Their conversation became a staccato stand off.

'Totally permanent?'

'Totally.'

'Business or personal?'

'By which you mean?' asked Powers seeing the opportunity to gain control of the conversation.

'Don't try to be clever, buddy. I ask, you answer. If you don't like that, then you can leave right now. Business or personal? Wife's young lover's would be personal.'

'Business.'

'Right. Male or female?'

Powers was tempted to say both but feared he'd lose him. 'Male.'

'Any preference for method?'

'No.'

'Good. Any protection?'

'You mean guards?' said Powers looking at him hard. 'Yes, he's protected.'

'Private firm?'

'No.'

'Political figure?' came the immediate question before Powers had completed even the single word.

'Political figure.'

'Riordan?'
'No.'
'Good, I like him.'
'Price?'
'Negotiable.'
'I've warned you, buddy.'
'Your price.'
'Time span?'
'22nd November.'

The significance of the date clearly hit Friggli hard but he showed no outward emotion as he lit another cigarette. 'I know who you mean,' he said softly, inhaling deeply. '*He* wouldn't have done that.'

'No, he wouldn't.'
'No interference?'
'No interference.
'Money up front?'
'Half up front.'
'$50m, $25 up front.'
'Agreed.'
'We don't meet again.'
'We don't meet again, but we talk by phone.'
'Agreed. The date might be impossible. Either no engagements or tighter security than usual.'
'Thereabouts, before if you prefer.'

Friggli nodded. 'Say before the end of November.'
'Agreed.'
'Method of payment.'
'Your choice.'

'Cash up front, small used bills. Balance deposited in Switzerland in a joint account. You give me a letter authorising withdrawals on my signature alone if the President of the United States dies before the end of November. On completion I'll give the bank the letter.'

'Suppose he has a heart attack or someone else shoots him before them?' asked Edwards nervously speaking for the first time.

Friggli looked dismissively at him. 'Maybe I'll pray. Either way we'll all have what we want.'

'Agreed. How do we pay you the first instalment and which bank?' asked Powers.

'Ring here tomorrow night, seven o'clock. You'll be told where to find instructions and,' Friggli hesitated and stared hard at them both, 'any interference, I quit. I might also quit if it gets too warm.'

'And our second instalment will be frozen.'

'Chance you'll have to take. I'll be in touch,' he replied, leaving them in no doubt that they were no longer welcome at his table.

CHAPTER SIX

'What d'you think?' asked Scott Pulsat as he and Steve Waite left the airport bar. Scott was a pleasant young man still finding his way in the CIA. His mind had won him several prizes at Yale before he had been recruited for his long term potential which was not in the field.

'I believe what he told us. But as he said himself, did he read them right?'

'Not something we can take a chance on.'

'No.' replied Steve. 'Call in and give them details of both parties and have tails put on them immediately, phone taps and postal intercept, home and office. They'll both have mobiles, so see what can be done about bugging their houses, their cars and their offices. Houses might pose a problem but get in there somehow and do it.' The order was crisp.

'What about the wives?'

'I doubt they are in on it. Men like that never involve their wives in anything, but we can't afford to take chances, so yes include them.'

'What are you going to do?'

'Organise everything we've got on them and their wives to be on my desk when we get back. I'd also like a list of who was at that party, but we'll never get every name.'

'So then we go back to Langley?'

'Yes, I want to hold an A2 and then probably set up a control centre in Washington, but that won't be up to me.'

'Will we stay on it?'

'You bet we will, I'm not going back on "Ns"!'

'What's the difference between an A1, A2 and A3?' Pulsat would not remain inexperienced for long. He was never afraid to ask questions.

'With an A1 we know for certain that there is an assassination attempt being mounted on the President's life. An A2 means we have grounds for being suspicious but that is all and an A3 is little more than an initial alert.'

'And you reckon this is more than an initial alert?'

'Yep. They are seriously plotting and we don't know how many others they have approached. We could be A1 before the end of the week. I've got a feeling about this one.'

Hamdi and Moncilo chatted for about an hour and although Hamdi knew his story was being probed, he was too tired to care. He told the truth and prayed. They would either believe him and help him or not believe him and kill him. There was nothing he could say to sway them if they did not believe him.

'You must have been at Oxford around 1968, Hamdi,' said Moncilo.

'That's right, yes,' Hamdi replied with a distinct tremor in his voice.

'Don't worry, I won't say anything.' said Moncilo kindly, showing both his compassion and his perception. 'I wasn't a Rhodes scholar but I was also at University College. It wasn't until 1972, but I heard a few wild stories. I'm sure most of them weren't true, they rarely are, but I can quite understand why you wouldn't want people here to be aware that you know a certain American politician.'

'Thank you, Moncilo,' said Hamdi. His fatigue was showing.

'Do you wish to sleep?'

'No,' he said wearily, 'I am enjoying our conversation and I want to know more about what's been happening. Even before we were rounded up and driven into the woods, I was not hearing very much news.'

'As you wish, but it is not good. The worst of it, I think, is that the Russians have signed a secret agreement to sell tanks and anti-aircraft missiles to the Serbs. They say the deal is worth £250m, although the Russian Foreign Ministry denies it altogether and it is causing political turmoil because Yeltsin was kept in the dark about it.

'The man from Janes Defence said on the BBC that

"what we are seeing is a deal which has not been sanctioned by Boris Yeltsin." '

'Anti-aircraft missiles, you say.'

'Yes, and tanks.'

'Are the air drops still continuing?'

'Not for several weeks now, why?'

'I was just wondering how Bill would react if an American plane was taken down by one of the missiles.'

'I think it would not just be the Americans who would react. The tension in the UN is great enough now and the Russian Parliament is still mounting pressure on Yeltsin to push the UN to drop the sanctions against Serbia and impose sanctions against Croatia.'

'If they did but know,' sighed Hamdi.

'No, my friend, I think they *do* know the truth,' replied Moncilo with sadness. 'It is deliberate. You must remember that there is no real power centre in the old Soviet Union now. All the states are fighting each other, if not literally shooting each other. The military is fighting the politicians in mother Russia itself and the politicians themselves are divided.'

'What about the British? I know they were worried about the airdrops jeopardising the safe passage of the relief convoys.'

'They are looking into the deal but have said that as they are not international policemen anything they learn will have to be passed to the UN.'

'Is there any doubt about the deal at all?'

'None and it can only get worse because there are a lot of semi-official, semi-government residual bodies left over from the break up of the old Soviet Union and they are doing all sorts of deals that Yeltsin doesn't know about.'

'And presumably a lot of equipment being returned to Moscow is getting lost in transit and finding its way onto the black market.'

'I am sure it is, but that is in addition to the weapons I am talking about.'

'What will happen, my friend?' asked Hamdi almost morosely of his new friend.

'Who knows. While they meet in New York and sit at tables talking peace, the Serbs launch new offensives against us. We have several radio operators around the country who call in to tell us of the atrocities and then we use our height and our more powerful transmitter to broadcast to the world.'

'Does anyone hear?'

'I think so because we sometimes hear later, even sometimes the same day, what we have said repeated on the BBC and there is no way that they could have the information from any other source and it is always given as unconfirmed. I think there must be reporters who listen, who then sell on the story.'

'But what about the Serbs and Croats, don't they hear? Won't they try to find the transmitter and destroy it?'

'I'm sure they must hear, but I don't think they care. If they found us of course they would destroy the transmitter, but they are not people who care about what the world says about them.'

Hamdi thought of Zena. She was a Serb. Although he had only known Moncilo for an hour his instinct told him he could trust him.

'You remember the old lady I told you of who helped me after the killings?'

'Yes, and I know she was a Serb and not all Serbs are bad. And some of our own people are no better than the people who killed your family, but surely that isn't the point. Whatever side they're on the people who carry out the atrocities are not normal. They are not like you and me, they cannot be.'

'I agree, but that wasn't my point. Here,' he said removing his shoe and handing Moncilo the papers. 'Zena also gave me these. I had to tear off the photograph, but they might have saved me if I had been caught by the Serbs. She was so troubled, so deeply troubled, and my fear is that some of our own people will seek revenge and kill her and others like her just because she is a Serb.'

'That is something you must live in fear of, my friend. There is nothing you can do and the comfort is that you would never know.'

'Little comfort,' replied Hamdi sadly as the radio crackled into life.

'We're under attack from mortars and heavy machine gun fire,' Despite the faintness of the voice the fear was clear. 'People are being killed while I talk to you, it...' the reception began to break up.

'Where are you? Who are you?' Moncilo's tone was urgent, although he knew there would be nothing he could do to help them. There was nothing anyone could do.

'...there are hundreds and hundreds already dead but we have no food and cannot fight, we have no guns, we....'

'Where are you?' Moncilo asked again but there was no reply.

The radio was silent.

'We don't even know who they were or where they were. They might have even been under Muslim attack for all we know.'

'That is not very likely with the few weapons we have.'

'I know,' said Moncilo, the weariness of the months sounding in his voice and showing in his face. 'In January there were thirty thousand people trapped in Cerska and, having taken the town, the Chetniks wandered freely through it looting everything and carting the spoils away by lorry load.'

'I had heard, but what can we do?'

Moncilo hesitated for a moment, almost afraid to speak his thoughts. 'Perhaps,' he said slowly, 'perhaps you could do something no-one else could do.'

'Me?' replied Hamdi surprised. 'What could I possibly do? I am a physically weak lawyer. I know nothing about war and my negotiating skills will hardly persuade the Serbs to lay down their weapons.'

'No, my friend, that is not what I had in mind. Now don't

misunderstand me and what I am about to say. I've read all about Bill Clinton's big heart and I even think it's probably true, but I fear that he probably decided to drop food aid more for his gain than ours. He alienated his allies by doing it but he was showing the world that he cared, that America cared and that he was his own man. That, I suspect, was as much part of the reason as any other — it showed the world that he would lead.

'In the event it was impossible to drop the aid reliably where it was needed and much of it even finished up with the Serbs.'

'We know that, but where do I come in?' Hamdi asked.

'You go and see him.'

Hamdi was stunned into silence.

'You know him. I doubt if there is anyone else in the whole of Bosnia-Herzegovina who knows him.'

'But that was years ago. He won't remember me.'

'No, but you'd not have remembered him unless you'd been reminded of him. We must remind him of you. You are the ace we've been waiting for, Hamdi.'

'What do I say to him?'

'We know that, whatever personal reasons I might feel he had, the aid drops were initially motivated by the reports of the mass killings and the starvation. I get the impression that he is a man who really cares but is easily influenced, especially by good and worthy causes and just can't say no. He ends up saying yes to everybody and just can't keep all his promises.

'We need him to persuade the other Western leaders that we *do* need arming. To make them see that they have enjoyed peace in Europe for over forty five years because both sides had weapons, that was the very argument of deterrence. The anti-aircraft missiles that the Serbs are getting from the Russians have a range of 375 miles, they feel safe from air attack. Bulgaria has moved Scud surface-to-air missiles to its border with Serbia so that it is safe against attack. We too must have a deterrent. Only then will the killing stop.'

'Your argument is powerful, but I'm having difficulty believing that I'm sitting here high up in the mountains listening to it; that we are having this conversation at all, that you have the knowledge that you do, while down below us people are being slain as we talk.' The conversation has given Hamdi a second wind, his tiredness briefly abated.

'There are those in the West who believe we should be helped. There are those in the West who believe that arming us would stop the slaughter. I know there are others who argue that it is a civil war, that it is not for them to intervene and that arming us would run the risk of escalating the problem, but they are wrong. We must remind them that Yugoslavia was not a natural country. It was the West who created it by bringing together people with nothing in common, people who had fought each other for centuries, people of different cultures, different religions. We must remind them that this is not a civil war, it is those nationals that they forced together, trying to tear themselves apart again.

'We must make them see that arming us is no different from deploying cruise missiles in England or SS20s in East Germany in the early 1980s. It is the fear factor.'

'Let me accept the principle for the moment. I could not travel that far and in any event how would I travel? I have no passport, no money.'

'The passport we can forge, the money we can steal,' said Moncilo who, seeing the look on Hamdi's face, continued, 'from the Serbs or the Croats.'

'Let me think. I am tired now, let me sleep.'

'You sleep, my friend, and I will arrange the money while you sleep.' said Moncilo smiling a knowing smile.

The A2 at Langley was attended by Steve Waite, Scott Pulsat, a Senior Field Controller and the Deputy Chief. If it went A1, the Chief would also attend as would another senior field controller.

'Right,' said the Deputy Chief. 'I've read the reports and

our man is someone we must take seriously. I trust his judgement, but I want to speak to him myself as soon as possible''

Tim Wood was nearing retirement and would never go any higher. Half of his emotions wanted the threat to be real so that he could go out on a high having thwarted it, but the other half was terrified in case it was real. They might not be successful in preventing it.

'I like your idea of being the chauffeur, Steve. I doubt they will say anything at all in front of you but it will give you a good chance to observe them. To form opinions of them, their mental states, their tolerance levels, which, if this is real, might prove all too important in the final analysis.

'Yes, sir.'

'All the surveillance is in place?'

'Yes, sir.'

'And it has produced nothing of interest yet?'

'No, sir.'

'I've authorised a Control Centre in Washington and you'll work inside the White House on instant duplication to here. I want two Duty Officers here monitoring everything the whole time.

'Knight has almost certainly been selling his wares where he shouldn't and I see, interestingly, that at one point we even thought about trying to recruit him. I want to know more about that and why we didn't.'

'Yes, sir.'

'Use as many men as you need on this one. These two are very much the sort of idiots who get stupid ideas into their head and then pride forces them to carry on with them.'

'Does the President know, sir?'

'Yes, I've spoken to him personally and told him that we are holding an A2. I think it shocked him.'

None of them replied.

'Night or day I want to be informed of every single development, no matter how small.'

'What about the girl, sir?'

'Continue to keep her under observation as well, I don't

care who we put through it, I don't even want an attempt on the President's life.'

'Shall we relay the bugs in Alaska back to here and the Control Centre?'

'Yes, I want as many minds trained on this as possible.'

Lech enjoyed his meal at Langans but didn't stay long in Gerry's Club. He was feeling tired after the journey despite the fact that he had shortened his day by the flight. However it did him good to forget the reality of his life, even for a short while. He even found himself singing along with one of the songs from Joseph when the old piano was brought to life by a young actress who also had a wonderful singing voice. Gerry's is a regular haunt for many from the theatre after their make-up has been removed. He was back in his room just before one o'clock.

Gillespi also enjoyed his meal but was back in the Fox House by ten in order to spend an hour in the bar before it closed. He learnt nothing about the American with the Polish name, other than he had been a member for over twenty years and knew the previous owner well. There was nobody else staying that night and Karl closed the bar just before eleven and was gone within minutes. It left Gillespi alone in the building and it took all of two minutes to open Lech's suite door.

All he learnt was what he already knew, so either the man was who and what he said he was, or he was a professional agent who was good. His instinct was the former.

Breakfast was served in the dining area adjoining the bar. Gillespi was in the breakfast room by seven the next morning. He sat reading the Times until ordering an hour or so later and was reading the Telegraph when Anna, the Spanish cleaning lady, cleared away the tables just after half past nine. Lech Zielinski had not appeared. 'Okay,' Gillespi said to himself, 'time difference, give him a day or two.'

That day Gillespi took a boat trip to Hampton Court and

the gardens at Kew which, much to his amazement, he found totally absorbing. He calculated that by returning to the Fox House at nine o'clock that evening, the American would be out eating and he would not see him. The bar was full and after a quick Scotch he retired for the night. He would be up at seven in the morning to start observing Zielinski, who he had fortunately avoided that evening.

'Ah, Karl,' said Lech as he returned from his evening meal in Tokyo Joe's 'no messages for me?'

'No, Mr. Zielinski, none I'm afraid.'

'Good, then all's well back home. I think I'll just have a swift whisky then make for the sack. I've just about got onto your time now and fancy an early night.'

It was almost nine when Lech surfaced for breakfast. The previous night all the rooms had been in use and now the dining area was crowded. Gillespi watched Lech for half an hour, by which time there were only two other people left in the dining area and so, wishing to avoid a conversation at this stage, he returned to him room where he waited watching television until half past one.

The bar was reasonably crowded and there were half a dozen people having lunch, including Lech.

Gillespi watched and listened to him for over two hours. He was not a professional and seemed concerned at not having received his anticipated phone call. Each time the phone rang Zielinski looked up expectantly. Tomorrow morning, he decided, they would start a nodding relationship. Slowly does it. He wanted to know his man, to be sure of him before he made contact.

The Club was closed at weekends, although members and guests could still use the rooms. It was late on Friday evening after overhearing Lech tell Ann that he would probably leave come Monday that Gillespi made his move. He suggested that they breakfasted together at the Ritz, which was only just across Piccadilly, on Saturday morning. Lech seemed glad of the offer of company; he was a troubled man. He had spent all day Friday at the Club waiting for a contact that never came.

Breakfast was uneventful but they agreed to do it again on Sunday and that was when Gillespi decided to make his next move. They were to meet at eight thirty, but Gillespi was in the Ritz by seven o'clock arranging for Lech to receive a phone call at nine fifteen. 'Now, repeat it to me again and you get £50 for your trouble,' Gillespi said to the porter.

'I ring the desk and ask to speak to Mr. Zielinski who is having breakfast in the dining room. When he comes to the phone I say, "I'm sorry there's been a delay but I will be with you by Tuesday," and immediately hang up.'

'That's right and if all goes well there's another fifty for you when I leave.'

Miles Waterford had been highly suspicious, as he'd told Steve Waite, of the long legged blonde he had seen in animated conversation with Brad Harworth shortly before she started talking to him at one of the drinks tables. What were those two up to? What was their game? Was the woman a friend, both men were rumoured to be ladies' men on the quiet, or was she there employed in case of need?

As she chatted away aimlessly he didn't listen, instead casting his eye around the assembled company. There were many from the arts, fewer from business, but all in all they seemed to be a thoroughly sound, good-natured group of people. One clique, to which both the Harworth wife, whom Miles particularly disliked, and the hostess, who was several parts to the wind, belonged, seemed out of keeping with the rest of the guests. They were the very sort of people whose behaviour gave the Democrats a bad name. He had no time for them.

'So tell me about yourself. You're obviously from out of town?' said Angie Tourle, desperately trying to strike up a conversation with Miles.

'Yep, I'm down from Alaska, the frozen north. We don't

see pretty young things like you running around up there dressed like that,' said Miles, striking out to see what response he would get. 'They'd sure catch a cold or two in an outfit like that,' he continued, waving loosely at her tight fitting, black silk evening gown which left no-one in any doubt that it was all she was wearing.

'Why now, I do think you're paying me a compliment,' she replied with a radiant and seductive smile.

'I'd not be too sure about that, but I've got to say you're a pretty little thing alright.'

'Sure sounds like a compliment to me.'

'As you wish,' said Miles, now convinced that this young lady had been told to provide him with all the comforts he needed. Hell, he thought, what the heck if he did indulge in a little pleasure. What possible embarrassment could they cause him by bringing it up later. He actually became quite excited by the fact that they had laid her on for him and even began to muse over whether or not it would be taped. He'd heard about things like that going on in the city. They never seemed likely to him until now.

The apartment was seductively furnished with silks and mirrors and they were no sooner through the door than Angie had slipped off her evening gown. She knew how attractive her body was and began to cup her breasts and lick her lips suggestively as Miles admired what awaited him.

'Not bad,' he said, 'not bad at all. But we don't go in for all this playing about and soft stuff where I come from.'

'You don't?'

'No, we don't' he said as his dress trousers and boxer shorts hit the floor and Angie gasped. Not yet fully erect, he was longer and thicker than any man she had ever seen. Her throat was suddenly dry as all her normal seductive build up routines deserted her and pure animal lust took over. She lunged at him with her hands, eager to hold it, eager to suck it and then to take it into herself.

'I told you we don't bother with all that stuff,' he said

pushing her playfully back onto the sofa. Angie smiled. She had never been so aroused, never ached so much for a man to enter her.

Miles threw aside his shirt, bent down and picked her up with his giant hands firmly supporting her back. She opened her legs as he drew her towards him and tried to close them around his back but they were too short. She came for the first of countless times almost immediately as he held her suspended in the air and drove himself in and out of her.

They indulged themselves for three beautiful days and night in the bugged apartment. Angie hid the tape when Miles had left. That was hers, for ever.

A week later Brad Harworth and Jeff Knight were on their way to join Miles at his cabin on Lliamna Lake.

'I've never been this far north,' said Brad as the plane circled the airport.

'Nor me,' replied Jeff. 'Shouldn't fancy it in the dead of winter.'

'No, must be pretty wild and inhospitable. Too many damn wolves roaming around the place.'

'Just like Washington!'

'Now those wolves I can live with, Jeff, but not the ones up here,' said Brad. He had felt uneasy about the trip since it was first suggested. Why on earth did Miles want them to travel two thousand five hundred miles to this Godforsaken backwater? Moreover, why had they agreed? Had they seemed over anxious by agreeing?

They were met at the airport by Waterford's chauffeur to continue their journey onwards to Lliamna Lake.

'You know, Brad, there is something exhilarating about this place, I can feel it already,' said Jeff as they sped through the flat plains of Alaska, staring out at endless tundra and stunted spruce.

'It does nothing for me,' replied Brad. 'Absolutely nothing.' He thought of the warm southern beaches and the skimpily clad young women who roamed them.

To reach the cabin they passed through some of the world's finest scenery. Lofty snow covered mountains, cascading waterways which tumbled south and west towards the Bristol Bay and the hungry ocean beyond. Neither of them appreciated any of it.

Miles was waiting for them on the veranda of the cabin. 'Welcome, boys,' he boomed, 'I hope the journey was pleasant.'

'Very good, thank you, Miles,' replied Jeff cheerfully.

'Well, come on in and let's get you settled.' Miles shepherded them into the warmth.

The cabin was spacious and comfortable. It owed its air of relaxed comfort to money. The rugs were rich and thick, the sofas deep and soft and the pictures that lined the walls could have graced a gallery. Like everything else in the cabin, they had been carefully selected to create the right environment, a welcoming homely atmosphere.

Miles had commissioned the building of the cabin to his own high specification five years previously. His original home, a few hundred yards along the Lake, was now used by his three staff.

'Right then, a drink,' said Miles as the two joined him in the early evening on the veranda. 'I'm afraid I don't run to the style that you fellas do in the city, but I trust you'll find me just as hospitable.'

'It's very good,' said Brad somewhat nervously. He felt completely out of place and wished to God he had never agreed to come.

'I doubt that you'll be lucky enough to run into anything as warm and friendly in my back yard as I did in yours, Jeff,' said Miles passing him a very large bourbon and watching both men's reactions carefully. They did not respond verbally but he learnt what he wanted to know; he had been right.

'Mind you, she was just as wild as some of the creatures out there,' he continued waving towards mountains beyond, but still neither man reacted.

'So, you want to know what I *really* think about the President?' said Miles deciding to force the issue at once. He wanted to enjoy his supper, not have it spoilt by double talk, and then enjoy his fishing tomorrow.

'That's right, Miles,' said Jeff. 'There's a growing feeling in Washington that he's no good for the country. But that's just one side of it and city life can distort opinions badly, whereas people like you, away from the hustle and bustle, can be more objective, see things in a better proportion.'

Bullshit, thought Miles. 'Sure I can see that,' he said refilling his glass and offering the others the bottle which they declined.

'So come on, Miles, lay it out, what's your view?' asked Brad.

'As I told you guys he's an asshole. A first rate asshole and I think he's controlled and driven by the wife woman. Always has been.'

'What makes you so sure?'

'Look, the guy's got balls, no doubt about it, and he's got charm, thinks on his feet, but essentially he's too nice a guy to be President. He's got the heart of a Samaritan but the political skill of a five year old. He's learning, sure he's learning and he's never better than when he's on his feet and up to his neck in it, he'll pull an answer out the hat and stun everybody. But that's just what it is, an answer, not a solution.

'She, on the other hand, plots and schemes. She *is* a politician. Just look at what she said when asked if she was ever likely to run for President, "We'll talk later." For God's sake, man' continued Miles getting to his feet, 'her damn husband has been in the job a dogwatch and she's answering questions like that.

'No, believe me she is the political brains behind the operation and it is a team, it is two for the price of one. All this bullshit about being a working mother who wants time to be with her family is so much crap, she's power hungry. You know when I was down with you people, I went to a few other places as well and I heard one Democrat say Congressmen come away as pleased with their meetings with her as their meetings with the President.'

'So you think she *is* running the show?'

'What sort of dumb question is that, Brad? How the hell do I know what is going on down there. You fellas are supposed to be in touch.'

'But it looks that way to you, Miles, is what I think Brad meant.'

'Sure it looks that way to just about everybody.'

'And isn't it the way it looks that matters?' asked Brad.

'Sure,' he replied expansively again offering the bourbon bottle around. This time Jeff accepted.

'Look, I don't know what you guys are driving at or why you're driving at it, but I don't buy all this bullshit about special missions or whatever it was you said back there in Washington. I don't like cities or even towns, if it comes to that. This is my home, this is where I feel comfortable and if you guys want to enjoy a few days fishing and chew over the problems in the White House that's fine with me. But don't think you'll get me involved in mad hat schemes to influence what happens, because you won't.' 'That's not at all what we had in mind' lied Brad, sounding more confident than at any time since their arrival, 'we do genuinely want to know what you think.'

'Well, as long as we've got that straight then let's have another drink or two before supper. I take it you two fellas both eat salmon?' asked Miles with a chuckle.

'Oh, yes,' they replied.

'Do you believe all you hear and read about Hillary, Miles?' asked Brad, refusing to be drawn away from the point in hand.

'I reckon the gist is right, after all some of her friends say things I sure as hell wouldn't want my friends saying about me in that situation. *He's* not so bad, in my book, but we want to see more guts, more backbone. He showed that by going to the Vietnam veterans memorial service. He was booed and abused but he went and he stuck to his views.' Miles was fishing a little to see if he could provoke a response.

'I thought all he said was he'd have written the anti-Vietnam war letter he wrote in 1969 differently if he wrote it now?' said Brad pointedly.

'Sure, but wouldn't we all,' said Miles. 'I thought what he said was that he couldn't run away from that letter but he might write it differently at forty six from the way he wrote it at twenty three. That was guts, it would be easy to say that he was wrong, that he's grown up and can see it now. That's what the guy did when he lost Arkansas.

'Now he needs guts to stand up to the wife woman and then he just might even make a decent President.'

'You keep coming back to her, Miles,' said Jeff helping himself to another bourbon although now several behind Miles with Brad still nursing his first.

'You bet I do! You know I read that even the liberal run media is starting to suggest that she can't keep it up. She'll have to decide whether she wants a career of her own or whether she wants to be the family type. "Parade", actually asked the question, "Who or what? Her family or her career?" And do you know what her TV producer friend, Linda Bloodworth-Thomason, is quoted as saying? "Hillary doesn't have to stay with Bill Clinton. She could go to the Senate or possibly the White House on her own and she knows it."

'I reckon one of the reasons that it took so long to get the Attorney General position filled is that Hillary insists on vetting every judicial appointment, just as she did in Arkansas.

'Now I'm getting hungry and I've had enough of politics. Bores me, politicians bore me, but if I read you guys right you're aiming at the wrong target.'

They were up at six the next morning and drove down to River Alagnak to fish. Brad and Jeff were both uncomfortable in their chest waders, which they had no choice but to wear all day.

'Not so bad once you get used to them,' laughed Miles, unusually enjoying seeing someone suffer a little discomfort.

He did not like either of them and most certainly did not trust them, especially Brad.

'Right, I'll show you how to catch giant rainbow trout and if you're lucky we'll have it frozen for you to take back to the city. Whether you eat it or stuff it and put it on the wall is up to you, but I'll teach you to catch it.

'First off you put one of these imitation mice on the line as bait.'

'What's it made of?' asked Jeff showing some genuine interest.

'Deer hair. I sit around the fire on long winter's evenings making them.

Jeff was impressed. 'And how do you catch the fish?'

Miles, delighted by his interest, put the rod into his hand. 'Release the catch on the reel, hold the line with your finger, so, and then bring the rod back over your shoulder like so,' said Miles easing the rod into position for Jeff. 'Now we want to cast as far as possible towards that far bank, so really throw yourself into it, but as soon as the mouse is airborne bring the rod back up and hold it high.

'Not bad, not bad for a first go,' said Miles, genuinely impressed as the mouse landed two thirds of the way across the river.

'Right, now hold that rod really high and reel it in so that you drag the mouse across the river. You're trying to make it look like a real mouse or a vole swimming in the current.'

Jeff reeled the mouse all the way across the river without a bite but was exhilarated by it. 'Brad, you wanna try this,' he said excitedly, turning towards Brad who was sitting on the bank.

'I think I'll just sit and watch you for a while,' came a sighing reply. 'This is something else,' whooped Jeff as he cast again reaching a yard or two further across the racing river.

Suddenly there was a swirling on the surface and Miles shouted, 'Drop the rod tip and whip it up hard!'

'Damn, you lost it, but never mind!' yelled Miles in a state of high excitement. 'As soon as you see that swirling, drop the rod point for just a split second and whip it up as hard and as quick as you can to set the hook. If you do hook it the take can be vicious and the fish will run with line — it might even strip the reel down to the backing — so be ready for it and hold on tight! Remember you'll have one hell of a strong fish on the end and there is a strong current as well.'

'Okay, okay' said Jeff. 'Let's do it again.'

Miles had caught three fish of between three and four pounds each before Jeff got another bite.

'You've got it,' yelled Miles, 'it looks big, now just hold it, hold it there.'

Jeff did exactly as he was told and could feel the power of the fish through his arms and back as it struggled to be free of his hook. 'This could be a double figure beauty,' said Miles with excitement, 'but you can never tell. I saw a guy once struggle for two hours with what we all thought would be a giant, but it was only just over three pounds. The river's fast and hard at the moment which makes it easier for the fish, but we'll land it, just keep that rod tip pointed high.'

It took an hour, by which time Jeff was totally exhausted, but Miles looked as if he had been awakened from some deep slumber, his adrenalin was flowing almost as fast as the current.

'About five pounds, I reckon, not bad for a first fish,' said Miles holding the fish in the palms of both hands to display it.

'Supper tonight or that opulent city study wall?' he asked.

'That depends on the size of the next one,' replied an excited Jeff who had just about started to breathe evenly again. 'Come on, Brad,' he called, 'I tell you it is fucking amazing.'

'I'm more than happy basking in your reflected glory,' replied Brad, who was actually busily trying to work out how they could hook and land Miles Waterford. They needed his money and it was plain that the video tapes of his performance or more accurately performances, with Angie Tourle would be of no use to them. Angie had suggested copying them and selling them to the hardcore porn market.

She had never before met a man with his stamina or physical power and doubted she would ever be satisfied like that again.

It was three hours before Jeff managed to hook into another bite; he had lost several and was becoming disillusioned. Miles during that time had caught a number of smaller fish, some of which he had put back to grow a little more.

The double figure weight Alaskan rainbow trout is an elusive fish but this, Miles believed, could be it. After an hour he took the line from Jeff, who was barely able to stand any longer, and it took him a further forty minutes to land the fish, all eight pounds six ounces of it.

'That's the one for the study wall,' he said proudly presenting it in the palms of his two giant hands to Jeff Knight.

'No, Miles,' he said exhausted, 'you landed it so it's supper tonight.'

'Won't hear of it,' beamed Miles. 'If I ever visit that study of yours again I expect to see it stuffed and mounted on the wall above the fireplace. You caught it, we all need a little help at times.'

'Thank you,' replied Jeff simply. He appreciated the genuine friendship and companionship of Miles Waterford. He had never known or experienced anything like it before. The man did not have an angle to play, he was not looking to score points, he was a warm and genuine human being who was clearly never going to be dragged into their sordid scheme. He began to feel ashamed at even trying to lure him into their net.

That night they enjoyed some of the trout they had caught and Miles' chauffeur took the prize specimen off to be stuffed and mounted. 'It'll be a couple of days,' said Miles, 'but I doubt if you'll be able to move much before it comes back, Jeff,' he continued passing him another large bourbon. Jeff was drinking almost as fast as Miles by then but Brad remained firmly entrenched in his shell, alone with his thoughts.

Miles was up and about as usual before six the next morning, but it was gone nine before Brad appeared and eleven when a very stiff Jeff joined them on the veranda.

Miles was grateful for the chance to speak to Brad alone, he disliked and distrusted the man and had decided that Jeff was being used by him. Brad had probably suggested to Jeff in the first place that he should have the party, and Miles wondered how many others apart from himself they had approached. Their real interest could only be his money, and he had recognised several other very wealthy individuals at the party.

Miles Waterford was never a shy man, although his caring nature sometimes made him look as if he were. He was, however, as capable as Brad Harworth of being both direct and concise. 'So what's the plan, kill him?' he asked bluntly as Brad settled down on an old wooden chair.

'You don't approve?'

'You bet I don't approve!'

'You don't think he's a menace to this country, to the whole goddam world,' replied Brad losing his temper at what he saw as the complacent arrogance of a man who had never had to work for anything in his life.

'Now that I don't say. I've told you that I think he's an asshole and that the wife woman is largely to blame, but that's not to say that I go along with bumping the guy off. What right have you to decide that the world is a better place if you kill him? Suppose, just suppose for a moment, that you succeeded and then found out Al Gore was worse. What then, kill him as well?'

'There's no way Al Gore could be worse,' responded Brad, losing his temper, 'apart from anything else, he would not have what you keep calling the wife woman pulling his string.'

'Maybe not, but that's not to say he'd be any better and then she might run for the White House on her own and knowing how soft the people of this country are, they're just as likely to elect her out of sympathy. What then, another killing?'

'You don't understand, do you? Stuck away up here in the hills with your fish and your money you have no idea what is really going on in the world!' Brad spoke the words with particular venom.

'Maybe I don't and maybe I want to keep it that way, but I sure as hell know that you don't go around killing Presidents just because you don't like the way they run the country.'

'You fool,' said Brad with evil in his voice, 'we didn't like the way Bush or Reagan ran the country but we didn't plot to kill them. They did not pose a threat to the nation ....

'And in your opinion Clinton does?'

'Too bloody true he does and the point is that it's not just my opinion and it's not just in this country. It's worldwide.

'Look at the balls-up after balls-up in appointing the administration, the times he has been forced to back down from appointees, the air drops into Bosnia. Look at the broken election promises, he's even managed to get himself into an argument about the Freedom Space Station. He just decided on his own to change it, but I doubt he'll get the plan through Congress if only because the smaller version will provide so many fewer jobs during the construction stage. Our partners are furious, Congress won't agree and he'll have to back down again and America will be humiliated.'

'Is that what really troubles you, America being humiliated?'

'Well, I sure as hell, to use your terminology, am not excited by the prospect. Are you?'

'No, but I sure as hell am excited by the prospect of America being honest and making honest mistakes and not by a group of puffed up pen pushers deciding to take the law into their own hands and kill the democratically elected President because they don't like what he does or the way he does it. I reckon that would cause America more than a little humiliation, as well as get her compared to some tinpot banana republic. Don't you?'

'Didn't when Kennedy was assassinated.'

'Is that right? Well, I don't agree with you, buddy. To me,' said Miles standing and shouting angrily at his guest, 'that was the most humiliating day in the whole damn history of this country.'

Suddenly the anger had gone. Miles let out a huge sigh, closed his eyes for a second and shook his head. 'Enough of this talk. You are my guests and I'll extend you hospitality in return for the hospitality you extended me, but I'll have no more talk of treason in my house.

'And, what's more, that hospitality will not extend to having you seduced by some half baked society tart who keeps what little brain she has between her legs. I wouldn't like to guess how many of you softies she's screwed before but she now knows what it's like to be actually fucked, and I reckon you guys might find yourselves a bit lacking in future.' He laughed as he went inside for another bottle of bourbon.

Neither Brad nor Miles spoke of their conversation to Jeff during the day but he was aware of the tension and knew something must have happened. He was too stiff to move much and too mentally exhausted even to want to know what had happened. His concern was to rest so that the next day he could go fishing again. He was bitten.

Supper was a subdued affair but as the bourbon flowed Jeff relaxed and felt less troubled by the atmosphere. 'What chance another go tomorrow, Miles?' he asked.

'No problem, you just say the word Jeff and we'll be off.'

'I thought we might think about making our way back tomorrow,' said Brad knowing there was no mileage in staying and wanting to return to civilisation.

'Up to you,' said Miles benevolently. 'You're more than welcome to stay as long as you like, fishing or no fishing.'

'Come on, one more day, Brad. Why don't you try the fishing yourself? I might ache all over but I feel years younger, my adrenalin hasn't run like this ever. Besides, I've got to wait for *the* fish.'

'Okay, I'm happy to stay over another day, just the one, but I'll hang around here. You two do your little boys stuff.'

'As you like,' said Jeff, 'but if you don't think me rude, Miles, I'd like to turn in so that I'm able to fish tomorrow.'

'You go right on ahead, Jeff. I'll wake you at half five, rashers and eggs and we'll be off by six.'

'I might as well hit the sack as well,' said Brad with little sincerity. 'I doubt we'd find much to talk about into the small hours, do you, Miles?'

'I doubt it, Brad.'

'What on earth went on between you two before I got up this morning?' asked Jeff as they approached their rooms.

'We had a philosophical conversation in which we didn't see eye to eye.'

'I'm not surprised. He's not our man and we must just hope that he doesn't find out what we really have in mind.'

'Why?' asked Brad fearing the answer would accord with his own thoughts on the matter.

'Because I reckon he'd turn us straight in, that's why.'

'He worked it out in your study, confronted me this morning and you're dead right he wants nothing to do with it.'

Jeff Knight went cold and suddenly felt the sweat start to form on his brow. He had been wondering for much of the day how he had got himself into this position with Brad as well as many others in his life. The great outdoors had made him look closely at himself and start to question his life and the way he behaved.

'And what else did he say?'

'Nothing more. But I think he might turn us in, which means we've got to deal with him before we leave here.'

'What d'you mean, deal with him?' asked Jeff.

'Kill him,' replied Brad starkly.

'Oh, no!' replied Jeff horrified. 'No way, man!'

'And what if he turns us in for plotting to assassinate the President?'

'There's no evidence. We've not even said that to him. All

we have to say is that he's misunderstood our questions. Look, Brad.' Jeff lowered his tone, bit the anger out of his voice, 'people all over this country and abroad are asking each other the sort of questions we've been asking him. Doesn't mean they're plotting to kill the President. Tough it out, he'll give us no trouble.

'Tell you what. While we're fishing tomorrow I'll tell him that you've got a little carried away, been fantasising a bit and that he's brought you back down to earth. What d'you say?'

'You can try it, but I tell you it won't. He'll have to go.

'Are you going to do it then?' asked Jeff Knight pointedly. There was no reply.

CHAPTER SEVEN

Miles smiled to himself as he replaced the receiver after the message from the staff cabin. Steve Waite had taken Charlie's place as the chauffeur for the airport trip while Pulsat had supervised the bugging operation. Every word had been recorded.

Brad Harworth spent a sleepless night wondering which way to play it. What Jeff had said was true, there was no evidence of any conspiracy, but would Waterford need that? They had misjudged the ebullient, larger-than-life figure. He was a man of honour, a man who would sacrifice himself for what he believed in and a man who would hold no truck with those who abused their positions of power, influence or wealth. But, he kept reminding himself, there *was* no evidence. Jeff was right, Waterford must have misunderstood their motives. But these faint reassurances did not help him sleep.

Even if they were able to put the Waterford episode behind them, that still left him with the major problem. How to remove Bill Clinton. In his own mind, whatever arguments the Waterfords of this world put forward, he still knew that in the interest of the world generally, Clinton had to be removed. Maybe removing Hillary would achieve something, it would certainly leave the President in control, but the real fault he considered lay in the fact that Clinton was not a man of conviction, whatever he had done and said about Vietnam. Clinton's stand on that was not in his view conviction, but fear. Brad Harworth knew what that fear felt like, he had experienced it and was grateful for the minor wound on his first expedition that had seen him sent home after three days in Nam.

Jeff Knight slept somewhat better, the pain of his aching body having begun to subside. He saw Miles Waterford as a fair man, one to whom he could talk and with whom he could reason. He was sure he would accept that Brad had got carried away out of a sense of frustration and that there had never actually been any intention, let alone a serious one, of assassinating the President. He was looking forward to his fishing the next day, and had already decided that he would come again. As he started to doze off he began to rue the fact that he had spent most of his life chasing dimes and women, not always in that order.

Jeff woke about three, his mind troubled not by what Waterford might say or do following his conversation with Brad, but what Brad might do. Waterford he thought was safe, but the fact was that Brad was deadly serious about the President, he was determined to see him assassinated. Did he, Jeff, have a responsibility to stop that happening? He was unable to see it as accepting a responsibility in the way that Garson, Gillespi and Hankin had in their moments of doubt leading up to 1963, but then the security of the nation was not his responsibility. His job was to make and sell armaments.

Miles Waterford slept like a log, he always did. He'd started to like Jeff Knight, but the other asshole was getting to him. If he had thought he was serious about assassinating the President — or capable of doing it for that matter — he would have clapped him in irons there and then. He had them for trapping bears that came too close to the cabin in winter.

The problem with people like Harworth, he told himself, was that they gave other people ideas, people who might be able actually to do something. Harworth frightened him. He would have to see what he could learn from Knight while they fished.

Brad was still considering whether or not to lift one of the giant hunting knives from a wall and plunge it deep into the man as he slept, when he heard Miles moving around the house. It was four forty five and he was up for the day. The opportunity had passed. Brad breathed slightly easier. He simply did not have the guts and now he had an excuse for not even trying.

By six Miles and Jeff had left the cabin and Brad knew they would not return before mid afternoon at the earliest. He decided to sleep again and by seven thirty had drifted off. He woke at eleven in a cold sweat, his body shaking and the sheet soaking wet. Although he'd not been dreaming he knew well enough the reason and decided at once to shower, dress and then ring Angie. There was more than one way to kill a man.

'Hi, Brad darling, how are you?' she said in her usual whine.

'Fine, just fine thanks, Angie. And you?'

'Okay, but a little bored, no action. How's my big friend from Alaska, does he remember me?'

'Oh he remembers you all right, honey and that's what we've been talking about these past few days.'

'That's nice,' she purred and then feigned embarrassment, 'but I hope he hasn't told you two *everything* we got up to.'

'Oh no,' replied Brad to her disappointment. 'Look, Angie we're coming back sometime tomorrow, but I won't let Bridget know and I thought you and I could slip away to the bungalow for a few quiet days. What d'you say?'

'Sounds lovely to me, Brad darling.'

'You get yourself a ticket for Tampa and I'll fly right on down there to meet you.'

'When will you be there?'

'That depends on when we leave here, but if you go today I'll be there within a day or two. You get the place ready and I'll be there just as soon as I can.'

'Okay, Brad darling and give the big man a kiss from me!' she said tantalisingly, knowing how much it would rile Brad. She'd had seven men in the last week and all she longed for was the great beast from Alaska. She was afraid that sex would become one big bore from now on.

Miles and Jeff enjoyed another stimulating day and although Jeff caught more fish neither of them caught anything over three pounds. 'That's the way it goes sometimes,' said Miles. 'Now if you were staying up a bit longer we could have a try for some salmon, maybe try the Kanektok River or even take a boat out on the Lake.'

'I'd love to, Miles, but I really must get back.'

'Okay, I understand, but,' he paused and looked hard at Jeff, 'you promise me this nonsense with Brad is over and if he talks about it again you'll either stop him or tell him you'll turn him in?'

'Yes. Life looks so different after a few days up here. It's all too easy to get sucked into the whirlpool back home. It just happens, develops, evolves without me being aware of what is happening.' Jeff sounded sincere.

'Sure, but that can happen up here as well you know. Wherever you are each step is so small that you don't notice how far down the track you've gone. You just have to stop sometimes and look. You guys almost had me in that study of yours, I was almost sucked in.'

'Really?' asked Jeff suspiciously.

'Really, I promise you. It was that close, but something just pricked me, held me back, woke me up. No idea what, but something did.

'I'm glad, it did us all a favour.'

Brad spoke little at supper that evening and Jeff was too tired and stiff to be much company so the meal was a quiet affair, but both Jeff and Miles consumed enough bourbon to ensure that they slept soundly. The two city dwellers left for the airport just after ten the following morning but it was not until Waite had left them that Brad told Jeff he was flying straight to Tampa to meet Angie.

'I wanted to talk to you about Clinton, Brad,' said Jeff.

'What's to say? Waterford hasn't got the balls and now he's talked you out of it.' Brad's tone was terse.

'Not so much talked me out of it, as made me see that we were stupid to think about it in the first place,' replied Jeff calmly, ignoring Brad's tone.

'Stupid you say,' said Brad angrily, 'That jerk is destroying this country and you say we're stupid to try and stop him. That sounds pretty stupid to me, Jeff.'

'Look, Brad, I don't want us to fall out and I don't want to have to turn you in, why....'

'You don't want?' yelled Brad so loudly that the crowds around stopped talking and stared at them. 'Do you mean to tell me that you would actually turn me in?'

'Yes, Brad,' he replied softly, 'I would. It's just not right and I'd have no choice.'

'Then I'd have no choice but to tell Uncle Sam about some of the little deals that Jeff Knight hasn't declared and I'm sure the CIA would be very interested to know who those deals were with,' whispered Brad venomously. ''How do people feel at the moment about arms being sold to Iraq and Libya amongst others to shoot and kill Americans? I doubt the members of the golf club would be quiet so keen to have supper at the Captain's table then, would they?'

'Look, Brad, I just don't want you to do anything that you'll regret, that's all.'

Brad was unmoved. 'To use the big bastard's expression, bullshit. You've just got cold feet and that's it. But don't think I have and believe me I'll see you behind bars for what you've done, so help me I will. And if I don't get him first you might find yourself in distinguished company.'

'What?'

'Oh yes, Jeff, you're not the only one to forget a few details on you tax declaration. The taxpayers of Arkansas picked up the bills for food, transport, electricity, housekeeping, entertainment and even Chelsea's nanny as a security guard. The press are about to push him on it all.'

'Then he'll have to go anyway, why kill him?'

'Don't be a fool, Jeff. He'll sort it out. Uncle Sam won't take the President to Court.'

Jeff said nothing.

'And you must know that Perot now has ten million supporters across the country and that come the mid term elections Los Angeles will not look like a one off freak result.'

'Okay, Brad, I'll say nothing, but I want no further part of it, alright?' Jeff replied trying to hide his fear of Brad's threat.

'That's fine, Jeff, but one word to anyone and I'll blow the whistle on you so loud that they'll hear in those far away places who use your weapons with your name ground out.'

'Okay, okay,' replied Jeff irritably. 'You've made your point, okay.'

'And if anything should happen to me either before or after the assassination or if I am even questioned, the finger will point at you, so you had better hope no-one else decides to rat on me, got it?'

'Got it,' said Jeff as he slowly walked away from the man who for over a quarter of a century had been his friend. He knew now that he had never known him any more than he had known himself. It was odd just how much a fish could change a man's life.

Brad was also tired and worried, but not worried about Waterford or Jeff Knight. He was worried about how he was going to get Angie to agree to her role and then get her close enough to the President. As sure as Miles Waterford drank bourbon, Bill Clinton did not intend to go near any stray women before the late fall of 1996 at the earliest.

'Good,' said Steve as Brad replaced the receiver after his call to Angie. 'Scott, get someone to find that bungalow and wire it for sound and pictures, every room. I want it infested with bugs. He's going to tell her exactly what he's up to as soon as he gets there. We must beat her to it, this is the break we need.

'How d'you know that?'

'Experience. Instinct.' Steve did not expand on the two words and Scott accepted them.

The tails at the airport picked up Brad and Jeff as they went their separate ways while Steve and Scott had listened in to their earpieces to the acrimonious conversation between the two men. The decision to bug their clothes and baggage had been a difficult one, it ran the risk of discovery, but the information they learnt at the airport that morning justified it and the alert went from A2 to A1 immediately.

'I thought you'd have asked for that last night,' said Scott.

'We weren't certain then that Harworth was going to

continue on his own, but I'm in no doubt now. I've been watching the man. He's a selfish, self opinionated, cowardly little shit and he's dangerous. Now he's told a few people what he plans to do he's got to find a way of going through with it. Not because he must achieve it, but because his pride won't let him do what Knight has done.'

'What do we do about Knight now?'

'Nothing. He might have changed his mind, but until we've wrapped this up he stays in the frame and under observation. Just because he's changed his mind once doesn't mean he won't change it back again. Harworth might still need his help and he's obviously got enough dirt on the guy to make him help.'

'What about us moving in first to use him?'

'I've thought about that. As soon as we get back to Washington we'll have the A1 on the linkup and see what the Chief reckons, but my view is no.'

'Any special reason?'

'Essentially, the man is weak. He doesn't have the arrogance of Harworth and I'm not sure he could handle it. As it is we're in touch with him, we know everything that goes on and with any luck both houses are now fully wired. Let's use him on our terms without the risk of him taking fright.'

Gillespi watched Lech very closely as he returned to the table but he was in total control. 'Nothing wrong, I hope?'

'No,' said Lech, 'just a message from my son-in-law to tell me that I've got to ring Uncle Sam about a new Trust I'm setting up.'

Whatever else Lech Zielinski was, he was not from the Agency. It was at least five hours earlier in the States.

After breakfast they strolled together in Green Park and stopped at the Grapes in Shepherd Market just after twelve for a pint of bitter.

'Odd stuff, this English beer. I've never really been able to get used to it and yet they drink gallons of the stuff!' said Lech, who had relaxed considerably since his phone call.

'I know, almost as much as tea and I don't like that either,' replied Gillespi, taking Lech's glass. 'But what say we have another just to try and understand what it is they see in it!'

'Why not, just one and then we can wander round to one of the restaurants in the market for lunch.'

It was four o'clock when they returned to the Fox House Club, both bloated and in need of a rest. 'I've got a little work to do and I must ring home so if you'll excuse me I'll just make my way on up to my room,' said Lech as they stood in the hallway.

'Of course. The bar's closed, so I'll do the same. I need the sleep. Not as young as you, you know!

'I'm going to have a quiet night in and watch TV. No doubt I'll see you over breakfast tomorrow.'

'No doubt,' replied Lech as he reached the door of his room and opened it.

Gillespi lay on his bed looking at the ceiling, just thinking for several hours. He didn't have to move before Tuesday and could easily string it out beyond then if he had to, but was there any need? Was there any point in getting to know the man any better? If he was what he seemed then why wait? If he was not what he seemed, then he was unlikely to make a slip now and the risk he had taken over lying about the phone call made no sense. A professional would have given an innocuous reply and with less detail. His seventy seven year old mind slipped into sleep as he lay there.

It was just after eight when he woke and he looked out of the window to see the street awash with water and the rain still pouring down. He wasn't hungry, he'd eaten well already that day, so he undressed for bed and watched TV until he fell asleep again.

Both men were up early for breakfast on the Monday and Lech asked Gillespi if he'd like to join him on a sight-seeing tour of London. He was planning to catch one of the open-top buses that ran from outside the Ritz.

'I'd like that, I'd like that very much,' Gillespi said, grateful for the continued chance to observe Lech at close quarters without arousing suspicion. They dined apart that night but at breakfast on Tuesday morning Lech was edgy again. Gillespi slipped out to while away the morning to a coffee shop and returned just before two to find Lech sitting anxiously at his lunch table, having only picked at his calves' liver.

'Hello, not feeling so good?'

Lech looked up, startled. 'Oh, hi. No, not hungry today. Don't know why.'

'Mind if I join you?'

'Karl,' said Gillespi waving towards the butler, 'a bottle of house red and a couple of glasses please, and I'll have a rare steak.'

'Certainly, Mr Somerfield.'

'Here,' said Gillespi as the wine arrived, 'take a glass of that and tell me what's bothering you. It started with that phone call on Sunday at breakfast, didn't it?'

Lech looked hard at him. Who was this man he had spent most of the last four days with? Whatever made him ask a question like that?

'Lech, I was in the Mounties, I was never a great detective but I know that it's most unlikely that your son-in-law would ring you in the middle of the night on a Sunday morning to give you a routine message. That is, if he had known where you were. Granted you might have left a message for him, but you seemed surprised when they paged you. You wouldn't have been if you'd been expecting the call. And yet you have been expecting a call here, haven't you?'

'That obvious, huh?'

'Every time that phone rang on Friday you jumped. But yesterday you were relaxed and went out, even suggested it to me, but today you're sitting here anxiously again. Now tell me it's none of my business if you like, but if I can help, please, I'd like to.'

'No,' replied Lech wearily, 'I was hoping to meet someone who would solve a mystery for me, for us all really, and perhaps throw some light on something current for me, but it looks as if he's not coming after all.'

'Was it important?' asked Gillespi gently.

'To me yes, very important. I wanted to know the truth.'

'About?'

'Something that happened almost thirty years ago.'

'Why after so long?'

'If the truth is what I think it might be, then history might be about to repeat itself and I'd like that.'

Gillespi acted puzzled. 'I've no idea what you're talking about. But why would you like history to repeat itself?'

'To save others from the suffering that my daughter and wife endured.'

That one Gillespi genuinely could not understand. What had Kennedy's death got to do with the suffering of Zielinski's wife and daughter? His steak arrived and he decided to lighten the conversation while he ate but returned to the issue as soon as he had finished.

'How did you wife and daughter suffer?' he asked.

'Cancer, leukaemia, both of them.' His tone was soft, remorseful.

'What could repeat itself that would prevent suffering?'

'It doesn't matter, I've got to sort it out alone. Look,' said Lech picking himself up mentally. 'I don't want to burden you with my troubles, how about some cheese and a few ports to wash it down?'

'Sounds good to me,' said Gillespi seriously wondering if he had pierced Lech's meaning together correctly. He decided to let the conversation drift again and it was well past four o'clock when they settled down to their coffees in the first floor lounge and club room.

'The only thing I can remember of any major significance thirty years ago was the assassination of Kennedy,' said Gillespi as he sipped his coffee. 'And like most people I know exactly where I was at the time.'

'Don't we all,' replied Lech immediately suspicious.

'Where were you, Lech?'

'Me? I was at work, signing a deal to buy out the Fifth Chicago Drug Company. We had just signed the papers and a secretary burst into the room having been told not to interrupt us under any circumstances. My first reaction was to sack her there and then, but when she gave us the news and wheeled in the TV so we could watch the aftermath, I promoted her. And you, Ted, where were you?'

'Ted Somerfield did not exist then.'

'I'm sorry?' said Lech puzzled.

'I was sitting in a small motel room with two other men watching the television from twelve twenty to until just after it happened. I can remember it as if it was yesterday. I can still feel the tension. Those other two men, Lech, were Carl Hankin and Mike Garson.

'So you are...,' began Lech slowly.

'Gillespi. And I'm sorry to have put you through the last four days, but I had to be sure. In theory, as I shall tell you, I had nothing to fear from the firm, but you never know in that business, you just never know, especially with a new President keen to make a name for himself and to do something to draw the flack from some of the things he perhaps should not have done.'

'I understand. I don't mind at all and if the man I've shared the last four days with is the real man, then I'm pleased you are so cautious. I wouldn't want anything to happen to you.'

'So where shall I start?'

'At the beginning?'

'No, that I can't do. But here is a letter which does start at the beginning and if you'll give me your address I'll see you get it when I die. You're a good few years younger than me so it should work out that way.

'I'll start from twelve twenty two on 22nd November 1963 when the three of us were closeted in that room, waiting, just silently waiting.'

'You've done well, John,' said Powers as they drove away from their meeting with Friggli. 'He's just the sort of man we needed.'

'But where will we raise that sort of money? Even to us it's big bucks.'

'Half of it I have,' he said quietly in a tone that Edwards had never heard before. It was confident, assured, but it was also gently.

'You do?' was the surprised reply. 'Where from?'

'Let us just say a number of well-wishers. You keep ahead in this life, John, by starting ahead. I started fund raising when Clinton was nominated in July last year, but I hadn't expected to need so much.'

'So why did you agree?'

'You do not argue with men like that, you pay his price or you look elsewhere and the problem is that if we'd said no or we wanted to think about it, any other potential assassin that we might have found would have known the going price even by now. And you know what happens when you buy cut price staff.'

'So where do you find the rest of the money and quickly?'

'For starters, you've not contributed yet, John and neither has Matt Andrews,' he ended, sounding thoughtful.

'Okay, but that won't raise $25m, and Friggli won't wait long.'

'I'll make a few phone calls. Give me a week, at most.'

Edwards was more than a little worried about what *his* anticipated contribution was. A million dollars he could live with, more than that would be difficult.

'We meet Matt tomorrow evening in New York,' said Powers triumphantly as he replaced the receiver and picked up his mineral water. 'He'll be good for $5m and I've got you down for $2m, okay, John?'

'He agreed that easily?' said a stunned Edwards.

'He might even decide to be a little more generous after we've discussed what he read in Ali's folder, we'll see,' replied Powers smugly. 'Your contribution satisfactory, John?' he added with a wry smile.

Edwards swallowed hard and sank his drink in one. 'Yes, yes, fine.' he replied timidly.

'Cash by the end of next week, here are the details,' said Powers handing him a small typewritten note giving details of a bank account in Bermuda.

'No problem,' responded Edwards starting to sweat a little and wondering just what Powers had in his file on him. Was it a double bluff, did he really know anything? He was scared to challenge him. That was enough to make him pay.

The three men met in the Sheraton Hotel and exactly on time Powers rang Friggli. 'All arranged,' he said returning triumphantly to the table. 'We have three weeks to raise the money and I've arranged the delivery. But he starts work tomorrow,' he added.

Andrews and Edwards looked at Powers, completely lost by the final comment.

'What does that mean?' asked Andrews, who was more subdued than Edwards had ever seen him and and barely touched his whiskey. His tone was mildly aggressive, mildly enquiring, mildly disbelieving.

'You can't assassinate a man just like that. The success of the operation depends on detailed planning, which in turn depends on detailed reports, observations and research. We've only got a few months — the thinking is that the CIA spent years working on the Kennedy assassination.'

'Always assuming it was them,' interrupted Edwards.

'Who else was it? Who else could have closed so many doors? Who else could have arranged for so many different people in authority to do their jobs so ineptly? It was the CIA and anyone who doubts it is a fool.' There was no room in Powers' words for disagreement.

'So who will the world think it is this time?' asked Andrews swilling his whiskey around in his glass but still not actually drinking it.

'I've not decided yet,' replied Powers looking evilily at Matt Andrews, 'maybe you.'

Andrews stared at him. 'You just might not live as long as the President if you don't start taking some care,' he said slowly and menacingly.

'Then, Matt, a file will be posted to every police authority and newspaper in this country from the smallest settlement to the Washington Post. You'd better pray I live, Matt, or it could be very embarrassing for you.

'Come on, drink up, you're lagging behind today,' concluded Powers, with another of his evil smiles.

Edwards was becoming increasingly nervous, but throughout this conversation said nothing. He was in it up to his neck. He knew it and he knew he had no choice. Harry Powers had been setting them both up for years, as no doubt he had the other unknown worthies who had already contributed to the fund and those who were about to do so.

It was early afternoon when Hamdi awoke in the mountain camp and stretched this weak, tired body. There was no-one about outside the makeshift cabin and he helped himself to a glass of water. Food was reasonably plentiful, mostly game caught in the mountains, and although the water had to be boiled from the snow it was in good supply.

Was Moncilo serious? Could he actually make an appointment to see Clinton and explain the position to him? Would Clinton listen? More to the point, would he act? Could he persuade others? If not, would America act alone?

How would he make the contact in the first place? He'd have to remind Clinton of their days at Oxford together and make sure that whatever message he sent reached him. He must receive thousands, tens of thousands of letters a week that would take staff ages to sift. That was no good. He could not think straight, his mind, once so sharp and agile, was that of a tired old man, listless and slow.

He sat there for a while struggling to think clearly. Before long Moncilo returned, looking pleased with himself.

'How do you feel?' he asked.

'Honestly?' replied Hamdi smiling weakly.

'Honestly.'

'Hungry.'

'That we can do something about, my friend. We must

feed you up, your mission is being arranged even as we talk.'

'It will never be possible,' said Hamdi choking on his words as he spoke them. Where had the self-belief gone? Where was the fight that had taken him from his tiny village to Oxford?

Moncilo looked at him sadly, seeing before him a broken man but one who could, with a little help, soon mend himself. He *had* to mend himself, for the sake of the Muslims.

'Come,' he said, placing a friendly arm around Hamdi, 'you must eat and we will tell you what is happening. We have achieved much,' he continued positively, 'but you will achieve more. You will speak to the President of the United States on our behalf, on behalf of our people.' His voice was strong, purposeful and clear. Hamdi drew comfort from it. He wanted to be positive, he wanted to succeed.

'Thank you, I'd like to know what has happened.'

'We will have the money tonight. It is to be stolen from a Serbian bank.'

'You can do that?' asked Hamdi, taken aback by the casualness of the remark.

'Yes, we can do it. It is dangerous and no doubt we will lose some men, but we can do it. We *will* do it.'

Despite his mental and physical state Hamdi realised that Moncilo had deliberately mentioned losing men. It was meant to motivate him and it did.

'And the passport?' he asked positively.

'It is being prepared now and after we have cleaned you up we will take the photograph.'

'Good,' replied Hamdi knowing that his cheeriness was an act and that Moncilo knew it was an act, but he had to start somewhere. The act must become a habit, the habit must become instinctive nature.

'The biggest problem will be getting you out of the country, but your Serb papers will help you with that. It will be dangerous but the safest route out for you, as a Serb, will be through Serbian occupied country, so we will also put a picture onto those papers.

Hamdi shivered. False papers in case of need were one thing but to deliberately walk into the arms of the Serbs as one of them was another.

'What have you in mind?' he asked.

'We can move you at night from one group of people like us to another until we get you across the River Drina. Once you are over it you will be in Serbia where, as a Serb you will be safe. The difficulty is getting you to the Drina because of Croatian activity between here and the river.

'Once you are in Serbia your journey should be risk free. You must make for Ulcinj where we have friends who will take you by boat to Italy. From there it is easy. You will be escorted to the American Embassy in Rome and they will arrange for you to be flown to Washington to meet the President.

'You make it sound easy,' said Hamdi with a genuine smile.

'It is my friend. In theory at least we have radio contact with people along the southern coast who are sympathetic and will help us.'

'We trust them, they have helped us before,' said the big man who had first questioned Hamdi. 'We also trust our information man here.' he continued, wacking Moncilo heartily on the back with his giant hand. 'He is more informed than anyone.'

Moncilo smiled. His only source of information was the BBC but he listened to it all day and night. Every little titbit of information he remembered. 'He is right, and in turn they have friends in Italy and, once at the Embassy, I am sure that if you tell them your story the President will agree to see you. It will be good publicity for him, I doubt that David Gergen will want to miss out on the opportunity. He has made quite an impact since he was appointed and a bit like Carville did during the election, he decides and Clinton does. There have been several little staged events since Gergen was appointed and they have all been successful.'But first I have to cross the river. And then how do I get to Ulcinj?' Hamdi was struggling to accept that it was possible, but equally determined to be positive.

'Neither will be easy and both will be dangerous,' replied Moncilo, his tone becoming more serious, more concerned, 'but it is possible and there is no other way.

'I will do it. If I have to I will threaten to expose matters from Oxford, even if I have to invent them. I will make Bill Clinton see me.'

'That, I hope, is not necessary, my friend. We want him to be sympathetic when he sees you. He has enough problems with the past haunting him — he recently even found a half brother he knew nothing of.'

'Really?' replied Hamdi in disbelief. 'How do you find out these things?'

'It is all on the radio,' laughed Moncilo. 'But, yes it is true. The child was conceived by Clinton's father's first wife in 1938, although they had divorced by then.'

'So they might not have the same father.'

'It seems that they have from what was recorded at the time. The first wife is still alive, aged 75, living in California. She says he is William Blythe's son and has said so since he was born.'

'But there are people in America who don't know this, how do you?'

'It did come to light during the election but was ignored by the Democrats and the press don't seem to have run with it. Far more interesting, from the gossip standpoint, is the fact that the woman, a Mrs Adele Coffelt, claims that after he divorced her, William Blythe married her younger sister before he married Virginia Cassidy, Bill's mother, in 1942.'

'Incredible,' said Hamdi, finishing his stew, 'and that was wonderful. I've not eaten like this for months.'

'Good, we must feed you up and we must teach you things you will need to know for your journey. A week should be enough. We don't have time to waste — you must be mentally and physically prepared.'

'But who goes without food to feed me up?' asked Hamdi anxiously.

'No-one, my friend, fear not. Up here in the mountains we can eat by catching wild animals, even some fish. In the valleys, in the towns and the villages it is different, but up here it is not a problem.'

'What was that I've just eaten?'

'I honestly have no idea. I went to Oxford, I speak English well so I listen to the BBC. I can organise and so I run the administration and make the contacts around the country. I would starve up here alone! Others catch wild animals and turn them into food. It is always stew but I never ask what it is, it is probably better not to know!'

'It works well.'

'It works well and you know the President of the United States, so you will talk to him for us. It is back to old days for us all. Each man doing what he is good at for the benefit of the community as a whole.

'Now I must teach you things you will need to know for your journey. We must spend at least an hour a day, you must eat regularly and you must rest. We can only do so much in a week, but we must do all that we can.'

Jeff Knight did not enjoy the flight home from Alaska. He knew what Brad could do to him. It would ruin him and he could spend the next twenty years, maybe the rest of his life, in prison. But Waterford was right, assassinating the President was not the answer, it could never be the answer and it would only bring disgrace to America.

'Hi honey,' said Sally-Anne as she greeted him in her usual alcoholic frenzy. 'Good fishing trip? I've sure missed you,' she teased, rubbing her left hand across her bosom.

'Yeah, great,' he replied, having no inclination to satisfy her needs. He had frankly expected her to be exhausted, having taken advantage of him being away, but clearly she did not get as many callers as she used to. Looking at her, that was understandable. It was also something else that he had thought seriously about while wrestling with the trout on the Alagnak River.

'What d'you catch, honey? Nothing nasty, I hope!'

The last thing he wanted was a scene or a half drunken attempt at sex. She was well on her way, he thought. A few more large gins and she would be asleep for hours.

Brad Harworth sat on the plane unable to eat or drink; his stomach was thrashing about like one of those trout Jeff had hooked. He simply didn't have the money to arrange the assassination himself, and was relying on Jeff to introduce a benefactor. At first Miles Waterford had seemed perfect. A simple country man with more money than anyone could spend. A man who was patriotic and could be made to see that he was doing it for America. Either Brad was losing his touch or the simple country boy was far from simple. He chose the second option, not because it was necessarily right but because his ego could not consider the alternative.

As soon as he reached the airport he rang Angie and she came to collect him.

'My it's good to see you, darling. You know I've missed you.'

'And I've missed you too, believe me I have,' said Brad, being honest for probably the first time since he had left Washington, other than when he was lambasting Jeff at the airport. 'What say we have some food and an early night. I'm flat out and I'd like to get back to my prime before I learn what the big man taught you.' There was that leer in his eyes that made Angie go all tingly.

'Why no, honey, let's get right on at it. I've been saving myself for you for three whole days and I'm feeling rampant. I'm sure all that country air up there must have done the same to you.'

The last thing that Brad Harworth felt like at the moment was screwing Angie Tourle but she was now the only way he could see himself having any hope of pursuing his increasing obsession to assassinate the President. He had no choice.

'Okay,' he said as he opened the door of the bungalow he kept for his various liasions. 'Let's go for it, baby!'

Before he had put his case down she was out of her thin white cotton miniskirt and undoing the buttons of her silky blue blouse. As usual she wore no underwear and as she stood there, her soft blonde hair flowing down over her beautifully formed breasts, Brad felt the excitement race through his body. The light silhouetted her smooth young body but as he reached forward to embrace her she dropped to her knees and began to unbuckle his belt. With a swift movement that came from experience, she slipped his trousers down.

Slowly she moved her tender hands up from his ankles, past his calves and over his thighs to his buttocks. She ignored the bulge that was pulsating in his jockey pants and, lifting and unbuttoning his shirt, began to nibble away at his navel as she gently ground the palms of her hands against his buttocks. Standing, slowly she removed his shirt and played teasingly with his nipples before biting them hard. Pin pricks of blood surfaced. Angie purred with satisfaction and licked them like a thirsty cat.

He held her head to his chest but she wriggled free, running her tongue around his tensing stomach muscles. He could bear it no longer. He put his hands beneath her bottom and lifted her clean off the ground and onto the living room table. They French kissed as she sat there, legs dangling off the table while he fondled her breasts and she slipped loose his jockey pants, which he kicked away.

It was his turn to work his way, more gently, down her body with his mouth. He lingered over her ample breasts while she held him close to her, her legs interlocked behind his back. It was twenty minutes before he reached her lower hairs and began to excite her with his tongue.

Lying back on the table with her feet held high she then drew him into her, and an hour of passionate love making began, after which they lay warm and relaxed side by side on the large white leather sofa.

'I'd forgotten just how good you could be,' he said to her as she kissed his lips gently.

'Life's become too normal, too routine,' she whispered in his ear. 'We need more excitement, more experiment. That hillbilly was a powerful man whose physical ability and strength enabled him to do things that no man I've ever met could do, but it was still only a variation on the text book.'

Brad laughed. The very thought of it, the text book! Loverboy Waterford. Had he instructed her in the art of Alaskan love making in the same way he had instructed Jeff in the art of trout fishing?

'Something I said?' she said.

'Yes,' he smiled, 'the thought of Loverboy Waterford with a sexual text book!'

'Oh don't misunderstand me, I learnt a few things. That's what makes me realise how boring my screwing has become. He wasn't that special. Although I wouldn't mind betting he could write a few text books on sex as well as fishing! Makes you wonder what they really do on those long winter nights up there in the frozen north.'

'That it does,' he replied gently cupping her left breast. 'Angie, I want to ask you a serious question,' he said gently.

'What is it,' she replied warily, drawing away from him slightly.

'It's important.'

'Hey, Brad, we screw, occasionally we make love, most times we enjoy it. We don't talk seriously, that's not my scene.

'This involves screwing. Screwing at the highest level.'

'And what does that mean?' she said, laughing as she nestled down onto his chest and slipped a hand down into his groin.

'What d'you think of the President?' He expected the question to stun her but she replied instantly.

'A shit.'

'A shit?'

'Yeah, a right shit, but I wouldn't mind screwing him all the same. That woman's not what a man like him needs, which is why he's had to look elsewhere.'

'Then what makes you say he's a shit?'

'All politicians are shits, especially Democrats and especially Democratic Presidents.' Her words were harsh, uncompromising, and they shocked Brad.

'So he's not a shit for his own sake but because of what he represents?'

'If you like, but why all the questions? she asked, in a direct and forceful tone he'd never heard her use before. She climbed over him onto the floor, to stand legs apart, hands on hips, looking down at him.

'Angie, can I trust you?' he asked seriously.

'That depends,' she replied, equally seriously.

'I think Bill Clinton is a danger to this country and a danger to this world and I plan to assassinate him.'

He saw the muscles in her body tense but her stance never changed. 'The plans I was laying down have got to be changed because I've been let down by two people who have chickened out. They've not got the balls for it.'

'So why are you telling me this?'

'Will you help me, Angie?'

She didn't speak for a moment but rolled him onto his back, knelt astride him on the sofa and lowered herself on to him. Squeezing his thighs together with her own she flicked her head back so that her long blonde hair fell down her spine. Pushing firmly downwards she said, 'You want me to help you assassinate the President?'

'Yes,' he replied between breaths.

'When?' she asked, rising up now, hovering over him.

He simply grunted in reply.

'When?' she asked again.

'As soon as possible.'

'How?'

'We'll have to work that one out.'

'Well I doubt if I'll get the chance to do it like this. I fear he's had to give all that up for a while, but I'll find a way, if you can get me close to him.'

'Why?' he asked, unable to hide her surprise at the reaction.

'Unsettled family business. Let's just say I don't like draft dodgers or Presidents who send men to fight when they've never done it themselves'

Brad Harworth had no idea what she was talking about, but he knew enough to see that she meant what she said and that he should not ask. He knew enough to lie back and do his duty for America.

CHAPTER EIGHT

The Control Centre in the White House consisted of two basement rooms, each about twenty feet square, with no windows but the most efficient and silent air conditioning that either of them had ever experienced. The rooms were interlocking, the outer housing all the equipment for the surveillance, the inner was furnished with desks, plastic wallboards and the linkup to Langley for the A1 conferences.

'Well done, Steve,' said the chief. 'We found and wired the bungalow before the girl got there. My instinct tells me that he's likely to tell her more than he tells his wife.'

'From what we've seen goes on at home when he's away they look about as faithful as each other, sir.'

'Yes and that worries me. We've put tails on all the men Mrs Harworth has seen in the last few days but if she keeps it up at this rate for another week we'll have to bring in the army!'

'Is it worth the effort? They look like her toyboys rather than anything to do with him, sir.'

'They look like it, I agree, but one of them may just be spying for him. In relationships like that it's dangerous to assume anything or to overlook anything. For a while we tail everybody, but we'll run that from here. You keep close to the two of them.'

'Do you want us to fly to Tampa, sir?'

'No, the sound and pictures will do. If you're needed down there we'll worry about that later. You've got to know them a little — I want you to watch, listen and interpret. You understand them better than any of us.'

'Do you think we should change our stance on Knight, sir?'

'No, I go along with your view in your report. It's early days yet, All Harworth has is the desire — he doesn't have the money, the means or the opportunity. All we've got to do is to keep so close to them both that if any one of those looks like falling into place we can pounce.'

'Then we'll carry on as we are, sir.'

'Keep it up, Steve.'

The screen went dead.

'Do you think he will find the money?' asked Scott.

'I think he'll keep looking for a way to carry out the hit, whether that means finding the money I'm not sure. If I were him I would look at the opportunity and then find somebody else with their own reason for wanting to carry out the hit,' replied Steve.

'What? Terrorists, Saddam, something like that?'

'Possibly, but remember a lot of people are none too happy with the President. There could be any number of pressure groups all over the country who want him dead and some of them are nutters.'

'Should we check them out first, stay one step in front of Harworth in case he goes down that track?'

Waite hesitated. The idea was good, but the list would be endless. Where would they start, where would they stop? But then the risk of not doing it was too great. It had to be done.

'Yes, get them working on it at Langley and detail it in the next hourly report to the chief.'

It took Gillespi an hour to bring Lech to the point where he had left Hankin having agreed to his terms.

'But you didn't stay.' said Lech, stating more than asking.

'No,' was the succinct response.

'Did you ever have any intention of staying?'

'To be absolutely honest, I'm not sure. I wanted to believe Carl, I think I did believe Carl, but I still had this nagging doubt at the back of my mind.'

'So what did you do next?'

'Like all troubled animals I went back to my own back yard where I was safe and felt comfortable.'

'New York?'

'Yes. I told my mother I'd lost my job. She thought I was a salesman, which fitted in well enough because Hankin had told me to take six months off.'

'Really?' asked Lech surprised. 'I'd have expected them to want to keep very close tabs on you for a long time.'

'I'm sure they did, but I could also understand that they didn't want me mixing with other agents who were bound to ask what I knew about Mike's death. The very fact that I was at Hankin's funeral would have raised some awkward questions. We never worked together officially, had no reason to even know each other.

'On balance it made sense and, although it was not their intention, it also gave me time to think quietly and logically. As long as I kept a low profile and didn't make any waves it was unlikely that they would move against me during those six months. They could have killed me very efficiently and anonymously in Santa Monica and didn't. Why do it in New York, where it would be more conspicuous?'

'I can see that, but why didn't they just kill you?' Lech was suspicious.

'I don't know.'

'So you just sat the time out?'

'Yeah and I really enjoyed most of it and so did Mum. In the end it was a blessing because she had a stroke and died the following April. We spent the last few months of her life together. I was there when she died. That wouldn't have happened otherwise. She died that night when she had the stroke, before the ambulance arrived, so there was no way I would have even got to see her if I'd been working.'

Lech smiled sincerely. He understood and Gillespi knew he understood. There was no need to comment.

'So when did you decide?'

'At her funeral, oddly enough. I just thought, there is nothing for me to stay here for now, so why don't I away to a whole new life in Brazil?'

'What about the people watching you?'

'They were only kids then, they'd been top drawer at the outset, but as the months went by and they perceived the chance of me slipping away to be less, they reduced both the quality and the quantity of the surveillance.'

'Even after your mother's death?' asked Lech, surprised.

'Yes, because the kids didn't think it significant enough to report. I'd have gone straight back to maximum cover — it had to be a high risk point — but they missed.'

'So what did you do?'

'I packed a bag and left,' replied Gillespi curtly.

'Not just like that,' said Lech emphatically, 'Tell me about it.'

'Yes, just like that. They were in pairs, three eight hour shifts a day and there was probably a bike rider stationed nearby but I never actually saw him. The worst shift is midnight to eight when at about three or four o'clock the night starts to drag, so that's when I left.

'I invited some friends in for a few drinks one night and made sure that there was enough booze to keep the party going well into the early hours, if not until breakfast. Once they were well tanked up I asked several of them to do me a favour and go for the odd cab ride from about midnight. Told them it was a bet. Just around the block and back ten minutes later, but the result was that from midnight there was a never ending string of cabs coming and going and people in and out of the basement flat the whole time.'

'And you just slipped away unnoticed?'

'That was the idea and it almost worked. In fact it did work, but the kids had radioed in what was happening and control told them to make sure I was still there. I'd only just left, obviously nobody knew what I was up to and whoever spoke to them at the door said I'd just gone out for a ride round the block in a cab. They were on to it like a shot, and every cab was pulled in — even in New York there aren't that many on the roads at three in the morning, and not much other traffic either

'We were approaching the airport at Manhattan when I saw the roadblock ahead. They'd moved fast, very fast.'

'What did you do?' asked Lech, always happy to think on his feet in a meeting but having no experience of situations like this.

'I remembered the golden rule. Never panic, they might not even be looking for you.'

'But they were.'

'They were, yes,' replied Gillespi, obviously finding the memory painful to talk about. 'I shot the patrol man approaching the cab and told the driver to drive through the road block.'

'With a gun at his head?' asked Lech.

'It wasn't necessary, besides which I had to take out the second patrol man as we crashed through the car.'

'Also dead?' asked Lech.

'Dead men don't shoot back or radio a position. It gave me just a little time. I forced the cab driver to take me into the shortstay carpark, ripped out his radio and locked him in the car. I guessed I had maybe ten to fifteen minutes before every policeman in the airport would be looking for me and every desk would be told to watch out for me.'

'They'd assume it was you?'

'They'd know it was me, with two dead patrol men.'

'So what did you do?'

'Rushed up to the PanAm desk and bought a rover ticket and jumped the first plane out, Seattle. They were taking the steps away as I hit them, but it was enough, they lost me.

'Once I was free I assumed the disguise of one of the passports they didn't think I'd still got and flew to Rio, having visited half the airports in the South on the way. It took time and care but I had the advantage, even Rio was not set in stone. I was not actually aiming for anywhere.

'What about money?' asked Lech, nothing if not practical.

'I always carried $10,000 in those days and I had an account in Switzerland which was still a secret.' Gillespi leaned forward a glimmer of nostalgia showing in his smile. 'In those days they really were secret.'

'So you settled in Rio?'

'No, I stayed there for several months, lost in the crowd, but then bought a little place near the coast at Sao Mateus. A town large enough to be lost in, but not so small as to stand out and be easily found in.'

'What made you go to Mexico?'

'I was found, seven years ago. I think they looked hard for me in the early days, but as the years went by and I didn't rock the board, the perceived threat diminished and they started to forget about me. In any event there were theories everywhere about what really happened and I'd have just been another one.'

'Despite being a CIA man?' asked Lech with surprise.

'I think so, yes. After all Jim Garrison — the former New Orleans District Attorney, remember?' Lech nodded, 'had started making waves in, I guess, about sixty six, and it was open season on theories. Perhaps the best cover up of all, who knows. It was Hankin's real death that stirred it up again. He'd written a letter to the chief which was posted on his death. Told all that he knew and asked him to take whatever action he felt right. He also enclosed a copy of my letter to him, which I'd posted in Miami on my way to Rio, in which I'd said I didn't want to be involved any more but would not release details of what I knew. Not that it included the all-important information, i.e. who controlled us. At best all I could have done was to convict myself of treason, as I said in the letter.

'The chief decided to do nothing, but took the view that if I'd been quiet for almost twenty years then I meant what I said and was not a security threat and put out word to find me. It took them nearly four years, but in the end they tracked me down and told me they were no longer interested in me.' Gillespi had taken a liking to Lech. Not enough to tell him that he had been put back on the payroll, just in case a would-be assassin did approach him, but enough to suggest that he would not be unwelcome at Langley and could make contact.

'So why'd you not go back home?'

'Maybe they really weren't interested in me that day but it's too easy to have an accident in New York, too easy for someone to overstep the mark, so I settled on Mexico and I've been very happy.'

'Until I came along?'

'Yeah,' he said wearily, 'you did worry me a bit. New ideological President, I thought. Democrat, having a few problems, what better way to win back a few lost friends than expose the truth about Kennedy and parade one of the plotters. He'd want me alive but at my age the thought of being held captive and put on trial is worse than the thought of the bullet. I was concerned, which is why I put you through what I did, I'm sorry. His apology was sincere.

'No, you were very wise and I'm glad you did it. I respect you for it.'

'Thanks .... So what else d'you want to know and how well did you know Oswald?' asked Gillespi, lightening his tone.

'Not that well. We spent a bit of time at school together and he dragged me off to David Ferrie's Civil Air Patrol, but we never had much in common. His letter was a complete surprise to me.'

'But you didn't act on it at the time. Why not?' asked Gillespi.

'Didn't want to put the family at risk. Hey, a bunch of guys who have just taken out the President aren't going to lose any sleep about removing me from the scene.'

'True. So you just sat on it until your daughter died?'

'Yes.' The reply was cold. Gillespi could not fail to miss the change in tone.

'Tell me,' continued Lech, 'did they ever carry on the operation?'

'What, more Oswalds?' the question was guarded.

'Yes.'

'I don't know and that's the truth.' His words carried conviction but although he was ageing, Lech was well aware that he was still a professional. 'My guess is yes, but when Bush was at the White House the whole programme was probably scrapped, even as early as when he was first Vice-President.'

'How would that have happened?'

'Bush was unique, a President, a Vice-President before

than who had connections at Langley. People all thought the CIA were involved in some way. He'd have found out and, if the programme still existed, made sure it was scrapped.'

'You don't think it could have been too secret for that?'

'It's possible, but every instinct I have tells me it was probably continued at first, but not for long.'

'But you don't know, there could still be a deep-seated contingency plan for assassinating a President if the Secret Service thought it necessary?' The question was direct and forceful.

'There could be, yes, but in my opinion it is unlikely. Why the interest?' The question was also direct and equally forceful.

'Do you think if there was still a programme that they would be likely to move against Clinton?'

'Maybe,' replied Gillespi guardedly, 'but why the interest?' This time the question was sharper.

'You've been straight, George, so I'll be straight with you. I fear this administration might cost America, cost the world, more lives than any administration ever, and it's all down to ideological dogma.'

Gillespi was lost, it made no sense. 'How?'

'We live in an age of technology, an age when everything in life is faster than it's ever been before. We live in an age when expectancy, already high, increases daily. It's there in every walk of life but none more so than in medicine.'

Now Gillespi nodded. 'Okay, go on.'

'If a man's car goes wrong he has always taken it down to the garage and expected a mechanic to tell him what's wrong and put it right. Reasonable when you think about it because it was the mechanic, or someone like him, who put the thing together in the first place.

'But today, if a man has something wrong with his body, especially if it's not self-inflicted, then he expects to visit the doctor and have it put right. Fifty years ago, he didn't think like that, but he has come to do so because of the success that medicine has achieved since the last war. Remember penicillin was not even discovered until during that war.'

'So what are you driving at, Lech?'

'The cost of research, the cost of developing and testing new drugs is astronomical, and it can only be funded by profit. There is no magical pot for research. Today's research costs are funded by yesterday's profits and today's profits will fund tomorrow's research.

'I know profits are huge, I know how huge, I make them! But I also know that we put it back. A profit this year is of no use to the industry, let alone an individual company, unless we can maintain and increase the speed of advancement. It's not just drugs, it's equipment, facilities and premises. Just look at what the medical industry puts back into the economy. Even the stockholders, who get very good dividends, eventually put it back into the companies through rights issues when the industry needs more cash for advancement.'

'And you're afraid that Mrs President's purge will not result in better health care for all at a cheaper price, but a run down in investment and a slow down in advancement?'

'In one. There's no doubt about it, but you can never get ideological liberals, especially the more intelligent and intellectual ones, to understand the need for profit to invest. They seem to think that the profit just sits there on the table doing nothing while some rich bastard looks at it! Even invested in a bank or other stocks the profit is still working for the good of the country and if I, a simple Polish immigrant, could see that when I left school, I don't understand why an educated woman can't see it. It must be down to ideological blindness.'

'And you believe that the slow down in investment will mean lives being lost that would have been saved if investment had continued at a greater pace.'

'Of course it would, any fool can see that. The more you invest, the more experiments you can carry out. The more experiments you carry out, the quicker you find the answer. It's not a case of inspiration, but of intelligent development and elimination using what you learnt from the last experiment.

'Just look at cancer. If all the money spent in the last ten years, most of which has been raised in that time, had been available as a lump sum ten years ago, then everything that has happened in the last ten years, all the advancements, would have happened years earlier. It's like Edison and the light bulb, which took about eleven thousand experiments to discover. He was asked after seven thousand odd experiments why he didn't give up because it was obvious it would never work and do you know what he said?'

'No.'

'I've not failed seven thousand times, I've succeeded in identifying seven thousand ways that it won't work. The quicker I can progress through the next seven thousand experiments or however many it is, the quicker I'll find out how it *will* work.

'Speed in the medical business, whether it is the develop-ment of drugs or space age equipment, is money, and it is the very money that the First Lady wants to stop us generating.'

'Your argument is powerful and I sympathise with it, but surely the counter argument is that all the profits do not go back into research and she's actually trying to provide a base level of medical benefit, a safety level, before pushing ahead with the research that will lead to cures for illnesses that don't affect everybody. She wants everybody to be able to walk into the doctors as they do in England when they feel unwell without worrying about the cost.'

'But she won't achieve that by starving the industry of money to invest for development.'

'Think of it like a car, Lech. If you like, she wants people to be able to have the car looked at and routine work carried out for free and to worry about how to repair a broken crank shaft another time, because relatively few crank shafts actually break.'

'But people don't die of colds in America any more or of

broken legs that they can't afford to fix. People die of cancer, of heart disease, of AIDS and of old age. One day we'll be able to cure them all and that day will be sooner if we keep making the profits and keep developing the drugs and the equipment, and that includes old age. Just think of the operation that was necessary for a gall stone until recently, now they zap you with the machine and you're done.'

'Lech, we could talk about this for days and I hope we will, but right now I could use another drink. Come on, let's go back down to the bar.'

'Okay,' said Lech, bringing the conversation back to his main concern, 'but in your opinion it is unlikely that a contingency plan exists as it did with Kennedy to remove a dangerous President and if it did you don't think they'd activate at the moment against Clinton.'

'Right, but we'll talk some more before you start getting any mad notions. I can see where you're leading and it's not good, Lech, however you feel. Believe me.'

Despite the conviction of Gillespi's words, they cut no ice with Lech.

Harry Powers sat alone in his office late that night feeling more than a little pleased with himself. He had just raised the final million dollars and had not spent a dime himself. Even the cost of the dossiers which had been compiled over the years had been paid for by the stockholders. Looked at in total even they had seen a return on their money from corporate advantages gained from the accumulated information over the years.

As he sat looking out across the twinkling lights of the city at night from his vantage point high above them all, Powers reflected on a life of cut and thrust. He had enjoyed it but wished Esme had survived to share it with him. She had shared his passion for a deal, she had shared his drive and she had supported him any way he asked in his quest for success. She deserved to have shared it with him.

Their home had been vibrant, always full of imagination

and excitement with everyone playing the game of life to win, not for themselves but for the common good. They all knew there were no prizes for second place. The conversations were stimulating and inspirational and guests, whether for the evening or the weekend, left exhausted by the high mental activity. Often views differed but no-one was ever bored and people looked forward to enjoying the mental stimulation. But never once had either of them or the children looked at anything as an attack on them personally. In Harvard terms maybe the atmosphere was not intellectual, but the thought that was stimulated and the positive ideas that flowed freely were dynamic by anybody's standards.

The children had excelled but after Esme's death, although he had tried to keep them at home, the only fair answer for them had become boarding school. No doubt with time it would have happened anyway. But with him away so often overnight, the home life that Esme had maintained so well had gone.

Grown now, the children were all setting out on their own lives — the law, the military and medicine. He was proud of them, any father would be, and they had taken with them that priceless capacity to reason and debate, to think and argue without being offended by the opposite argument, however it was presented.

Marriage to Barbara was different. He had drifted into it slowly over a period of eight years, but it had provided company, companionship, someone at home when he was there. That, he often told himself, was why they had married. It had given her, a spinster past her best, a secure base, companionship for her if he lived and money if he didn't. He enjoyed her company in a general sort of way but everything in life was a problem to her. She would fret and worry about details that no-one else even knew existed and spent so long planning things before she did them that the opportunity was past by the time she actually took action. She had no vision, no faith or belief in anything including, sadly, herself.

It was impossible to have a real conversation with her because she felt she was under threat the whole time and took every disagreement as a personal attack. To Barbara, having the factory tidy and efficiently run was more important than producing the goods. He had often tried to explain to her that a tidy, efficient factory was an important aspect of any production operation but it was not a substitute for the product. At the end of the day, competitively priced goods coming out of a scruffy, badly run operation was better than a smart setup that produced nothing. She could never see it, the tiniest problem always masked the greatest opportunity.

Friends told him that he had changed in his six years of marriage to her; his sparkle had gone and his quest for new horizons had disappeared. Now he would have to keep his greatest ever achievement from them, at least until after his death. What Esme had known, along with a few close friends, was that his own brusqueness and curt approach to business life was an act. He was a performer of great class and skill who could and would play any role required of him, but he was now denied that which he had most enjoyed, a family life where no-one scored, but everyone laughed and pulled together. As a result, what at work had once been a tough and uncompromising act had taken him over and habit had made it his normal behaviour.

Esme had matured to be just like her mother, something he had hoped for and gambled on when they had married in their early twenties. Had she developed her father's character their marriage would have failed without a doubt, but her mother was still around at the age of eighty and he visited her regularly. They both enjoyed the stimulation of conversation, thought and provocation and he never ceased to marvel at her grasp and knowledge of current affairs which, mixed with her redoubtable memory and experience of life made her quite inspirational at times. His regret was that his three boys did not see much of her. They had passed through the granny era and were at that stage where old and young were anathema. They were yet to discover the pleasure of maturity.

Powers decided it was time to update the other two.

Edwards answered the phone rather sleepily. Powers heard a television in the background.

'John, Harry.'

Edwards looked at his watch, it was not as late as it felt.

'Harry, I'd just dozed off.'

'Then this will wake you up. We have the money.' His tone was efficient but Edwards could just detect a hint of excitement, perhaps even of jubilation.

'Harry,' he said his voice rising as he spoke, 'how did you manage it so quickly, that's fantastic news!'

'I thought you'd be pleased,' replied Powers with condescension.

'Yes, so what now?'

'We deliver the cash and wait.'

'Do we have any contact at all?'

'Yes, I have agreed a message system for me to contact him by phone and adverts will be placed in the Washington Post personal columns if he wants to contact us.'

'I'll have to order it.'

'Don't bother, I've done it and if anything should happen to me you'll receive an envelope that tells you how the system works.'

'So there's nothing more to do?'

'Not a damn thing, except pray it works.'

'Night, John.'

'Night, Harry.'

There was no reply from Matt Andrews. The slob was in a bar somewhere thought Powers. Perhaps he'd treat himself to a little something to drink, a glass or two or burgundy, but before that he made a call to the number he had been given for Friggli. It was a different number from the one he had rung previously and although only answered with "Hello." Obviously Friggli *was* in a bar.

'Is Enzo there, please?'

'Who's calling?' was the gruff response.

'A friend,' he replied curtly.

'Hang on,' came the disinterested reply.
'Hello,' said Enzo cautiously.
'Your terms and times will be met,' said Powers efficiently.
'Good.'
'And the communication?'
'As I told you before, okay?'
'Okay,' replied Powers but the phone was already dead.

After his call from Harry Powers, John Edwards also decided to have a drink, but for different reasons. He was getting nervous and there was nothing to tie Powers into the plot. Enzo only knew him, and he knew who had introduced them to each other. As he sipped his whiskey he lit up a large cigar and sat pensively looking out across the pool to the hills beyond.

It was over an hour before he came to a conclusion and sat at his desk to write his difficult letter. Having sealed it, he wrote a short note to his solicitor asking him to open the enclosed should he die other than by natural causes and, in any event, after his death once Harry Powers and Matt Andrews were also dead.

He retired to bed but did not sleep. The time before Friggli struck was going to be anxious; the big question was, how much more anxious would the ensuing months be?

On an A1 alert the members of the committee met routinely throughout the day either in person or, as in this case, by satellite link up.

'We have some additional information which I don't like,' said the chief after they had reviewed all the detailed information collated since the early morning meeting. 'It is a variation on your theory about nutters, but we are dealing with very sane people, or at least one very sane and powerful person.'

'A separate operation, sir?'

'I fear so, Steve. A man called Lech Zielinski who controls one of the country's biggest pharmaceutical companies is currently in London and he is contemplating an assassination attempt on the President.'

'Are we to assume, sir, that he has nothing to do with the other two?'

'We don't assume it, Steve, we know it.'

'How do we know, sir?'

'I have someone close to him who he's confiding in. He believes that it is little more than frustration and that Zielinski can be talked out of it, but as it stands we have another line of assassination zooming in on us.

'What worries me most, Steve, is that you and Scott might be right and there could be countless groups beginning to think in the same way.

'I want you to stay at the top of the pile, but also stay on Harworth and Knight personally because you've started to know them. You can pick your men to run with every likely group, to investigate, tail, whatever, but all the information feeds back to you and is duplicated here. Can you handle that, Steve?'

'As long as I'm not charging around the country and Scott is with me, sir, yes, we can do that on a twenty-four hour basis. There might be more than one potential paymaster, but leaving aside the nutter, who would commit suicide to do it themselves? There can't be many potential assassins and we've already started pulling names'.

'How many so far?'

'Seventeen and they're all being checked out now. I was thinking about being heavy handed about it. What you tell me makes me think it's the best way to go about it, sir.'

'Let the world know that we know something is afoot, you mean?'

'Yes, sir.'

'I can't see it doing any harm. Whether it scares anyone off is another matter. There will be several who will walk away if they know we are making waves, but there will be others who will look at it as an additional challenge. To complete the job despite our interest.'

'It'll raise the stakes, which will also put pressure on

Harworth because I don't think he's got any real balls, sir.'

'What worries me most is your theory about him teaming up with some terrorist organisation because he hasn't got the money to buy an assassin.'

'Which puts us back with the nutters who'll die to achieve their goal. There's no way of tracking them. Look what happened to Rajit Ghandi, sir.'

'No-one would get that close here, the check points and the dogs would detect the bomb.'

'I'm not as confident as you about that, sir.'

'We increase the searches.'

'Yes, sir.'

'I think we have to change our approach now, Steve. To date we've assumed that there was no immediate threat because we knew the plan was embryonic. We must now assume that, whilst that is true for Harworth, it may not be true for another party.

'Step up the security on the assumption that someone could now strike at any time. I'll arrange for you to see the President in an hour. He won't like it and I suspect Mrs Clinton will like it even less, but you'll have to charm them or bully them as you think fit.'

'What about her, sir?'

'I don't think she's in any direct danger. There's no political upside to taking her out.'

'Kidnapping, sir?'

'Unlikely in my book, but explain it to her anyway. You know what to do, Steve, you've been on the courses and if you have any problems ring me day or night on my private number.

Enzo left the bar immediately he had spoken to Powers, without even finishing his drink, and returned to the hovel he called home, a bedsit in Brentwood. He immediately poured himself a large whiskey, drank it, poured another, sat on his bed and began to weep.

What would his mama and papa have said about

his life now?

They'd been so proud when he had graduated from the military academy in the top five per cent of recruits. They knew then that he was going to make something of his life. What had gone wrong? Of course, he knew what had gone wrong. That woman in Madison Square Garden. That one night stand, over eight years ago, coming on nine.

What upset him most was that it was Clarissa, not him, who had suggested that they should both be tested for AIDS before they married, despite the fact that they have been living together for five years. Five years since the week after his trip to New York in 1984. They were only getting married because they both wanted children so badly and suddenly his world had fallen apart.

He didn't have the courage to face her and had simply packed all his things one day while she was at work and left, but he had done so knowing her test was negative. She had tried to find him, friends had told him that she wanted him back with her anyway, but he was unable to face it. Unable to bear the thought that he could kill the one person in the world who meant everything to him, he had decided to make a clean break of it and to bear his loss. He could but hope that she would recover.

It was soon afterwards that he was asked to join the snatch back gang — an out of work ex-marine would always be in demand in the Brentwood area of Los Angeles. Word travelled fast. He had enjoyed the work at first and it was something his folks, now dead, would have approved of. It was almost fairy tale stuff, saving the little ones as his mama always called them. But this latest assignment was different. It was purely for money and his mama would not have approved. She did not approve of the Mafia, she did not approve of the crime syndicates and whatever the President may have got wrong, and who was to say that he had, she would not approve of him killing him.

He wept some more, drunk his whiskey in one and poured another.

Enzo had four brothers, three sisters and twenty eight nephews and nieces and so they would receive almost one and a half million dollars each. That his mama would approve of. He decided to finish the bottle and sleep. Tomorrow he started work, which would mean cleaning himself up and staying sober until the job was finished.

In his mind he had already started planning but, contrary to what he had told Edwards' friend, he would not really start seriously on the operation until the cash was received. He would incur expenses getting to Washington but it was not just because he could not fund them himself. Officially, his first job was to establish the President's movements in November. But there was something more pressing than that. Before he did anything, Enzo wanted to know who he was being employed by. Edwards was clearly only support cast and pretty nervous about the whole thing.

Brad and Angie spent a week in Tampa and for the first three days made no further reference to their conversation concerning the President. Brad, stunned by her willingness to help, was afraid that she would change her mind if he pushed the matter too fast.

'So how do you get me close to him?' she asked suddenly as they sat outside a bistro one evening having supper.

'It has to be some sort of social event or fund raiser.'

'But neither of them will come to any of your parties, maybe that's because he's afraid of people like you.' The statement sounded daft at first, but as it sank in Brad actually wondered if it contained a grain of truth.

'No, that's not the reason, but we have to get you invited to something he will go to or better still something at the White House itself.'

'The White House!' she squealed rather too loudly.

'A reception of some sort.'

'Why don't we set up some charity event, something that will make him look good?'

'You have to have a line on him to do that. He gets

hundreds of requests a day to open this and be Patron of that. No, the only way forward is to get into something that he will be at anyway.'

'My sister might be able to help,' said Angie rather matter of factly.

'Your sister! I never knew you had a sister.'

'Yes, a lot older than me. Twenty five years older than me in fact.'

'What, a half sister?'

'No, a whole sister. I also had an older brother but he died,' she said giving away nothing of her motive for her mission, 'and I was the replacement!'

'You mean you were meant to be a boy?' Brad said roaring with laughter.

'Yes, the son to replace Simon. I wouldn't have made a very good boy, would I?' She winked at him.

'No. What does your sister do?'

'She works for a Political Lobby company. That's all I know. Don't know what she actually does but I imagine she could help.'

Brad could not believe either his luck or Angie's dumbness. Why on earth had she not told him this days ago? 'That would be very useful. We should meet her,' he replied, barely suppressing his excitement.

'Then when we've finished enjoying ourselves here we'll ride on up to Washington and visit Beccy. I've not seen her myself for almost a year.'

'No, let's go tomorrow.'

'What's the rush? The job will wait unless someone else beats us to it, which will suit us just as well and I've not had enough excitement yet to start running off to Washington. I don't want to stop until I can't take any more, so when we leave is up to you, honey.' Her tone was mocking but he knew she meant it.

When Brad finally arrived home after his week in Tampa he immediately had a blazing row with Bridget over the facial adviser's bill which was waiting for him.

'What the hell does the guy advise on for sixty three hours in a month? And what sort of advice is worth forty dollars an hour? yelled Brad as he stared down at the bill for $2,520 plus tax.

If she had recognised the account, which like all previous ones should have been addressed to her and not Brad, she would have taken it from his post and paid it, as she had all similar bills over the years, from their joint checking account. She was as livid as Brad.

'I've not noticed any change in your face,' he yelled at her, 'and no doubt you'll be off to the plastic surgeons soon for him to write out another damn great bill. Isn't screwing the arse off you enough for these guys? Do they have to charge me as well?'

Of course, she suddenly realised, that was how Louis, the facial adviser, moved his clients on when he bored of them. Send the bill, a big bill, to the husband by mistake. The bastard, she thought, the Sicilian bastard. She was going to give him one last session he wouldn't forget in a hurry and he wouldn't be using his over-developed equipment for a while after that.

'It takes a long time to truly understand a face and consider the options, the best ways to enhance the skin and bone qualities, not to mention testing the preparations.'

'Bullshit!'

There was no point in concealing it so she drove her own nail home. 'What about the money you spend on your little tarts, like that Angie Tourle to name just one,' she yelled back in anger. 'She's no better than a whore. You pay all the expenses and buy her clothes, cars and apartments, but that's no different to paying her cash. Face facts, Brad, we're neither of us able to pull like we used to and we both have to pay for it one way or another most of the time.'

'You speak for yourself,' he yelled, slamming the door behind him and throwing the facial adviser's bill into the trash can as he left.

Jeff Knight had not had a happy week. He had gone to New York for two days and returned to find Sally-Anne unconscious and suffering from alcoholic poisoning. There was no telling how long she had been like it, but her stomach was empty of solids and the hospital thought it was probably several days since she had eaten anything.

For over twenty hours it was touch and go but slowly she began to show signs of improvement. 'It will take many months, if not years, to get her well again, Mr. Knight,' said the doctor. 'But the first problem is the drinking. We have to address that immediately.'

'I know,' replied Jeff sombrely. 'It's been bad for years. Several bottles of wine a day every day, perhaps a bottle of gin to top it up, but in recent months it's gotten worse.'

'That is serious. We'll do the tests when she is stronger, but are you sure she drinks that much?'

'We get through twenty bottles of gin a week and I don't drink the stuff. There's no way she drinks it all — she's always having people in to gossip — but she must drink over half of it and the wine goes down just as rapidly.'

'But you drink that as well?'

'Yes.'

'So what would you say she drinks in addition to the gin?'

'It must be ten, fifteen bottles of wine a week. We never have less than two bottles with a meal and I have three, maybe four glasses.'

'Let us look upon this incident positively, Mr. Knight', he said with kindly purpose. 'She will be in here for at least ten days and then we can send her on to a place to convalesce for maybe another ten days. In that time she will eat properly and she will start to dry out and, most importantly, we'll be able to cope with the withdrawal problems.'

'Unless she discharges herself,' said Jeff.

'Do you think she will?'

'You never know, she's very strong willed.'

'But not when it comes to saying no to the bottle.'

'No,' replied Jeff reluctantly, wondering how much of the situation was his fault.

'If she did try to discharge herself we might be able to get a Court Order, with your help, to say that she was a danger to herself and should not be left alone. Would you be prepared to do that?'

Jeff thought before he replied. Sure he liked a drink or two and there were those, his mother for one, who said that he was an alcoholic and drank too much. Technically, no doubt he did, but even some of the surveys now showed that alcohol every day, far from being bad for you, had beneficial effects, despite some of its downsides. Sally-Anne was another problem, it was like hard drugs. She needed help.

'Yes, I would,' he said slowly. 'If you think it is necessary, you just tell me what you need me to do and I will do it.'

'Good, thank you. Now first of all I think we have to be very gentle with her, very kind to her, lots of loving. Whatever happens, don't mention the problem — you must stay on her side in her mind. It is me, us, she will want to fight, she must have a friend. You.'

'Okay.'

'And then we take it as it goes, hour by hour at first and then day by day. She's on a drip now which will stop the dehydration and get some nourishment into her. We will probably have to include some alcohol in the near future, or the withdrawal problems could be acute, but you leave all that to us. You just support her and make sure that we always know where to get hold of you in a hurry.'

'Would it help if I made some preliminary arrangements in case we need to apply for a Court Order?'

'No, we'll deal with that at the time if we have to. Pray we don't have to, but there really is nothing we can do in advance anyway.'

Jeff did not reply. The doctor placed a limp hand on his shoulder before walking off and Jeff turned towards the exit. What a mess he had made of his life.

CHAPTER NINE

'I can't get over how calm everybody is,' said Scott after one of the early morning A1s. 'We've been on this for weeks now got nowhere and yet no-one gets excited.'

'That's not really true, Scott. What has happened is we've proved to ourselves we can think in front of the game. Look at Angie's sister. We'd identified her, found her and had a tap on her before she came up in the conversation. If we can stay in front like that then I'm happy.'

'You think the President is safe?'

Steve knew what was really behind the question.

'I might be seven years older than you and not have your education, Scott, but that doesn't mean that I want to stay in the field all my life either. If we screw this one up we're both down the tubes and that matters to me just as much as it does to you, believe me.'

'Sorry, I didn't mean to sound selfish?'

'Don't worry. The hardest part of this job is staying level headed. Not when all hell is breaking loose, that's easy, but when we go through the placid times with not much happening, no apparent progress. Don't let it get to you. If we've achieved nothing else we've rattled a few cages and made a few people think, that's never a bad thing. Maybe, and the problem is we'll never know this, we've even scared someone off, who knows. Get yourself some sleep, and then we'll review the entire situation from the very start to see what we've missed. There's bound to be something. It'll do us both good.'

On Hamdi's third day at the mountain camp the scouts returned in the early afternoon with a band of injured children who had been found wandering in the valley alone.

'The doctor, the doctor,' one of them kept saying, 'the doctor.' The others were in too great a state of shock to even give their names and Hamdi helped nurse them throughout the afternoon and on into the evening.

One little girl had been badly hit by machine gun fire and her left arm was almost severed. Hamdi felt totally helpless and useless as he sat there mopping her brow, trying to make her comfortable. 'There is nothing we can do, my friend,' said Moncilo as he joined him. 'She is dying. But you must tell Clinton of this, you must tell him of our suffering, the pain, the death.'

'I will, my friend, I will,' replied Hamdi. The sight of the children was the final push he needed. He felt immediately stronger.

'The doctor, the doctor,' the girl murmured as the other child had done, who had since died. 'The doctor.'

'What about the doctor?' Hamdi asked.

'He will help me,' she said weakly.

'Where is he?' asked Moncilo.

'With us,' she said with her last breath.

They both wept, Moncilo not for the first time. Unlike Hamdi, who was soon to leave them, it was not for the last time either.

'There's a doctor down there somewhere, we must find him,' said Hamdi.

'It is impossible,' said Moncilo, 'If he is not dead he will have moved on.'

'We do not know that. We do not know why or how he was separated from the children. Even if he was hurt, he may not be dead. We must look for him.'

'Hamdi, you don't know this area,' said Moncilo in a fatherly manner. 'We would never find him and night is on us now, which only makes it harder.'

'But we *must* try,' replied Hamdi forcefully. 'Not you or I, we would be hopeless, but as you said others know the woods, the mountains, the valley. They could find him. Night means nothing to them, it is an advantage. Just think how useful it would be to add a doctor to the skills in this camp.'

'You sound like an Oxford graduate when you speak like that, my friend.'

'I am an Oxford graduate and so are you, Moncilo. You are the organiser. It is your duty to send out a search party. These people rely on you. Imagine how you would feel if there was no food,' he finished emotionally.

'You are right, my friend, and you are making good progress. Two days ago you would not have argued with me like that. Come, we will organise a search party now.'

'No, I'll stay with the children, you do it.'

It was almost four o'clock in the morning when the search party returned carrying the doctor, who had been shot in the leg. They had found him semi-conscious in the undergrowth a few yards from where they had found the children. He had concealed himself so well that they had missed him twice. It was mid-day before he was able to tell them what had happened.

'We were fired on by Serbs but I knew that most of them would not kill a group of children on their own so, although I had been hit, I crawled away from the children and told them not to tell the Serbs about me at all. I told them to leave me. Your men were very lucky, they only missed the Serbs by minutes. The children were too afraid to speak when your men found them.'

'It was the dying words of a little girl that brought us to you,' said Hamdi with the emotion creaking in his voice. I'm a lawyer, he thought, I'm not cut out for this type of thing.

The doctor's injuries were not as bad as they might have been. He had only been hit once, and the bullet had passed straight through his calf leaving a clean wound. Inside a few days the intellectual caucus had grown to three but Hamdi was due to leave soon — the handovers had already been arranged.

'I admire you,' said the doctor, who was called Andrei, 'but will it be possible for the world to help you even if they want to?'

Hamdi latched on to Andrei's precise words immediately, 'What do you mean "to help *us*"'

'I should include myself now because I am here, but I am Rumanian. I was simply working here when the troubles started but could not just leave all my patients. Some were Serbs, some were Croats and some were Muslims. I did not expect to be a victim but I was, I am. All three groups commit atrocities, but my job is to heal people, whoever they are.'

'I am sorry that you have suffered because you have helped our people,' said Hamdi, 'but what do you mean about it being possible to help us?'

'Look,' said Andrei sympathetically, 'I'm not a military expert but I can use my common sense and wasn't blind to what went on around me before this war started. Just suppose for the moment that someone, say the Americans, agrees to supply you with arms. How will they get here? Small arms will be no help, they will only lead to more face-to-face fighting when your villages are overrun, which will mean more deaths. You will still not force the Serbs or Croats to retreat, because of their heavy armoury. The Serbian Army is the fall-out of the old Federal Army, which they dominated. Not only do they have the equipment but they know how to use it. They have also been trained. Have you?'

Hamdi and Moncilo recognised the truth when they heard it. Andrei concluded, deepening their depression. 'Nato has vast resources of redundant heavy weapons, tanks, armoured personnel carriers and artillery, but you will also need spares and ammunition, all of which will have to be delivered to you if they are to be of any use. You have no sea border, so any supplies would have to be by road, rail or air. You simply do not have the runways capable of taking the giant transporters that would be needed to deliver tanks and other artillery weapons. And even if you did, the Serbs have the anti-aircraft capacity to shoot them down.'

Gloom was now descending on Hamdi and Moncilo like the rain on a summer's afternoon of cricket at Oxford.

'You look despondent, I am sorry. You save my life and I dispel your dream.'

'No,' said Hamdi, 'carry on. These are arguments we had

not thought of and I must be able to counter them.'

'How?'

'As yet I do not know, but carry on, please.'

'So an air drop is not possible. That leaves the road and the railways, both of which have to pass through either Croatian or Serbian held territory. You know how difficult it is for the convoys of food to pass safely. It could not be done with heavy weapons, and it is heavy weapons you need, unless those supplying them were prepared to escort them.'

'You mean deploy tens of thousands of troops to fight the Serbs and the Croats in order to deliver to us the weapons we need to fight the Serbs and the Croats for ourselves?'

'Yes, but it would not just be a case of the weapons. As I say, it is also the spare parts and the ammunition which will be in constant demand. I have said nothing about training, but who here knows how to use a western tank? Even anyone from the old Federal Army would find it difficult because they were trained on Russian tanks — I understand everything's highly technological now.

'I wish you luck, really I do, because I agree that the only way to stop the bloodshed is for the Croats and the Serbs to realise that they stand to lose as many lives as the Muslims by attacking them. But I cannot see it happening.'

That night the enthusiasm which Hamdi had built up for his mission was severely tested, not least because he was furious with himself. As he had said to Moncilo earlier in the day, it was their job to think, to anticipate the problems and to overcome them. After all, they would not be pleased if the trappers did not bring back enough food.

For most of that night while the doctor slept Hamdi and Moncilo talked round and round the practical problem, equally cross with themselves for not anticipating it. It was no use blaming the conditions under which they operated: they were both professional men.

It was almost four in the morning when they conceded to their tiredness, 'You should not do this,' said Moncilo. 'You need sleep.'

'I wouldn't have slept anyway.'

'Perhaps not.'

'And I'm not sure that I will even now. We have not found an answer, yet.'

'We will, my friend, we will.' He smiled. You believe so, or you would have not said, yet.'

Hamdi was not sure how far he could take or should take Moncilo into his trust and the latest twist had only confused him. If Bill Clinton was not prepared to help the Muslims, Hamdi planned to kill him. He'd no idea how, and it might take a long time, but he knew he would do it. He knew it would not be possible at the initial meeting and that he would have to work hard at getting and staying close to him after that, but he was prepared to do so. He had no family to live for and, as he had seen it until that afternoon, they could still have been alive if America had ignored the siren voices and given the support his people so desperately needed earlier in the year. He was sure that George Bush would not have allowed the situation to develop as Bill Clinton had — no-one would ever convince him otherwise of that — despite the logic of what Andrei had said.

His sleep had been restless and short, but his mind was clear when he woke. His transition from the state he'd been in days earlier made him marvel at the ability of the human body to repair itself. He would say nothing to Moncilo, but if Clinton would not help, he would kill him, however long it took to create the opportunity.

'Cheers,' said Lech to Gillespi, handing him his drink as they returned to the bar of the Fox House from the lounge.

'Good health,' he replied swigging his Scotch.

'So, to return to the subject in hand, you would say that one way or another there is no threat to Clinton's life from the Secret Service.'

'Nor from anywhere else. You can't get near a President now. That episode with Reagan was the final attempt. Short of bombing the White House and hoping to catch him in the debris, I'd say there was no way to do it.'

'But he goes out, he gives press conferences.'

'True, but the security is one hundred percent.'

'Nothing is one hundred percent, George, nothing.'

'Lech,' said George kindly, 'I appreciate your anger at the administration, but you cannot seriously consider an attempt on the President's life. We got away with it thirty years ago but we were on the inside and look at the trouble we had. We also used a freelance to fire the killer shot and had the KGB deal with him.'

'You're joking,' said Lech slowly.

'Not at all, Lech. It was a military operation that took years to plan. It even took us three months to implement once we decided to go live, and that was with all our resources and inside knowledge.

'You couldn't do it, and at best you'd spend the rest of your life in jail. If you tried to do it in the wrong state they'd execute you. What good would that do for your Trusts? What good would that do in you battle against Mrs President and her reforms that you see doing so much damage to medical research? You should fight the way you know how, the way you're good at. Don't daydream about killing the President, it will only distract you from your main task.'

'But once I'd got someone in place to do it, I'd leave it to him.'

'There's no easy way to say this, Lech, and remember I've done it. I've organised someone to kill a President and we did it. We succeeded and we didn't get caught. You'd be mad to even contemplate it and you're mad even to talk to me like this. How'd you know I won't tell the CIA and then one morning there'll just be a knock on your door and that will be it, you'll never walk the streets again?'

'I don't. It's a chance I decided to take.'

'When?'

'When I started looking for you. I decided then and nothing you have said actually gives me cause to change my mind. You won't turn me in.'

'You don't know that,' replied Gillespi sternly.

'Ah, but I do. Don't forget that I've spent a lifetime doing deals, looking into men's eyes, watching their body movements, muscle movements and forming conclusions. Correct conclusions. That's why I own what I do.'

'Yes, I do and you're right, I won't turn you in.'

'But you won't help me either?' The question was very softly spoken, very gently delivered.

'No, Lech, I won't help you, and not just because I'm an old man but because I now believe, as I've done almost since the day, that we were wrong to do what we did then. Just think about it. Think about all the other people who feel like you do about a particular subject. Are they all plotting to kill the President?'

'That's not the issue. It's not just that I disagree with a policy which I also think is dangerous, it's that he's rudderless, he has no backbone. I actually think he has a big heart, but that's not enough. We need strong dynamic leadership. Out and out mistakes made positively are better than the present oscillation.'

'That might change, given time to settle. Rightly or wrongly the American people chose a lightweight to replace a heavyweight and a party that had no Presidential or ministerial experience of note to draw on. I think Gergen is changing it, and he'll force Clinton to change some of the personnel who are clearly out of their depth. It was bound to be a difficult birth.'

'Difficult's not the word I'd use.'

'Okay, but let's talk about it, let's look at all the other people who could feel as aggrieved — maybe even more aggrieved — than you, starting with the queers. You've already mentioned them.'

'What about them? They deserve all they get in my book.'

'Maybe. That doesn't concern me. But Clinton either made a promise or left them believing he'd made a promise that he'd make changes in their favour in the armed services, but he hasn't done it. That to me would seem to give them a pretty good reason to dislike him, but not enough to kill him.'

'But that will affect only them. Don't you see that what I'm talking about will affect millions of people for decades to come, many of them not yet born? You can't compare that with not being able to be gay in the Marines, even if you were promised that you would be able to.'

'I accept the argument, but that is not what I am saying. What I am saying is that *they* won't see it like that. They were promised — or thought they were — that they could be gay in the Marines and now they've been told they can't. Now you may think your cause is more worthy, it may actually be so, but they wouldn't.'

'So you'd leave well alone and let them destroy the pharmaceutical industry. No way!'

'No, Lech, you fight your corner, but not by shooting the man! It won't solve anything and there must be dozens of pressure groups who feel as you do about their particular interest. It's not just the gays — what about the scientists working on star wars who've been sacked? They could even argue the greater cause, like you.

'What about the blacks? The civil rights activist? First of all he says he's appointing Lani Guiner to champion their cause from the inside, then he backs off and they're all screaming for blood!'

'But he could never have appointed her, she's been recommending that voting arrangements should be changed to give blacks greater influence in legislation, out of all proportion to their actual numbers. She even wants them to have a veto in some situations, which would transgress the Voting Rights Act. It doesn't compare, George.'

'Lech,' said Gillespi wearily, 'we've known each other only a few days but I like you. *Please*, for your sake, forget it. Fight it another way.'

'Sorry, George, I can't do that.'

Enzo woke early and lay in his crumpled bed for almost an hour, thinking. The room which had been home for him for over two years was little bigger than the average garage, but he had crammed his whole life into it. There were pictures on every last centimetre of wall. He knew as he lay there that he would never return, would never stare up at that nicotine stained ceiling again. This was really the point at which he would die, the point at which he would leave his life behind.

How many people, he wondered, were actually HIV positive? Surely the vast majority of them had no idea. How long would it be before he became seriously ill, before he turned the gun not on the President, but on himself? It didn't matter he assured himself. He would complete his task and after that the next generation would have a solid start in life, that was all that mattered to him now.

Then suddenly with one bound he was up and washing for the last time in the cold water that tricked from the ageing tap into the chipped basin slung under the one small window. He shaved, cleaned his shoes with his bedsheet, removed his only suit from the hook on the back of the door, dressed and left. He took nothing with him.

Having the money put in a left luggage locker seemed corny, but it worked. He collected the key, which had been left with Carlo in the bar, opened the locker and there was the suitcase, exactly as arranged. He sat in the toilet cubicle for nearly twenty minutes just looking at the cash, before putting fifty thousand dollars in his pocket, locking the case again and hailing a cab to take him to his sister's apartment, where he left the suitcase with her for safe keeping. She asked no questions and he knew it would be completely safe.

'You look very smart today, Enzo,' she said eyeing him up and down in a typically Italian motherly manner.

'Job interview,' he replied with a broad, enticing smile.

'Good luck!'

'Thanks.'

On his way to the airport he posted a letter to the bank in Switzerland and then boarded the flight for Washington.

The White House information desk were very helpful. 'It's subject to change of course,' said the jet black haired young lady in a Southern drawl, 'but the President's itinerary from September to December is set out in this Press Release.'

'Thank you.'

His luck was in. In four days there was a large reception which would almost certainly require outside staff, if not outside caterers, and the President was to host a Kennedy Memorial Buffet Lunch at the White House on 22nd November. With any luck it would involve the same outside workforce.

Having checked into a large but nondescript hotel in the suburbs, he spent three days buying a selection of clothes and disguises from a wide variety of outlets and theatrical costumiers. Come the fourth morning he had aged ten years, walked with a limp and wore the tired uniform of a private from the Vietnam war with a single campaign medal ribbon. He was outside the service entrance gates to the White House by half past six.

He did not have to wait overlong to learn what he needed to know. He then made his way slowly back to his hotel, from which he emerged after lunch in a finely tailored suit, sporting a thick black bushy moustache and a stetson. The offices of Harbuckle Inc had the presence that one would expect from a well-established family business that held lucrative contracts with the White House for catering.

'Good afternoon, sir. How can I help you?' said the receptionist warmly.

His accent was pure Texan. 'Thank you, yes. My wife and I will be renting a house up here for the latter part of the year and my daughter will be twenty-one while we're here. We'd like to do something special for her, and I'm looking into the catering.'

'Of course, sir. If you wouldn't mind taking a seat I will arrange for Mr Harbuckle to be with you immediately.'

'Why, thank you, ma'am, that's right civil of you,' he replied, touching the stetson. He knew all she would remember, all anybody would remember was the moustache, the hat and the voice. All the exaggerated items.

Mr Harbuckle was indeed with him immediately, impeccably dressed in morning suit with trouser creases that would have put the Military Academy to shame. The business having been established in 1893, the Mr Harbuckle before him was clearly one of the longer serving family members. 'Would you care to step this way please, sir.' he said crisply and politely as he held open the polished wooded door.

'I thank you, sir,' boomed Enzo touching his hat again.

The room was pleasantly decorated without being overpowering, and had a warm friendliness which immediately relaxed the customer.

'Charles Harbuckle, sir,' said the old gentleman as he passed his card across the coffee table.

'I thank you,' said Enzo, 'Jim Welbeck.'

'And how may we be of service to you, Mr Welbeck?'

'Our daughter will be twenty-one in the fall and we'll be living up here in Washington at the time. We thought it would be a nice surprise to give her what you might call a grown up party as well as the affair on the ranch back home.'

'Certainly, Mr Welbeck. And where are you likely to be holding the gathering, sir?

'Why, we're looking at renting a Georgian mansion and were thinking of a real Washington dinner party, making the whole affair something very special.'

'And for how many people, Mr Welbeck?'

'Say around two hundred.'

'It will have to be a very substantial property, sir.'

'Oh it will be, Mr Harbuckle, it will be.'

'A dinner, you say?'

'Yes,'

'Have you set a budget, sir?'

'No, because frankly,' said Enzo leaning across towards Mr Harbuckle in a conspiratory manner, 'it's not the cost that concerns me so much as security.'

'Security?' Harbuckle replied with just a trace of surprise in his voice.

'Yes, sir, security. Back home the lads and lassies'll have a cook-out and I doubt there'll be a soul over twenty-five at it. But here it will be more refined. It will be our friends who celebrate with us those happy twenty-one years, and some of them are important people, people who can't just walk down the sidewalk in the way you or I can.'

'Politicians amongst them, perhaps?'

'Most definitely, yes,' replied Enzo nodding frantically.

'That will present no problem at all, sir.'

'That's what I'd heard, Mr Harbuckle, which is why I've come to see you. Now I'll be leaving all the matters on the catering itself to my dear wife, but before we get that far I need to satisfy myself that you are able to provide the service that I need.'

'I can assure you we can, sir, and I will be more that happy to arrange for you to have references to that effect.'

'Well, that's mighty generous of you to say so, but a tough old southern bird like me never did go much on references.'

Mr Harbuckle's expression never changed. If he felt insulted, he neither said so nor showed it. 'Then might I ask what you had in mind, Mr Welbeck?'

'You see the problem with references, Mr Harbuckle, is that you only ever get good ones. I'm sure Billy the Kid would have had impeccable references because they would have come from someone he had asked to give them. No, sir, what I like to know to satisfy myself totally, is how you vet your staff, both in the kitchens, including the preparation and those that come to house and wait.'

'I can assure you, Mr Welbeck, that our procedures are quite thorough and that we have never experienced any problems at all, but I could not reveal to you the internal workings of this company. To do so would, as I am sure you will appreciate, Mr Welbeck, be gravely irresponsible and actually jeopardise the very security of which we are so proud and which you yourself value enough to have come here.

Please, Mr Welbeck, be assured that we have never experienced any problem at all. I can only repeat that, and my offer to have references made available to you. I am sure that those of whom you could enquire are of a standing that will speak for itself and cannot be compared to any associates of Billy the Kid.' The tone and manner of his words was still crisp and courteous.

'Well, in that case, Mr Harbuckle, I'll have to consider the matter, speak with Mrs Welbeck and get back to you. I don't doubt what you tell me, and if the referees are of that standing, then I'm sure we will be able to take matters further with you.

'I'm greatly obliged to you for your time, Mr Harbuckle.' said Enzo, getting to his feet.

'Not at all, sir,' Harbuckle replied as they left the room. 'I have every confidence that we will be able to accommodate you to your entire satisfaction, and I look forward to speaking with you again.'

'You are most kind, Mr Harbuckle, and I'm sure I'll be back to you without delay.'

'Have a nice day, sir,' said the receptionist as he left the front office.

'Miss Walters,' said Mr Harbuckle to her once Enzo had left the building, 'did Mr Welbeck leave you with a business card or any form of address?'

'No, Mr Harbuckle, nothing at all.'

'Thank you, Miss Walters. Would you be so kind please as to contact Sergeant Mulligan and have the call put through to my office.

'Yes, Mr Harbuckle.'

Perhaps, thought Enzo as he settled into the back of the cab, he had been naive to think it would be that easy. He had an advantage that assassins rarely enjoyed: no objection to being caught or even killed. Indeed he almost had a preference for being killed, but he still had to have access to his target.

He dined alone at a corner table in the hotel restaurant

that night. Perhaps he should aim at another day, look for an easier opportunity than the Memorial Party when security was bound to be stringent through sheer emotion, if nothing else. The gun itself would be no problem, but it would take time to have it made and he would have to go abroad for it.

Guns themselves attracted no interest at all in America, they were an everyday item, but his requirements were unusual and nothing was ever absolutely secret. He knew people who could do what he wanted, knew them well, but the risk was too great and he guessed he might have already made one mistake by visiting Harbuckle's. He could not afford another. The problem with going abroad could be getting the gun into the country, or worse, from Europe onto the plane — unless he treated it as a test run at concealing it.

The following morning, Enzo left the hotel to buy a set of leathers, a crash helmet and the latest copy of Autobike. It took him just over an hour to age his purchases so that they would be inconspicuous and a few minutes to identify half a dozen potential motorbikes in the magazine. The third and fifth calls were answered and, with two appointments made to view that afternoon, he enjoyed a light lunch in his room watching a movie channel.

He suffered his first serious craving for alcohol that afternoon. He resisted the temptation. He purchased the second motor bike he look at, for cash, because it had the large pantoons. Immediately he rode out of the city to Harbuckle's depot. For a catering company the security was impressive — he'd seen cash vaults less well protected.

The compound was surrounded by a sturdy wire mesh fence approaching five metres high, with returns pointing both inwards and outwards to create a vee-shaped gully along the top of the fence, about a metre across at the widest point and three quarters of a metre deep. Through the gully ran two strands of barbed wire and a single strand of gleaming wire mounted on rubber bushes. The sturdy mounting posts, which were at five metre intervals, projected about two metres above the top of the fence line and each had four powerful floodlights mounted at their pinnacle, two spraying light into the compound and two into the surrounding roads.

Ten metres in from the perimeter fence was another lower fence about two and a half metres high where every mounting post carried a camera. The gate house, built of brick, stood centrally in a quad with double gates fore and aft either side of it. He counted six security guards.

The building itself was a simple frame construction clad with steel panels covering about two thousand square metres, with no windows and two sets of double entry and exit doors. There were numerous carbuncles around the exterior walls, which Enzo assumed were vents to remove the heat and smell of the cooking which obviously took place inside. He found it hard to believe that this was just a huge kitchen, but if they were catering for the White House in quantity he supposed they had to ensure that there was absolutely no risk of the food being tampered with. Wouldn't it have made more sense to have an inhouse operation?

To the right of the building was a fenced car park which could accommodate some two hundred and fifty cars. Inside was a larger version of the gate house with a passageway leading directly into the main building. He assumed that the staff had to pass through a security inspection in the smaller building before entering the main building and, from the three coaches parked adjacent to the smaller building he guessed they left from there to carry out their assignments, having again passed through a security check.

The whole operation was as impressive as Mr Harbuckle had been polite. The vetting process for staff was going to be equally impregnable. Resigned to his problem remaining unsolved, he gunned the bike into life and returned to his hotel to consider other options. There seemed little chance of becoming a caterer.

Rebecca Tourle was as attractive a woman for her age as Brad Harworth had ever seen. Still single, she had a vitality and confidence about her that he found totally captivating. There was no need to ask if she was good at her job, it was written all over her, despite her three nervous breakdowns and the fact that she still had therapy once weekly and would always have to. The underlying feelings of fear, of shame, of insecurity that had beset the family after Simon's death had never revealed themselves to the outside world. To other people she had always appeared as Brad saw her, to herself she could not have been more different.

Looking at Rebecca and Angie together Brad found it hard to believe that they could have had the same parents and upbringing. There were some physical similarities, but where Angie was shallow and nervous, Rebecca gave the impression of substance, real substance. She had a smooth, rich, cultured but nonetheless highly seductive voice as opposed to Angie's grating whine. If it were not for her ability to perform as she did in bed, Brad would not have been able to tolerate Angie. On the other hand, Rebecca appeared to be an entirely different proposition. The question he found himself asking immediately was, whether or not she was as good as Angie in bed, or could she, as with everything else as far as he could see, be better?

'So you would like to arrange for my little sister to visit the White House, Brad?'

'That I would,' replied Brad trying desperately hard to impress.

'And why would you want to do that, Angie?'

'Brad felt it would be a good idea for me to mix in a better social circle. He's thinking of running for office himself and has asked me to be a part of his staff team.'

Rebecca looked at Brad and raised her left eyebrow. 'It doesn't matter to me why you want to go to the White House party, but please, Angie, don't insult me with completely unbelievable stories. If you don't want to tell me, just say you'd rather not and we'll leave it at that.'

'It is probably my fault, Rebecca,' said Brad. 'Don't be cross with Angie, I've just asked her to do me a little favour.'

'As I said, I'll fix it. If you don't want to tell me what it's all about, I won't ask.'

'Thanks, Beccy,' said Angie with obvious relief.

'But, please, Angie, I have asked you so often before, don't call me Beccy.' Her tone was not strident, but was not one to argue with either.

'Sorry, I always forget. But Pop always called you Beccy.'

'Not until after you were born, and he had a special reason then. So, when would you like to go?'

'How soon can you fix it?' replied Angie.

'Well there's no immediate rush,' interrupted Brad, knowing that he had yet to work out how he was going to plan the operation. It was one thing to say you were going to assassinate the President and to hire a professional to do it, quite another to take on the organisation yourself. If only Miles Waterford had come across with the money.

'Sure, but we don't want to leave it too long, honey, a lot can happen and I might need to go more than once,' said Angie showing, for the first time that Brad could remember, something approaching common sense.

'Look, I really am very busy,' replied Rebecca, 'so why don't I see what dates I might be able to arrange and then you can see how it fits into your plans?'

'Thank you, Rebecca. I suggest you do that and then we all have dinner tomorrow evening,' said Brad, still trying to impress.

'Fine with me, but now I have to get on,' said Rebecca, unaware how unhappy her little sister was with the suggestion. Angie knew how quickly Rebecca would move on a man when she wanted him, and she had no intention of allowing her too close to Brad. Although she was unaware of what Bridget had said, Angie knew it was perfectly true — she was a kept woman, and she had every intention of staying that way. It was another motivation for agreeing to kill the President.

Dinner was a strained affair, Angie's conversational ability being limited. Talking at length was not something that she and Brad ever did; it was not something that she had done very often with anyone. But she was determined to prevent an interesting conversation developing between Brad and Rebecca.

It was not easy.

'Do you see much of the President, Rebecca?' asked Angie.

'No,' she replied condescendingly, as the conversation changed direction yet again just as it was becoming interesting. Brad was obviously screwing Angie, there was no doubt about that, but the question forming in Rebecca's mind was, how good was he? Angie was being very protective; she must be afraid of losing him. 'In fact I've only seen him once since he became President, he didn't greet me like a long lost friend. You know, you'll be very lucky even to get close to him at one of these White House parties, let alone talk to him. The only events that I can get you into, as you've seen from the list of dates, are the major ones, and there'll be literally hundreds of people there.'

'But I've got to get close to him,' said Angie, earning a reproachful glare from Brad.

'I've marked seven dates on which I think I could get you in and these three,' she said, pointing at the list, 'will be the smallest gatherings. Even so, they'll all be attended by at least two hundred to two fifty people.'

'I was going to ask you about this one,' said Brad, pointing to the buffet lunch on 22nd November.

'No chance,' said Rebecca. 'Invitation only, and they were all sent out immediately after the election.'

'What, before the Inauguration?' said Brad expressing surprise but not revealing that he and Bridget had received an invitation. It had not arrived until February.

'Well before. The Democrats will make a big thing out of the thirty years and, in view of the problems Clinton has had since assuming office, informed opinion is that he will use the opportunity as a relaunch.

'No-one in the know can see an out-and-out professional

like David Gergen missing an opportunity like that. They are bound to make something of it.'

'So there's no chance of Angie being there?' said Brad, failing to hide his disappointment.

'I wouldn't go that far, but I would need to have a pretty good reason to pull out the necessary stop. Even then there's no guarantee that I could do it.'

'What would constitute a pretty good reason?' asked Angie, sounding more intelligent than either of them were accustomed to.

'Nothing that I can think of, which is why I've said I don't think it would be possible. Look,' Rebecca said, drawing in breath, 'I'll do what I can, I've promised you both that, but I have a job and a position to keep, and I can only do so much unless I know the whole story. Then I can decide. Maybe it wouldn't make any difference, maybe it would.'

Brad knew that something had motivated Angie; he wondered if that same thing motivated Rebecca. If only he knew what it was, if only he had followed it up at the time. If only, he thought, the saddest two words in the entire language.

'Pop would have been able to get me into the celebrations,' said Angie, interrupting his thoughts.

'I wouldn't call it a celebration, it's a memorial lunch.'

'Whatever,' she replied with a shrug of the shoulders. 'He'd have been able to get me in.'

'How would that have been?' asked Brad.

'Our father was very well placed in the Democratic Party. If he were still alive today he would certainly have received an invitation.'

'And that,' said Brad, 'would be your angle if you thought it worth making the effort?'

'Correct.'

'It's for Simon really, Beccy,' said Angie slowly, 'Pop would have done it for Simon, wouldn't he?'

The two sisters looked lovingly at each other for the first time since Brad had seen them together. He said nothing. Angie was half Rebecca's age and, character-wise, they had nothing in common. Still, there was clearly a bond between them.

'Pop would have killed for Simon, he would for all of us, Beccy, you know that.'

'And we for him, Angie.'

'And we for him and Simon, Beccy.'

'I suspect you had better tell me what it is you're planning, don't you?' Rebecca said. 'And I suspect that I ought to know exactly who you are, Brad, and what is your real interest in Angie going to the White House. If I can get her in, then I can get you in, and perhaps you don't need her to do your job for you then.' Brad started to sweat a little. There was no way he was going to tell her everything, and he was certainly not going to commit the act himself.

'Are you a professional?'

'A professional?' he replied with surprise. 'No, I'm in textiles.'

'So you're not being paid to do something and then trying to get Angie to do it for you?'

'No.'

'Then what is your interest in the matter?'

'Patriotic.'

'But Angie takes the risk. You're obviously not a poor man, why don't you pay somebody to do the dirty work instead of using Angie?'

'I'm not poor, it's true, but I'm not in that class of wealth.'

'Suppose we were all three of us to go, together, what then?'

Brad swallowed hard. This was not what he had intended.

'Well?' she asked 'Why should Angie take the risks just to satisfy your patriotism?'

'She must have her own reasons. I did not pressurize her, did I, Angie?'

'That is not the point,' said Rebecca, before Angie could speak. 'Why should Angie take the risks to satisfy your patriotism?'

The venom of Rebecca's words frightened Brad as her

201

outward veneer of sophisticated control cracked, revealing her insecurity. 'You're a sleaze bag, you know that,' screeched Rebecca suddenly. 'Like all those other puffed up shits who sit around controlling other people's lives all day, you don't give a fuck as long as you get what you want and someone else takes the risk, someone else takes the rap.' Her outburst had turned heads, drawn attention to them 'Never you,' she said, almost spitting the words at him. 'People like you make me sick.' She was speaking more slowly now. 'No regard for other people, their lives, their families, their feelings, and if you get it wrong and screw up, what the hell, someone else will pay the price, as long as you don't have to. As long as you can still lord it over all and sundry the rest of us don't matter.

'You suit yourself, Angie,' she said finally, 'but I'm not sitting at the same table as this scum.' She stood up, sweeping an arm swiftly across their table sending crockery skidding onto the floor. 'I've screwed his sort for years. They're all the same. You'll learn in time the hard way, as I did. I hope he's good on the job — most of them aren't but they think they are. Take my advice, little sister, always make sure the apartment and the car are in your name and paid for.'

CHAPTER TEN

'Steve,' said Scott urgently as he woke him. They had set up campbeds in a room along the corridor from the Control Centre and were taking it in turns to sleep. The four machine operators also worked a shift system so that three of them were at their posts at all times. 'I'd say we had a break if we didn't know that it's nothing to do with Harworth, which makes it doubly worrying.'

'What?' asked Steve, wishing it had happened half an hour earlier because half an hour's sleep was worse than none at all.

'The Washington Police have just been in touch. The caterers who supply the White House have received a visit from someone who has made them very suspicious. He's been asking questions about security.'

'What have you done?'

'I've told them to bring the owner in here to see us.'

'In here to the White House?' said Steve with a laugh.

'I know you and I couldn't both leave, and reckoned it was better to see him together. According to Sergeant Mulligan, Mr Harbuckle has the highest level security clearance and spends half his life walking in and out of this place, so I guess it was the right thing to do.'

Steve detected just a hint of concern in Scott's voice.

'Yeah, Scott, no question of it. It just struck me as odd the way you put it.'

Mr Harbuckle arrived with Sergeant Mulligan and after spending half an hour with him, both Steve and Scott were seriously troubled.

'So what do we know about this man?' asked Steve once Harbuckle and Mulligan had left.

'He's no Texan,' replied Scott.

'Agreed, and he's clean shaven. Mr Harbuckle is a fastidious individual but what he remembers most are the three things he was meant to remember. And they're all false.'

'Height and weight are too vague,' said Scott.

'Olive or slightly tinted skin, that's about all we have to go on.'

'You don't think that was make-up?'

'No.'

'That's emphatic. Care to teach me?'

'Nothing more than a hunch. The features that were supposed to be remembered were so pronounced I don't think he'd have bothered with his skin. They were all quick, easy features.'

'So, South American, Italian ....'

'Don't say it, Scott, but yes, Mafia.'

'Do you *really* think so?'

'No idea, but it scares me.'

'Where do we start to look for this guy?'

'Are you serious?'

'Nothing else to do.'

'Mug shots and the impeccable Mr Harbuckle. My guess is that despite the disguise, we'd have an even chance of recognising the man again from a picture, and that's more than most people would without the disguise.'

'So I pull every olive skin and sit with Mr Harbuckle?' Scott laughed.

'No, pull the names, faces, yes. But then look at the background, see what you can build up.'

'And then I sit with Harbuckle?'

'Yep.'

Angie sat speechless in the restaurant as Rebecca strode from the room, brushing aside two waiters carrying laden trays as she went.

Brad remained tight-lipped at first but then beckoned to a waiter. 'I am truly sorry about this. The lady's husband has only recently died and she is still in a state of great distress.'

'We understand perfectly, sir,' replied the waiter with the anonymous politeness that all good waiters assume in difficult situations.

'If you would arrange to add the cost of the damage to my bill, then I'll be glad to deal with it,' continued Brad, endeavouring to recover his lost composure. A swift glance around the restaurant had left him relieved to see that there was nobody there who knew him. He was thankful for that at least.

'Most certainly, sir, and if you would care to move to another table.'

'No, no, we must be going. We must find my friend's sister, she needs help.'

'I understand, sir.'

How odd, thought Brad. No-one would have believed that Angie and Rebecca were sisters, but his wife and his mistress, now that they would have believed. Probably did.

'Come, my dear,' said Brad, ushering a steadying hand towards Angie, 'we must find Rebecca and help her.'

Angie looked at him but her smile was not there. Even the flirtatious eyes had none of their usual flare. 'They *are* in my name,' she said, 'and they *are* paid for.'

'What?' replied Brad obviously flustered.

'The apartment and the car are both in my name and they are both paid for,' she said slowly getting to her feet. 'And you can go stuff yourself, buddy.'

There was just one glass amongst the wreckage on the table that was still full of wine. She picked it up and poured it over him as she left. 'So long, sucker!'

'Perhaps, sir, you would like to come with me to clean up a little,' said the waiter as the other diners, trying not to miss a word nor a movement, gave the impression of being totally uninterested.

'Thank you,' was the dispirited reply.

Rebecca had hailed a cab and gone straight to her apartment, which had come her way in much the same manner that Angie had just acquired hers. For seven years she had been Edward's mistress while his wife slowly died, and no sooner was she buried than he had married his secretary. Bastard. To her, all men were bastards.

'Come on in,' said Rebecca to Angie as she opened the

door. 'Dumped him, then?'

'Yes.'

'So, you need somewhere to stay?' It was not a welcoming invitation.

'Tonight, yes. But the apartment and the car are in my name. I just don't want to make the journey tonight.'

'Hardly far,' replied Rebecca contemptuously.

'Far enough. Besides, I want to talk to you.'

'Talk away.' Rebecca lit a cigarette and watched her sister expectantly.

'Why did you do it?'

'Why?' she replied expansively, drawing on her cigarette and flopping down onto the sofa. 'The guy's a slimeball and he wants you to kill the President for him. What's in it for you?'

'How did you know?' asked Angie genuinely puzzled.

'Obvious,' replied Rebecca dismissively.

'And you disapprove?'

'Hell, no, Angie. I'd kill the President myself if I could. I'd kill all Presidents, especially Democrats.'

'Like me, because of Simon?'

Rebecca hesitated. Despite what people thought, Angie was not stupid all the time. She noticed the hesitation. 'What's wrong, Beccy?'

'Men are bastards, Angie. All men are bastards.'

'Pop wasn't. Not all men, Beccy.'

'All men, Angie, including Pop.'

'No!' screamed Angie, 'You don't know what you're saying.'

'But I do,' she replied starting to sob.

Their father had died four years earlier. Both girls had worshipped him, as he had them, but after his death Rebecca had received a letter from him. It told her not only of his affairs, but also the truth about Simon's death.

'Sit down, Angie, listen carefully, and if at the end you don't believe me then I'll show you the letter and you can read it for yourself.'

'What letter?' She was suddenly calmer. As if, by telepathy, the message had already been transmitted and received.

'Pop lied to us about a lot of things, and after the funeral his solicitor gave me a letter. He had had several mistresses over the years. He said Mom never knew, but who knows. Maybe she had lovers as well, I don't know, but that's not what hurt me. That's not what *really* upset me.'

'Then what did?'

'He lied to me about Simon's death. He *was* killed in a training exercise. Pop was so ashamed that his son died and it wasn't in action that he wrote the letter I found in his desk himself. He said it helped him to believe his son had been a hero. I think he had even co nvinced himself that it was true.'

'What difference does it make?'

'The accident that killed all those boys was an accident in that it wasn't intentional. But Simon caused it, he caused it by disobeying orders. Simon was responsible for killing them all.'

'And Pop lived with that knowledge all those years. My poor Pop.'

'No, Angie, he should have told us, or at least not lied to us as he did. We broke up, all three of us, after Simon's death but lying to us didn't help. I look back at it now and think we might even have coped better if we had known the truth.'

'But he only did it to protect you and mummy.'

'Did he? He didn't write that letter and tell me what he did to protect us. He did it to hide his shame, for his own selfish benefit.'

They sat in silence for well over an hour and it was Angie who finally broke it. 'Do you realise that I was going to kill the President because another President had killed my brother?'

'Does the slimeball know that?'

'No.'

'Then just forget it, walk away from it. You'll probably never hear from him again after tonight.'

Angie couldn't reply. She was very fond of Brad; it hadn't

just been the sex and the good life — she'd had that with all the others.

'Was he any good in bed?'

'So-so, but he's got a friend from Alaska who's something else.'

'So tell me about it.'

'It's his strength, his stamina, his ... he's just such a wonderful *animal*.

Angie began thinking perhaps she might make a trip up north.

Brad decided against going home that night. He booked into the Hilton and spent the night in the bar. Finally, just before seven in the morning, totally exhausted and barely able to stand, he staggered to his room and slept restlessly until midday, when he woke with an appalling hangover.

For the next four days he did nothing but drink and sleep. Even Bridget began to get concerned. He usually rang home every few days, whoever's bed he was in, but it was almost a week since she had heard from him. He had not been in touch with his office for five days. That was unheard of. Had she gone over the top in the facial adviser incident? She still needed Brad, she needed his money. Access to all his money, not just a pay off or the settlement following a messy divorce.

When Brad did return home, Bridget found it hard to believe that the dishevelled wreck that stumbled from the cab at lunchtime was him. 'Whatever happened?' she asked, with just the tiniest hint of concern.

'Got drunk.' was the stammered reply.

'Sarah, Sarah!' she called to the maid. 'Come and help me with Mr. Harworth.'

Having put Brad to bed, Bridget called the doctor. She was genuinely worried: it surprised even her.

'Nothing that a few days rest and some decent food won't put right,' said the doctor, having examined Brad. 'Lay off the liquor for a week or two.'

'I'm grateful to hear that. Thank you, doctor.' Bridget's

relief was genuine, but it didn't arise out of love.

Meanwhile, Sally-Anne Knight was craving for the same self- indulgence and threatening to discharge herself from hospital.

Jeff had sat by her bedside for three days and nights, holding her hand most of the time. He knew that if he hadn't been to Alaska he wouldn't have been there. How is it, he wondered, that life gets itself into such a twist? How do we get ourselves into such stupid situations? He had been contemplating assassinating the President. How many other people were harbouring equally futile ideas?

What was Brad up to?

That last single question returned to the forefront of his mind time and again, no matter how hard he tried to suppress it. What was Brad up to, and what should he do about it? Could he do anything when there was no proof? He was brought back to reality with a shudder as his wife suddenly started screaming.

'Jeff,' she sobbed when she was coherent. 'I've had enough of this damn place, they don't even feed you properly, they don't give you a drink when you want one. I'm leaving, you hear me! Get me out of here!'

Instantly he pushed the red button to call the nurse. He couldn't restrain her, he knew she wouldn't listen to reason. They gave her another shot and she sank back into a more relaxed state again.

'I fear,' said the doctor, 'that we are going to have to make that application.'

'Then we must,' Jeff replied unhesitatingly.

'With your help we can make it on the basis of a short term safety requirement for her own protection.' He paused, 'But I'm afraid I have some bad news for you.'

'Bad news? What?'

'One of my colleagues who visited your wife earlier in the week was a neurologist. He carried out some tests and also arranged for another colleague, a psychologist, to visit her. They are both certain that your wife is suffering from a serious brain disorder and that she may never be able to leave hospital.'

Jeff dropped limply onto the chair he had been leaning against. A few weeks ago he'd discovered real life again. He'd hoped to nurse Sally-Anne back to how she used to be before they had moved to Washington and joined the smart set. Her alcoholism was a blessing is disguise, that's what he'd told himself, a chance to rebuild their lives. How trite, how naive, could he be? He wanted to cry, but could find no tears. The pain was too deep.

'Never?' he repeated quietly.

'Maybe never, Mr. Knight, but certainly not for a very long time. Many years, I'm told, but it isn't my field. We'll get her physically well, then my colleagues can start their task.'

'Was it the drink?'

'Possibly, but people who never drink suffer mental illness too, Mr. Knight. We can't assume that there is any connection and, at this stage, you of all people must assume that there is not. If what my colleagues fear is correct, there will be times when your wife does not recognise you, as she didn't when she first started to come out of her coma. At all costs, you must remain her friend. She must always be able to turn to you, to trust you. Sadly, I fear there'll be times when she won't think like that, when she'll despise you and no doubt say hurtful things, but that is when she will need you most.'

'Is there any chance?' he asked feebly. He wasn't sure he'd taken in what the doctor had said.

'There's always a chance, Mr. Knight.' The doctor placed a hand on Jeff's shoulders, gently guiding him to the door. 'Look, she's going to drop off to sleep now. Why don't you go home, have a shower, have some food and have some sleep. Come back this evening. She needs you to be strong, not close to collapse.'

'And so, my friend, it is time to go,' said Moncilo, holding out his hand to Hamdi.

'But I will return,' he replied, clasping it firmly.

'I hope so, but first I hope you get to Washington.'

'I will get there,' he said taking a small package of food from one of the children. 'Thank you, this isn't stew!'

They all laughed. The atmosphere for once was relaxed.

After Hamdi's trepidation, the fifty mile journey that night towards Mostar was uneventful and by daybreak they were safely holed up out of sight. The day dragged increasingly slowly, and it took all of Hamdi's willpower to stop his spirits flagging. His guides — or were they his guards? — were simple peasants who had left the land to work in the hotels and bars when the tourist boom had started. They had found themselves forced less willingly into their new role when war broke out. He chatted easily with most of them, but was already missing the stimulation of his conversations with Moncilo.

Hamdi taxed his mind relentlessly for a solution to the problem raised by Andrei, but none was forthcoming. Perhaps that was the real problem; not that the west did not want to help them but, logistically they couldn't. There was simply no way to supply the equipment.

When they set off they had intended to make the journey in two nights. Once they reached Mostar, Hamdi would be on his own with only Zena's son's papers between him and death. They were making good time on that second night when, hearing a truck approaching from the south, they slipped quickly into the woods that lined the road.

'Several trucks,' whispered one of the others.

'At least five and they are slowing.'

Hamdi had never used a gun in his life and until he left the mountain camp, had never even held one. He gripped it tightly now as the small convoy drew to a halt about a hundred yards short of them. There were six trucks, five of them troop carriers, and one tank.

Although it was dark, there was some moonlight that night, and it shone along the path which the road carved through the trees. As the troops poured noisily from the trucks into the woods to relieve themselves, Hamdi could see that they were not smartly dressed or well disciplined. There was no order to them but, more worryingly, they seemed in no hurry to continue their journey, standing around in groups laughing, talking and smoking.

There was little or no undergrowth in which to hide, and the seven Muslims lay exposed to anyone who cared to see them. The trees at that point were sparse — it was the worst point for miles around to have been forced to hide. Hamdi's guards were accustomed to it and were not as frail as him. He lay there with his face pressed down hard into such undergrowth as there was, feeling the bumpiness of the ground everywhere it touched his body. It seemed to be all over.

After half an hour it was apparent that the Serbs were not in any hurry to move on. 'What if they stay for the rest of the night?' whispered Hamdi to the man next to him.

'Then we stay for the rest of the night,' he replied, not understanding why Hamdi had asked the question.

'But as it gets light they will see us.'

'Then we move. But if we had a decent gun we could take them all out, now, from here.'

'You mean a machine gun?'

'No, something a bit bigger. Don't lift your head, but can you see that gun mounted on the second truck?'

'Just about.'

'That'd do. It would cut through them in seconds before they even had time to raise their Kalashnikovs.'

'That many men?'

'There are no more than a hundred, hundred and twenty men there. No problem.'

'And we have nothing like that at all?'

'We don't in our group. There must be some in our hands, but only a few. If we were more men, say a dozen or so, and had better cover, I'd say we should take them on and capture not just the gun but the tank as well. Just think what we could do with a tank.'

'But you would need shells and spares.'

'Spares, yes maybe, but there will be shells in one of the

trucks, they would not take a tank out without spare shells.'

They spent another half an hour in silence during which the Serbs still gave no indication of moving on.

'We won't complete our journey tonight,' said the man next to Hamdi, who he had never spoken to before that night. 'When they go, we'll have to look for a place to rest up. This road will be busy during the day.'

'How do you know?'

'It's been looked after. Pot holes filled. That can only be because it is used, probably to move tanks.'

'You mean there could be more tanks along here even during the night?'

'I'm sure of it. But don't worry, Hamdi, once we can move we'll get back into the thicker area of the woods. We'll be safe there even in daylight .'

'Is there no way that we could overrun them?' said Hamdi.

'What, the six of us?' he replied with surprise.

'Seven,' said Hamdi with good humour.

'Even seven.'

'But they are sitting in groups and there is no-one on the big gun. What is the range of our weapons and how quickly do they fire?'

'Not far enough, and too slowly,' the man replied grimly.

'But it is less than twenty targets each and they don't even all have guns with them.'

'You can see that?'

'Yes, I've a clear view of them now.'

'To be safe, we'd need to be no more than twenty five yards away.'

'That is close,' said Hamdi thinking. 'How quickly could you get that close?'

'I don't know what you're thinking, but we've been told to look after you, to die to save you. You must get safely to America, Moncilo said so.'

'What else did Moncilo say?'

'Just that you were going to America and if your mission was successful it would help our cause more than anyone had

213

helped it before. He only wanted six men. We all volunteered, but so did others. We drew lots to come with you. We can't risk a shoot out and you not getting to America.'

Hamdi was unaware that they knew anything about his mission. Unaware that they were prepared to die for him. This made him think again. Until then he was thinking of walking up to the Serbs to distract them while the others got into position so that once he had walked on past the trucks, they could open fire. He would be safe, they would not shoot until he was well past the trucks.

'Look,' said Hamdi, 'even if I get to America there is no guarantee I'll be successful, and much could go wrong before then. That tank is valuable, that tank and gun could save lives now.'

'But,' began the young man next to him.

'But nothing,' replied Hamdi, having made up his mind. 'I am going to walk towards them …'

'No!'

'Listen, I'm going to walk towards them and they'll let me pass. While I'm doing that you and the others must get close enough to shoot them all. Once I have walked past the end of the trucks, you open fire.'

'But what if,' began the young man, but it was too late. Hamdi was on his feet, dropped his gun and began walking in the shadow of the trees along the road towards the Serb soldiers. The sooner they saw him the better, as it gave the others more time, but he had covered almost half the distance before one of them shouted.

'Stop.'

'What's the problem?' replied Hamdi in his heaviest Serbian accent.

'Who are you?'

'A hungry peasant.'

A torch beam shone on him and they could see he was unarmed and no-one moved towards a gun. 'Approach.'

'Papers,' said one of them as he reached the group, most of whom ignored him and carried on playing cards.

'An odd time to be about,' said the soldier, returning his papers.

'I have nowhere to go. The Muslims killed my family. What is time?'

'Okay, on your way,' replied the soldier, more interested in getting back to his game of cards than in Hamdi.

The others moved swiftly and silently through the trees at an alarming pace. They had only been trained in the hills, but they had been well trained. Three of them even took the risk of crossing the road.

As soon as Hamdi passed the last truck, he stopped and positioned himself so that he was out of sight. Immediately he had disappeared from view they opened fire. It was all over inside half a minute. A few of the Serbs reached their weapons and made an attempt to return the fire but with no impact.

'Quickly, quickly,' called the leader, 'we must move the bodies.'

Hamdi stood and looked down at the dead bodies strewn around the road, twisted and contorted, lying across each other as they had fallen. It had all been over so quickly. Some were blood stained, others showed no sign of having been shot. The man who had looked at his papers and waved him through lay on top of a pile of bodies with blood running across his face and dripping onto the road below.

He felt sick, he wanted to vomit, but it was not the sight of the bodies or the blood that turned his stomach. For all he knew they might have been the very men that had killed his family and friends. The knowledge that they were Serbs in no way lessened his abhorrence at the killing process.

But suddenly he had doubts about his mission. What if they were right, who argued that arming the Muslims would only increase the bloodshed? What then? Was it worth it? He remembered hearing a debate at Oxford about preferring to be Red than dead. Was not that the debate now? Would the killing actually stop if the Muslims surrendered, or were the Serbs determined to wipe them out anyway? Surely not, he could not believe it, but in his heart he knew it was that he didn't want to believe it: they would not hesitate.

As he watched the bodies being dragged from the road and concealed in the woods as far as the limited resources allowed, he remembered that he had instigated it. Until he had stood up and walked towards them, all those men were alive and breathing. He may not have fired a single shot, but he was responsible for their deaths.

As he stood there shivering, they realised that some of the Serbs were not dead. No-one checked the wounds to see how bad they were — they shot them.

He was violently sick.

'I will carry on by truck', said Hamdi as he rejoined them; he had taken himself into the woods for a few moments to recover.

'But one of us comes with you.'

'No, it isn't necessary,' he replied, looking up into the dark eyes of a man almost ten inches taller than him. 'It's bad enough taking a truck. You must go, you must get the other trucks and the tank to somewhere safe before dawn.'

'But one of us must come with you for the handover.'

Hamdi had no answer to that.

He reluctantly agreed. 'Alright.'

'Then take Alexi, he says you are mad, he will enjoy himself!''

'Alexi' called the giant and the young man who had been lying next to Hamdi appeared. He was no more than a boy, seventeen, eighteen at the most. Hamdi had been unaware of him before, he hadn't really looked at him, or any of them, that closely.

'You deliver Hamdi safely so that he can do in America what he has done tonight. Help our people. Good luck,' finished the big man, shaking Hamdi warmly by the hand and kissing his cheeks.

CHAPTER ELEVEN

Hamdi and Alexi made good time towards Mostar. 'Much easier than walking,' said Hamdi, trying for the third time to start a conversation with the young man who just a short while earlier he'd been lying next to him on his stomach in the scrub.

'I don't mind walking,' came the staccato reply.

'You must do a lot of it.'

'A bit, yes.' Another conversation stopper.

'Why did you volunteer to come with me, Alexi?' Hamdi asked gently.

'I was ordered, you heard it,' replied the young man, clearly puzzled by the question.

'No, Alexi, not tonight in the truck, but from the camp?' Hamdi maintained his soft, kindly approach throughout the conversation. He didn't find it difficult: it was his natural manner.

'That was a great honour,' Alexi replied proudly.

'Why?'

'Because you are the man who is going to America to speak for our people.' The difference in tone from Alexi's normal replies was beyond description, his pride oozed from every syllable.

'Who told you that, Alexi?'

'The whole camp knows,' he replied, slipping back into his normal tone.

'What else does the whole camp know, Alexi?'

Alexi was quiet for a moment and then replied very nervously, 'It is said that you were at Oxford with the President of America, that you know him, but we should not say that as it could risk your life.'

Hamdi laughed.

'You find this funny?' Alexi asked, more puzzled than ever.

'Not at all, Alexi, but it was supposed to be a secret.'

'That is why we do not talk about it, because it is a secret.'

'Thank you, Alexi!'

'Tell me, how old are you?'

'Almost seventeen,' he replied boastfully.

'Did this war interrupt your schooling?'

'No,' was the suddenly enthusiastic reply. 'I lived with my family in the mountains, we kept animals and farmed a little. My older brothers would go down to work in the hotels for the summer and I had to help at home.'

'Did you ever go to school?'

'A little,' laughed Alexi.

'Don't you regret that?'

'No.'

'Wouldn't you like to learn things?'

'But I do learn things, different things from you, but I do learn things. You cannot hunt and kill for food, you do not know how to mend this truck if it breaks down, you do not know how to use and maintain a gun.'

'Okay, okay,' said Hamdi laughing, 'you've made your point, very well. But you are an intelligent boy, what you've just said shows that. Don't you want to learn other things?'

'No.'

'What do you want to do for the rest of your life?'

'Kill Serbs.'

'There must be more to life than that, Alexi.'

'No.'

'Did they kill your family? You know they killed mine?'

'Yes, I knew. They killed mine too, I was up in the hills looking for some lost animals and I saw the smoke from the fire. They killed them all, my mother and father, my grandfather and all my brothers and sisters. Dumped them in the house, stole anything they wanted and set fire to the house.'

Hamdi found it difficult to reply but Alexi continued, 'They killed all the animals as well, not to eat but for fun. I hate them.'

'Do you think killing Serbs will make it better?'

'They want to wipe out all Muslims so we must fight them.

If we shoot all of them they will not be able to wipe out all the Muslims. The tank will be a big help, they will not expect it.'

Hamdi decided not to point out that one tank would not change the balance of power at all.

'Do you know what actually happened to me and my family, Alexi?'

'No.'

'Would you like to hear?'

'I don't mind.'

Slowly, painfully Hamdi started to tell the story but it was not until he reached the point about Zena that Alexi seemed to be listening. No doubt he had heard the rest of the story before, thought Hamdi. Different names, different places, same story.

'She did *that*?' asked Alexi, 'but why? If she is a Serb she should have killed you. I would have killed you if I had been her.'

'She has seen too much killing, Alexi. She has lost too many people she loved, killed by the wars. And for what?'

'That is not for me to answer,' he shrugged. 'My job is to kill Serbs, the more Serbs I kill the better.'

'What about Croats?'

'As well, yes, but especially Serbs.' He was just slightly hesitant.

'Because it was Serbs who killed your family?'

'Yes.'

'Suppose it was actually Croats?'

'It wasn't,' Alexi replied angrily.

'You can be sure?'

'Yes,' replied Alexi, becoming confused. 'What is this?' he asked. 'Why do you ask me all these questions? You should want to kill Serbs as well. Isn't that why you are going to see Clinton, to get tanks and heavy armoury for us to kill Serbs?'

'More so that they stop thinking they can kill us easily.'

'That will never happen. We must kill them. Kill them all and some of us must die doing it. I am not afraid to die,' he said proudly. 'You were not afraid to die when you walked towards them tonight. But if you don't want to kill Serbs, why did you do it? Why do you go to America if you do not want to kill Serbs?'

'I want to stop all the fighting, Alexi. I don't want the killing to carry on, whether it's Muslims, Croats or Serbs. I just want it all to stop.'

'What, and let them live? You're mad, you're not the man we thought you were. Perhaps I should kill you now if you are not going to help us.'

'Would that help?'

'Perhaps you are not a Muslim with false Serb papers, perhaps you are a Serb with false Muslim papers who is tricking us all.'

'How on earth did you know about the papers?'

'The ones that you used back there tonight, you mean? We found them when we searched you while you slept when you first arrived.'

Hamdi was amazed. He knew he was tired, but how could they search him while he slept? He had not slept that deeply for months. 'I don't believe you, Alexi, I would have woken up.'

'Not with the sleeping dose in your drink.'

'You drugged me? No!'

'Oh, yes, we do it to everybody. I did not go to Oxford, but I understand the plants that grow wild in the fields.'

'So Moncilo knew all along?'

'Oh, yes and that you were at Oxford when Clinton was there.'

'From my wallet.'

'Yes.'

'And still you trusted me?'

'Moncilo trusted you. He said he would talk to you, he would tell us if you were a Muslim or a Serb.'

'Suppose he was wrong?'

'We will know when you reach America. If Clinton is your friend, then he will help you. If he helps you, we will get our weapons and we will know that you are one of us. But if he does not help you then it would have been better that I killed you now.'

The maturity of the boy before him was a lesson to Hamdi. A lesson he told himself he should have learnt long before. Just because he was well educated did not make him superior or more important than others, he simply had different qualities to contribute to the community. The boy before him was an experienced man in some matters and in these matters he himself, for all his advantages, was no more than a child. It was exactly as Moncilo had said.

'It is not that simple, Alexi.'

'Firstly, just because we were at Oxford together does not mean that we know each other or that we are friends. And secondly,' continued Hamdi, realising that he was sounding exactly what he was, a lawyer, and that it was probably the worst impression to give but he couldn't help it, 'even if we were friends that does not mean that he will do whatever I ask.'

'I would for my friend.' The statement was uncomplicated.

'You would do anything for a friend?'

'Yes, anything.'

'But suppose it wasn't possible?'

'For a friend you make it possible.'

'But it can't always be done just like that.'

'For a friend it can.'

Now it was not the intellectual gulf that was a problem but the social gulf, the environmental gulf. 'What is possible in a village is not possible across the world in the same way, Alexi.'

'I do not understand. If my friend asks me to give him my goat because he needs it, I give it to him.'

'But what if your father tells you that you can't. Do you disobey your father?'

'If it is my goat then it is no concern of my father. If it is my father's goat then I should not be giving it to my friend.'

'Suppose it was the family's goat?'

'Then it would be for my father to decide, as the head of the family.'

Hamdi realised that he had made matters worse not better with his poor example. He was about to try again when Alexi spoke with urgency. The man had surfaced again and Hamdi knew he was now the child. 'Hold on,' said Alexi as the truck swerved off the partially-metalled road onto a dirt sidetrack, heading up through the woods.

Hamdi assumed that Alexi had seen something, 'What was it?' he asked.

'Trucks up ahead, coming towards us.'

'Shouldn't we go faster then?'

'No, it would create more dust and if they have seen us anyway it would make them more interested. An Army truck that is hurrying is either retreating, going to war or doing something that it should not be doing.'

Through his rear mirror Alexi kept a constant vigil on the road behind him as it slowly disappeared into the distance. By the time he saw the trucks passing the gap in the trees, the road itself had gone from view.

Alexi slowed the truck to little more than walking pace and kept his eyes constantly on the mirror. Hamdi had turned around in his seat to watch over the tailgate of the truck. 'They've gone,' he said.

'Wait.'

They waited and watched and about two minutes after the last truck had passed there came another single truck. Hamdi smiled at Alexi, 'A wise head on young shoulders.' Alexi did not reply but continued slowly along the dirt track.

'Why do they do that?' asked Hamdi, trying to engage Alexi in conversation again.

'They were well trained, better than the others we met. It means that they are safer, there will have been a big gun on that last truck. It is easier to protect the convoy against attack that way. Your plan would not have worked, would it?'

'No,' said Hamdi slowly. 'Is that what you were about to say to me when I jumped up and set off?'

'Yes.'

'I was lucky.'

'Yes, we were all lucky.'

'What are you looking for now?'

'Somewhere to hide the truck, we are only about three kilometres from Mostar. We will walk the rest.'

'I'll do whatever you say, Alexi.'

The young man smiled, appeased him with lip service; 'And I will respect what you teach me from what you have learnt. I hope you can get Clinton to agree, perhaps no killing would be better than everyone being killed.'

Surely he had not convinced him that easily, but then, thought Hamdi, as Alexi had shown several times, the fact that he was uneducated did not mean that he was unintelligent.

It took them twenty minutes to find a suitable hiding place and another fifteen minutes to cover the truck from sight.

'Come, we must hurry,' said Alexi, 'it'll soon be light.'

'Where are we going?'

'To a house. Once we reach the town we will be safe. Our troops control it now.'

'Will you stay?'

'Probably until tonight, yes. It will be too light when we reach it for me to return immediately.'

The house was larger than Hamdi had expected and completely nondescript. There were seven rooms in all. Alexi knew three of the four people who welcomed them, two of whom were women.

'I suggest you sleep for a few hours, have some food and then start making your way towards Ulcinj. You will have to walk a lot, but there may be trains and even a bus. Radmilla,' he said turning to a girl not much older than himself, 'will brief you. She has the details and the maps that you will need.'

'Thank you,' said Hamdi, aware once again how mature Alexi was in matters of war. 'What will you do?'

'I will rest and return tonight. With the truck it will be an easy journey. I'll do it in one night.'

By the time Hamdi woke in the late morning there was a feeling of enthusiasm in the air, which he detected as soon as he joined the others in the kitchen. Alexi smiled proudly at him. 'This is the man to thank. He inspired us,' he said proudly to the others.

Hamdi looked puzzled but assumed there had been contact from the mountain camp.

'Moncilo says to thank you but to tell you not to take any more foolish chances,' said Radmilla. 'The trucks and the tank will tide them over until you return with the real weapons.'

The little band applauded, much to Hamdi's embarrassment. He nodded and smiled nervously.

'Here, sit with me,' said Radmilla, drawing a chair from under the table, 'I will brief you while you eat.'

Another aged beyond her years through war, thought Hamdi as he looked at the war-weary eyes in her youthful face. He had learnt so much in such a short space of time, but would he be able to convey it? Zena had been right, it was the fighting that had to he stopped. Altogether, not just for a week, a month or even a year. He had to work towards something more permanent. That, he knew, was well beyond his immediate task, but he would return to it.

'Thank you,' he said, taking the chair. 'I thought you would be asleep, Alexi.'

'Not yet,' he replied blushing slightly as he smiled at Radmilla. Hamdi envied them their stolen moments of passion. Passion, for him, was over.

'Let us not waste time,' said Hamdi. 'I must eat and be gone.'

'Very well,' replied Radmilla as she reached for the pile of paper across the table, 'please listen carefully.'

The briefing only took twenty minutes. Hamdi was impressed by her clinical efficiency.

As the weeks passed by it was not only the inexperienced Scott Pulsat who was becoming increasingly frustrated by the lack of positive results. The Als were full of detailed and interesting information but apart from the Chief telling them that he was happy to forget the Zielinski threat, they were going nowhere.

'How long do we keep it up, sir?' asked Steve.

'I don't know. Harworth worries more now than he did before. He's been rejected three times, and men like that don't take kindly to rejection. He'll suddenly do something daft.'

'All he seems to be doing at the moment is sitting drinking. Knight is at his wife's bedside, London you say is dead.'

'But you've still got your unidentified olive skin who visited Mr Harbuckle.'

'Yes, sir.'

'No luck with the pictures?'

'No, sir.'

'What about guest lists?'

'We're working a couple of days ahead of each function and then picking up the changes. Vetting each one again, *whoever* they are, and showing Mr Harbuckle all the male pictures.'

'Good. It's the sort of work that will produce a break. We're all frustrated, but in my view you haven't missed anything yet —if you have, I've missed it as well. It's tough, but we must just keep up the drudgery.'

'Thank you, sir,' replied Scott, no longer trying to impress. He had learnt a lot.

Enzo sat in his hotel room seriously wondering whether or not to just take the twenty five million dollars and forget about the assignment. It was very different from the usual trade he plied. Normally an assignment began with constant surveillance to build up a picture of the captors, their habits and their security arrangements, in order to learn to think like them and identify their Achilles' heel.

This was different. He felt out of his league. His real task was to find and exploit a hole in the security of the most closely guarded man in the world. His only advantage was his willingness to die to achieve his goal.

Taking the last soft drink from the hospitality fridge in the brightly furnished room, he looked at the other bottles arranged neatly on the shelves. One, he knew, would lead to another, and then he would slip into his old habits. Once he had done that he would never achieve his objective; his attempt would be doomed to disaster from the moment he set off.

He lay on the single bed, gazing up at the ceiling as the curtains fluttered gently in the late morning breeze. He would not be beaten, he would find a way, but he had to start again.

The gun was not a problem, but to bring it into the country was an unnecessary risk. True, it would test his ability to smuggle it in pieces through detection equipment, but what was the point of getting caught entering the country? No, he decided, he would use his contacts at home to arrange the gun. He'd only need a hand gun.

In that single decision he had also decided either to die at the same time as Clinton or to be taken into custody. It had to be a close range hit, he was too out of practice for anything else. The problem was to get close. The problem was to get to the Memorial Lunch on 22nd November.

The dressing table drawer contained writing paper but nothing to write with. He cursed the fact that he did not even have an old pencil—so much for buying everything he'd need when he arrived in Washington. The desk clerk, a pretty little thing who, in another situation and years before, would have warranted further attention, was more than happy to oblige him with an embossed hotel biro.

Returning to his room, he sat at the dressing table and started to list the classes of people who would be in the room that day at the buffet. The first obvious split was into three groups — guests, staff, security — and he wrote each group name at the top of a separate piece of paper.

He looked upon security as being the easiest to identify and the least likely to afford him any opportunity for scope, so he took it first. There would be the usual White House secret service agents, who would no doubt stay reasonably close to Clinton throughout the part. Then there would be the gatemen, people manning the metal detectors and the sniffer machines, and probably a separate group assigned to search and check the staff. It was also a reasonable bet that every carpark attendant would actually be a gun-carrying officer. If there was any scope on the security angle that was where it would lie; in the carpark.

Having dismissed the security option he considered the staff. The obvious route he had already dismissed, Mr Harbuckle knew exactly what he was doing. 'Damn,' he said, cursing what he saw as his stupidity, 'the bloody press.' He started a fourth sheet and returned to ponder over the second. Guests were likely to have chauffeurs, but they would get no-where near the President. All the other staff would be permanent. Another blank.

The guests. Presumably, he thought, they'd all be Democrats with a close connection. He wrote just one word on the sheet: "Widows".

Finally, the press. How had he not thought of that even before the caterers? He had friends in the press but, more valuably, he actually had a valid press card of his own. It was only for a small local rag in Michigan, but it was legitimate. He would be a press photographer: that would solve all his problems.

He felt tired as he began to address his greatest problem, which was staying fit until the end of November, almost six weeks away. He had seen many AIDS sufferers and knew that he had moved into the final phase of the illness. He was no longer HIV positive, he had AIDS and it was not only affecting him physically but mentally as well. The pain from the glands in all parts of his body was becoming unbearable, but those in his throat and neck were the worst, causing blinding headaches which impeded his ability to think clearly.

He had been suspicious for several months of the slight loss of weight and the periodic feeling of nausea for no apparent reason, but alcohol had numbed the sensations. 'No!' he screamed at the bottles of spirit in the hospitality fridge. The sales pitch was reaching him. He turned violently away and hung his head out of the sixth floor window, breathing in the City air for several minutes before hurling himself back face-down onto the bed.

'One bloody mistake,' he yelled, 'just one bloody mistake!'

Time and again he had asked himself how it could possibly have happened. He had used a condom, he had done everything right. It had to be her, though, there was no-one else since he had been tested after his scare with the stripper from Julina's Bar; the three month wait after his drunken rampage that night had been agony, surpassed only by the ecstasy of the negative test.

Then he began to cry, pounding the pillows around his head with his clenched fists as he screamed, 'Clarisa, Clarisa.' Cupping the pillow in his hands either side of his head he buried himself in it. He lay like that for several minutes, sobbing uncontrollably, wishing he were dead.

Slowly he released his grip on the pillow and his hands fell limply above his head. He was exhausted, emotionally and physically. He longed to hold her, to kiss her, just to be with her. She was all he had wanted. Now he had nothing, and soon would be dead.

It was almost an hour before he was sufficiently composed to make his first phone call. 'Gary.' he said, all trace of his troubles dispersed as Gary Walton answered his phone. 'Enzo Friggli. How are you?'

'Mighty fine,' responded the small-time news proprietor with all his usual thirst for life. 'And you, you old rascal, how are you?'

'Never better,' lied Enzo, 'never better, my old friend.'

'And what do I have to do for you this time?'

'Hey, such cynicism!'

'You only ring when you want something, Enzo.'

'But I've given you some great scoops,' he replied honestly.

'True, very true,' replied Gary, who was now less interested in scoops, more interested in finding a buyer for his newspaper so that he could retire. On the other hand, maybe a scoop would produce a buyer. 'So, what is the scoop to be this time, Enzo?'

'That's not something I can tell you at the moment, but I can tell you it will be the biggest ever.'

'And what do I need to do to be the owner of this biggest ever scoop?'

'Just confirm if the White House Press Office rings you that I am one of your reporters and that I take my own pictures.'

'The White House?' said Gary showing his surprise. 'Sure thing. That's all?'

'That, my old friend, is all, I assure you.'

'Then I look forward to hearing from them. This might be the last time I can help you though, Enzo.'

'Why?'

'The paper's up for sale, I just want to retire, I've had enough.'

'Then I will make sure you get the inside story on this one, Gary. From the very beginning, names, dates, places, the whole lot, world exclusive.'

'I'm agog, Enzo. Speak to you again soon.'

'This will be a long one, perhaps a couple of months, so hang on in there, buddy. I promise you, Gary, it's much bigger than Watergate.'

'Then I'll wait to hear.'

The White House Press Office were most helpful when Enzo spoke to them on the phone next. 'Shall we say two fifteen on Tuesday next week, Mr Friggli?'

'That will be just fine.'

That was better, thought Enzo as he replaced the received. He would meet a press officer next week, conduct a background interview, get Gary to run an article and then obtain a pass for a lesser event. Time was tight, but he could do it and that way he would not look conspicuous. He would not appear to be homing in on his target date, which he was sure would be the subject of even tighter scrutiny than usual.

His Tuesday appointment was perfect. It left him four days before he had to be back in Washington. The man he had to see, Frank Austen, was in New York.

'Enzo,' said the wily little man as he looked up from his workbench, as always covered with bits and pieces of metal that to anyone else looked like scrap, but to Frank were his living; specialist guns. His main market was overseas, and he described himself to those who asked as being involved in exports and, on closer enquiry, would say, 'Hidden exports.' Dressed in one of his smart suits, they usually assumed that he was a banker. Nobody imagined him to be a gunsmith, and an extraordinary one at that.

'Frank,' replied Enzo, embracing the small man. The filthy little workshop at the rear of the down market motor repair shop beneath the railway arches hadn't changed. It wouldn't.

'And what brings you to see me?'

'What d'you think?'

'Special?' asked Frank, with a smile of anticipation. Frank Austen was a skilled craftsman, he enjoyed and relished a challenge. Routine bored him.

'Very special, Frank.'

'Good,' Frank replied, clearing away some rubbish from an old wooden box, 'sit down and we'll have a coffee while you tell me about it.'

The coffee was foul. It was always foul, though to Enzo's knowledge no-one had ever said so. He certainly would not.

'I'm looking for a hand gun that I can smuggle through a security check.'

'How good's the check?'

'The best.'

'What will be available to smuggle it in?'

'Me.'

'Not possible,' replied Frank, smiling ruefully.

'And,' continued Enzo, 'a commercial camera.'

'Now that is more interesting — that I can do something with,' said Frank cheerfully.

'I thought you'd like the idea.'

'When do you need this?'

'Two to three weeks.'

'No problem.'

'Have you got the camera?'

'Not yet, you tell me what you want and I'll get it.'

'Nothing special, but the more equipment, the easier it will be.'

'Just tell me what you want.'

'Will the camera have to work?'

'No, flash a bit maybe, but not actually take pictures.'

'Good.'

'How will you do it?'

There was only one thing Frank Austen enjoyed more than crafting his works of genius: telling people how he did it.

'There'll be time to assemble the weapon inside the security arrangements before use?'

'Yeah.'

'And how many bullets will you need?'

'That depends on what they are.'

'Well, how many targets?' he asked.

'One.'

'And the range?'

'Thirty feet to zero feet.'

'Zero feet?' asked Frank, perplexed.

'Possibly, yes.'

'Okay,' he said sounding uneasy for the first time. 'I can make a bullet that will ensure death if it hits the body above the waist from anything under ten, maybe fifteen feet.'

'Ideal.'

'But, Enzo, it will be a one chamber weapon.' His tone was sombre, more serious than Enzo had ever heard in all the years that he had known him.

'That's fine, Frank. In fact,' said Enzo very calmly, 'that's perfect.'

'So long as you're sure.'

'I'm sure.'

'Okay, then the gun will be in several pieces and you will have to practice putting it together in the dark. I'll conceal the pieces around the camera, some where metal is allowed but which won't show as anything more than a part of the camera, even on X-ray. The other pieces will have to be encased in lead.'

'What about the bullet?'

'A lead lined film canister. That's no problem.'

'So,' said Enzo putting down the untouched coffee, 'I'll go and buy the equipment, let you have it and then come back in what, ten days or so?'

'Fine, but first we need to arrange a fee.' Frank sounded like a banker when he said that.

'How much?'

'Fifty thousand dollars.;'

'Steep,' replied Enzo, genuinely surprised.

'This is obviously a very special job, Enzo.'

Enzo paused briefly. It would mean revisiting his sister but it was a welcome excuse — he could see the children one last time. He'd spend the weekend with them.

'Half now, half on completion.'

'As always.'

Within two hours Enzo had bought and delivered the camera equipment and was making his way to the airport. He was relaxed, remarkably relaxed.

It was several years since he had stayed with any of his relatives and although his sister was aware that something was wrong, she knew better than to ask. If he wanted to tell her she wouldn't need to ask, if he didn't want to tell her, then asking would only provoke a confrontation. She enjoyed his stay, as did they all but somehow she knew as he left that it was a last goodbye. Before the cab was out of the street her fears were confirmed by the contents of the suitcase which he had touched just once, immediately before he left.

The small room in which, after passing through seemingly endless security checks, he was greeted by the White House Press Officer, was neat and tidy, with plain white walls decorated with three pleasant prints, and plain pastel curtains. The round white melamine table was purely functional but the steel tubular framed chairs he found attractive.

'How can I help you, Mr Friggli?' asked the young man, who was in his mid twenties.

'I am writing a series of articles,' began Enzo, passing across his press card, 'on the change in society during the past thirty years. I wanted to start and finish the series with the White House under President Kennedy and the White House under President Clinton.'

'And how do you think we can help you?'

'The first article will be about the Kennedy days and the relationships between the President and the people and the President and the press.

'I have completed some of the research already, but I wondered if there was anybody still in the press office who would have been here thirty years ago. I know it's a long shot, but you never know.'

'There is one person.'

'Would it be possible to speak to him?'

'Her. Possibly. I'll see what can be done. She's on vacation this week.'

'That would be very helpful. I have several families in different parts of the country who have agreed to help me, and most of the articles will reflect how the family sees the changes in society over the last thirty years. Also how the President's life is different, to show that even he has been affected by the changes and is not able to ignore them.'

'You know that President and Mrs Clinton do not look kindly on the comparisons made between them and the Kennedys.'

Enzo had absolutely no idea of that. 'Yes, I was aware. That in part is what prompted the idea of the article. By writing it in the way that I am, I'll give the President the opportunity to put that message across, but gently. It would be me, not him, making the point that their lives and their life styles are different,'

'The President would probably appreciate that.'

'Will he be that personally interested?' asked Enzo, surprised for the first time since he had walked into the building into an honest answer.

'He may be, he just may be, Mr Friggli. Let me have a resume of what you propose to write and an outline of the articles, and I'll make an appointment for you to see Miss Culpan next week. I would hope to be able to let you know next week how we could help. Would two fifteen next Tuesday be suitable?'

'Yes it would, thank you.'

Enzo strolled slowly from the White House up Pennsylvania Avenue. Waffling his way past a relatively inexperienced young man was one thing, but putting together the information he needed was another. On the other hand, it could actually lead to a personal interview with the President. Now that would be a scoop for Gary.

Alone in his hotel room he struggled for hours with the task, unsuccessfully. There was only one solution he decided. Gary would have to write it, but what would he tell him? What would his cover story be?

He slept on it and flew to Michigan first thing the next morning, having paid up his room in advance to keep it.

'So what is this series of articles about how life has changed in thirty years?' asked Gary as soon as he saw him.

'So the White House has been in touch?'

'You bet they've been in touch. They don't let just anyone

walk into the President's office to interview him.'

'They offered, I didn't ask,' replied Enzo, with a soft smile.

'That's what made them wonder if you were real. You didn't seem too keen to see the President!'

'Didn't think it would be that easy.'

'Well the resume's not that easy either, which is no doubt why you've turned up here!'

'They told you?'

'They told me!'

'Can you help?'

'Sure, but what am I getting myself into, Enzo? I just want to retire and watch the horses run once a week, win a dollar, lose a dollar, nothing exciting, but it'll suit me.'

'Can't tell you that, Gary, but as soon as it breaks I promise you'll have the full story. The letter's already written to date, I add to it each day.'

'You ain't kidding me now, Enzo?'

'Gary, would I?' asked Enzo, vowing to himself that the first thing he would do when he returned to Washington was write the letter and thereafter keep it up every day. 'And there's also a letter with it even now that confirms you knew nothing about the job in hand, in case it should go wrong and be misunderstood.'

'Okay, you promise me?'

'Have I ever lied to you, Gary?'

'Probably, I've just never found out. Okay, I'll do it and then you buy me a steak, a big steak.'

'You've got yourself a deal,' replied Enzo, slapping Gary hard on the back.

That night in his motel Enzo wrote the promised letters to Gary and placed them in an envelope clearly marked to be opened on his death. He sealed them in another envelope and posted them to himself at the hotel in Washington. He'd decided the odds were he'd be killed as he fired the fatal shot, but he did not want to leave Gary exposed if for any reason he died before.

There was no need to return to Washington before the following Tuesday and so, having posted the resume to the White House press office, he flew to New York and enjoyed a few quiet days before calling on Frank Austen on the Saturday morning.

'Wasn't expecting you until next week, Enzo,' said Frank as he looked up from the oily old workbench.

'Passing with not much else to do. I leave here Monday evening, but until then I'm at a loose end, so I thought I'd see how you're getting on.'

'Very well,' said Frank, passing him the camera case. 'Here, find the gun. There's a small X-ray machine in that cupboard if it helps.'

It was not going to be obvious to the naked eye and so Enzo passed the camera, its case and stand through and through the machine. He could find nothing. Then he tried to unscrew pieces of the stand leg. Finally he tried to unscrew anything and everything, without success.

'Okay, Frank, it's a work of art. Show me.'

First Frank removed the rubber base of one of the stand legs and then detached the leg from the camera mounting place. Carefully he pushed the telescopic legs back inside each other until the top of the bottom section was protruding from the top of the leg. They he gently unscrewed the top four inches to produce his gun barrel.

Enzo smiled.

Slowly but equally surely the entire gun emerged from the camera, the final piece being the trigger mechanism which was concealed in the operating mechanism of the camera itself.

'What's more,' said Frank as he removed the trigger, 'if you operate the camera it does actually appear to work. The shutter clicks.'

'Brilliant,' enthused Enzo.

'So let me see you put it together.'

Enzo declined the offer, 'I'll watch you first.'

'Fair enough,' Frank replied and as he spoke the pieces quickly moved through his experienced old hands to produce a small hand gun with a single chamber.

'A work of art,' said Enzo, 'a pure work of art.'

Frank nodded, dismantling the gun as quickly as he had assembled it. 'Now practise. I want you to be able to do it with your eyes shut.'

'So do I,' replied Enzo.

He spent two hours practising until he literally could do it with his eyes shut.

'Good,' said Frank. 'Now we must practise getting the pieces out of the Trojan Horse. Learn the sequence, it will make life easier. I assumed the gun would need to fit into a jacket pocket and that you would need to assemble it in the john.'

'Yeah,' nodded Enzo.

'Right, so move that box against the wall and sit on it,' said Frank, opening the door to the garage workshop and bringing in a large sheet of oily plywood. 'They use this under cars, but it will suit our purpose as a wall,' he said, using another box to position it alongside Enzo seated on the old wooden box. 'Off you go.'

Enzo dismantled the parts and assembled them into a gun thirty times before Frank was satisfied. 'Fine,' he said at last. 'Now we'll have a beer. You're buying.'

For most of Sunday Enzo sat in the park reading and learning by heart the resume and Gary's questions for Miss Culpan. Reading had never been easy to him but this was one time he had to do it. Properly.

Miss Culpan was nearing retirement but was very attractive, in a spinsterly sort of way. She wore no rings, but Enzo round it hard to believe that she had spent her entire life as a lonely spinster.

'I am impressed with the resume, Mr Friggli. An odd name,' she said, changing the direction of her conversation suddenly, 'in fact it made my colleague suspicious and so he rang your paper.'

'I know,' replied Enzo, 'it's Italian and causes me trouble from time to time. If I really was up to no good, now wouldn't I use a common name?' His smile was as charming and as infectious as usual.

'Exactly what I thought, Mr Friggli.' She smiled back. 'Now, as I say, I found the resume very helpful. If you'd like to fire some questions at me I'll see what I can remember from thirty years ago.'

It was five o'clock when Enzo left the White House, having recorded all Miss Culpan's answers. That night he added another page of his babyish handwriting to the ongoing letter, wrote a line to Gary and mailed him the tape of the afternoon. The first article was going to appear during the last week of October, written by Gary himself.

CHAPTER TWELVE

Both the doctor's diagnosis and prognosis proved to be accurate: a few day's rest, good food and no alcohol had Brad Harworth back into fighting form. He had been under considerable pressure for months, and the obsession with Clinton had paralysed his ability to think at all, let alone clearly. The rest had changed all that. He even made love to Bridget and they enjoyed it.

'We haven't done it like that for a long time,' she said lying back and lighting a cigarette.

'Not together, you mean!'

She laughed. She was relaxed: they both were.

Brad had no intention of changing his ways or his lifestyle any more that he was sure she did, but that was no reason not to enjoy a better relationship with her.

'How many have there been, Bridget?'

'You *really* want to know?' she asked, turning to look at him.

'Just roughly.'

'What to see if you're winning?'

He wasn't sure if she was teasing or not. 'If you like, yes.'

'I honestly don't know. Over the years there must have been about thirty that have lasted, but I couldn't even remember all the couple of times, let alone the one offs. You?'

'Not as many ongoing, but countless others.'

'I like you like this, Brad.'

'But it wouldn't change us,' he replied sternly.

'I wouldn't want it to. Would you?'

'No, but I'd like to enjoy more times like this.'

'To do both?'

'Yes. Then we will,' he replied as he pulled her on top of him and they began making love again.

He decided, during that brief and none too passionate performance, to take her into his confidence.

'I've got something to tell you,' he said as she lit up another cigarette.

'What? Let me guess. Despite all the other women I'm still the best!'

'No,' he replied. 'I'm planning to have Clinton assassinated.

'Darling, how exciting!'

He'd not known how she would respond, but she succeeded in shocking him. 'You think so?'

'You're not serious, Brad. You were always a dreamer.' Her words were cold, she was unimpressed.

'But I am serious,' he replied.

She turned to look directly at him, drawing herself into a squatting position and crossing her legs Indian style. 'You are seriously going to assassinate the President of the United States? I don't believe you.'

'Not personally, but I've been trying to arrange it.'

'You mean talking about it but not actually doing anything about it?' Bridget laughed. It had always been her who made things happen. Brad was never one to get his hands dirty.

'No, I've been working at it very hard but so far I haven't been able to raise the money.'

'That's not why you latched on to that Waterford man from Alaska?'

'Yes, how'd you know?'

'I don't miss a thing, darling, not a thing. You were wasting your time, but no doubt he enjoyed a few romps in the sack with your little tart Angie. He was never likely to come across, but I wouldn't mind him coming across me once or twice!'

'Your trouble, Bridget,' he said crossly, 'is that you're coarse.'

'Now I've upset you,' she said with mock regret.

'You don't believe me, do you?'

'Oh, yes. I believe that you have been trying to put something together. I just don't think you've got the balls to carry it out.'

Not so slowly, their attitude towards each other was returning to normal.

'You reckon?'

'I know.'

'Well at least I'm trying to do something about the goddam mess he's leading this country into instead of just screwing around all day.'

'You mean as well as just screwing around all day. But I don't reckon it's such a bad idea, in fact it's a good one.'

Not for the first time in his life Brad looked at her in amazement. 'You don't?'

'No, I don't.'

'Do *you* want to help?'

'It will make life a darn sight more interesting than sitting around here all day,' Bridget said teasing him, but he missed it. 'Tell me where you're at.'

'Well,' said Brad as he started to outline the history and finished with explaining how it was that he had arrived home in the state that he had.

'You didn't really expect that silly little tart to bump off the President, did you?'

Put like that the question did cast a serious shadow over Brad's judgement. 'No, I didn't until she agreed so readily. I still don't know why.'

'Whatever made you even ask her?'

'I need a way to get to him and she's a pretty girl.'

'Forget it, Brad,' laughed Bridget. 'Even if all the wild stories about his womanising are true — and I doubt it — he's out of all that for the next few years. You're a fool, Brad. *You* have the way to get close enough to kill him, the problem is that if you don't want to do it yourself, you've got to find someone else to do it for you.'

'I've no idea what you're talking about, Bridget, but even if I did I still haven't got the money to hire an assassin.'

'You don't need any money, Brad. Think!'

He was now sat up on the bed, his legs stretched out in

front of him, crossed at the ankles. She had lost him completely.

'There are two problems, Brad. One, to get close enough to kill and two, to carry out the act. Now if you can't afford to hire someone to carry out the act, and I accept that it would be a little foolish to do it yourself, you need to find somebody who has their own reasons for wanting to kill Clinton, but can't create the opportunity. Agreed?'

'Agreed, but who?'

'Try Saddam Hussein for one! He was not over excited when those rockets hit Baghdad.'

'Brilliant, but what do I do? Ring him up?' Brad laughed.

'You had a dossier compiled on Jeff Knight, didn't you?'

'Yes,' he replied, showing enthusiasm.

'And I'm sure he was supplying arms to the Iraqis. All you have to do is get the man who compiled the dossier to put you in touch. My guess is that they will pay him for you. You have ready access to an assassin and probably one that is ready to die in the act.'

'Why didn't I see it before?'

'Because, darling, you're thick!'

He ignored her remark. It might be true. 'But what about access, you said I've got it. I've got no way to get that close to the President.'

'But you have, darling and it's on the mantlepiece in your study.'

He thought for a moment. 'The Memorial Lunch? How does that help me get an assassin into the White House?'

'It's for two, isn't it?'

'You and me, yes.'

'And do you think the man on the door or the security check will know me? Those passes that came last week were by security delivery and we had to sign for them. We have to send them back with a photograph and a signature. We make it someone else's.'

'But they have to be back in ten days.'

'So we have to move fast.'

'But that would implicate me if I take an assassin in with me to the lunch posing as you.'

'I'll have been kidnapped, darling. The terrorists will be holding me to ransom and they will kill me unless you help them or if you go to the police.'

'It sounds a bit like Hollywood to me.'

Bridget was finding it hard to accept that Brad was taking her seriously. The obsession had obviously destroyed any judgement he'd ever had. She decided to run with it. 'Trust me, it'll work, darling. You speak to that man who spied on Jeff for you today and by the end of the week we will have it all in place. Saddam will arrange a female assassin for you and some captors for me. We might even both enjoy some pleasure with our temporary friends.'

'You *are* coarse, Bridget.'

'I know, but I fuck well,' she replied coarsely to emphasise the point. 'You've got work to do, darling, so get on with it,'

Brad dressed and went downstairs to his study while Bridget lay on the bed and lit herself another cigarette.

The opportunity opening up before Bridget was too good to miss. If she played this right she would rid herself of Brad and keep all his money. She knew his Will still left it to her. He had changed it three years ago, but she had seduced his solicitor the night it was signed when Brad had been rushing off to see Angie. While the man slept after the love making she simply stole the new Will from his case and replaced it with the old one. Much that Bridget did might, as Brad had said, sound like something out of Hollywood, but so much of it worked.

She smiled. To her, her idea was brilliant, as Brad had said. If her sole purpose or even main idea was to assassinate Clinton, then it was brilliant for that alone. But to catch Brad in the net as well, that was her real target. She had little doubt that the private detective who she knew, and had slept with a few times but not as one of the thirty, would damn Brad for a few thousand dollars and a few hours in bed with the promise of more.

'He'll set up a meeting this afternoon,' said Brad, returning to the bedroom unable to conceal his excitement at the detective's response.

'What did you say to him?'

'That I wanted to make contact with someone from Iraq as I might be able to help them with one of their overseas objectives.'

'Their what?'

'I thought it was quite good myself,' said Brad misunderstanding her question.

Bridget ignored his answer. 'Will he be going with you?'

'No, I don't think so. Why?'

'I think it might be safer for you, darling. He is experienced in dealing with these people, you're not. I wouldn't want anything to happen to you, darling. Not after we've rediscovered ourselves today. I think he should go with you, just to be on the safe side.'

'But then he'd know what I'm up to. Is that wise?'

'You pay him don't you? You've used him for years, you must be one of his best clients. He needs you, Brad. He's not going to worry about the business in hand. I'm sure he's been aware of off the ball arrangements you've made before.'

'But this is slightly different.'

'No, darling, just bigger, so the payoff will have to be bigger. This is a very simple world and we only have problems because people, and that includes Governments, don't understand how simple. Everything, but everything, Brad darling, has a price. Pay his and you'll have no problems. I'm quite sure that if you tell your new friends that you have had to make a large payment to the introducer, they'll re-imburse you. They'll be very grateful to you.'

The arrangements seemed too easy to Brad. In two days he'd had two meetings with the Iraqis and the following day met the assassin herself, who signed her security pass as Mrs Bridget Harworth.

'Your wife must be taken into custody by us tonight, so

that it happens before you return the pass,' said the Iraqi officer who was organising the arrangements from their side. 'I suggest that our operative now returns to your house with you and remains completely out of sight from everybody, including servants.

'Is that possible?'

'Yes.'

'And you are to be moody, restless, break appointments, drink heavily, get up late, not shave, all the things that a man under stress would do. You do not matter to us; if they catch you and execute you that is not our concern. However, for your own safety you must live life as it would be. This, as I read in one of your western novels, is the Theatre of the Real.'

Brad was taken aback by the man's phraseology but his message was both loud and clear. More importantly, it made sense. The only question in his mind that mattered to him was whether or not this attractive young lady sitting opposite him wanted to spend the time alone. Brad would never change. However, he asked another question. 'How will you kill him?'

'That is not your concern.'

'But I do not want it to go wrong. Won't we be detected at the security check on the way in?'

'That will not happen.' The statement was final.

'That's it,' said Scott as Brad returned to his bedroom, 'shall I send in the watchers to pick them up?'

'No,' said Steve. 'We can't listen in at the meeting with the Iraqis. We know when they plan to strike, so we'll hold off until then. In that way we get more people in the net. We get some Iraqis as well and the woman posing as Mrs Harworth will have to be equipped in some way for the hit. The evidence will be stronger.'

'So we wait?'

'Yes. We wait and watch. But we'll call an immediate A1 to update and look at broader strategy. Remember, we've still got no further with the olive skin other than that he's nothing to do with Harworth. If it wasn't for Harworth, we probably wouldn't be looking for him but we can't sit back congratulating ourselves for uncovering one assassination plot while there's still another moving smoothly ahead unchecked.'

'If it is a plot and if it is the only other one.'

Steve nodded solemnly. 'No news of any of the nutters I suppose?'

'None.'

'As the Chief said, we've just got to keep up the slog. We'll get another break soon.'

'We'll have to start giving you two long stay discounts,' said Ann with her usual good humour to Lech and Gillespi as they sat chatting over coffee. 'Where to today?'

'Today we're off to see Bath.'

'Not in one day, it's eleven thirty now!'

'No, we'll be staying over, but don't let those rooms go!'

'Wouldn't dream of it. Enjoy yourselves.'

'Thank you.' said Lech.

'You know I really am enjoying myself, Lech. Who'd have thought it,' said Gillespi as they left the Fox House Club, 'we've come together with nothing in common and twenty years between us, and yet the chemistry works.'

'We do have a tentative something in common, George.'

'We do?'

'You organised the assassination of an American President and I wanted to organise the assassination of an American President.

'As long as it is, *wanted* to organise, then I'm happy with that!'

'Make no mistake about it, George, I'd cheer louder than I did when Kennedy died if someone killed him. But I was mad even to contemplate it.

'The problem is one of helplessness. I can't actually get to reason with the people who take the decisions and you wonder sometimes just who is advising them. I'm sure the

246

problem's not just in the States, it must happen in every country. People in a bar can talk more sense than comes out of Government Departments and if you put the people in the departments into a bar they talk more sense themselves!'

'Must be what they serve in the bar!'

'Maybe! But I was just so frustrated and to make it worse I know you cannot even reason with the ideological liberal mind — it's too clever, too intelligent by far. Totally impractical.

'I know, I've met them!'

After the overnight stay in Bath the two men travelled to Scotland, Wales and the Lake District. Eventually, they decided to return to London.

'You know I might almost be suspicious of you if I hadn't had such a hand in the itinerary,' Lech had said as the obvious date to return home had emerged — 22nd November.

'Do you really think I would try to keep you here until after the thirtieth anniversary?

'No, but I think you'd like to stay here until then yourself,' Lech replied with humour.

'Now there you are right. But I'm under no illusions about you. I was a professional secret service officer and my mind will always work in the same way. If *you'd* fixed the date, I'd be wanting your phone lines tapped in case you were setting up the hit and using me as your alibi.'

'How d'you know I'm not? Lech had replied with a wink.

'I don't.'

Sally-Anne Knight spent three weeks in the hospital being treated for the after effects of her final drinking session. She was then moved to a neurological hospital.

'Where are they taking me, Jeff?' Her voice was weak, her spirit broken.

'To a special hospital. You need more time to recover.'

'You'll be there with me?'

'Yes.'

'All the time?'

'Most of the time, yes.'

'Thank you.' Her pathetic gratitude touched him deeply.

Her room was very pleasant, a far cry from the image of mental hospitals, more reminiscent of a holiday villa in Florida or California than a neurological hospital in Washington. The walls were papered with a light pink floral pattern, restful yet engaging, with matching chinz curtains. Even the furniture had character to it and the bedlinen was colour co-ordinated.

'Nice,' Sally-Anne said as the porter and nurse lifted her from the wheelchair onto the sofa. 'Very nice.'

'Yes and the sofa makes into a bed, so I can stay some nights if you'd like that.'

'Please, Jeff, please.' Her voice was that of a frightened child and it scared him.

'I promised the doctor that as soon as you were settled in I'd look into his office for a chat. Is there anything you need or shall I do that now?'

'No, you go along now.'

The doctor had warned Jeff that at times Sally-Anne would not be able to cope with even the most simple question like that. He dreaded it. It had not happened yet.

'Being perfectly straight with you, Mr Knight, I'm not sure that there will be very much that we can do for her. There is severe damage to the brain, undoubtedly caused by alcohol, but that is not the only problem. I won't bore you with the medical intricacies, but she has symptoms usually associated with a congenital brain disorder to which we do not yet know the cure. We're close, but I fear it will not be in time for her.'

'How long do you think she has?'

'Hard to be precise. If we could treat her for the disorder, then I would be confident that we could keep her alive, talking, thinking and appearing reasonably normal, if a little slow witted, for as much as a year, maybe even two. The problem is, once we start to lose her, how long do we continue?'

It was not actually put as a question but Jeff understood all too clearly that he was being asked something the doctor was not allowed to ask out loud, never mind do.

'However, with the added problems of the damage actually inflicted to the brain, her capacity to respond to treatment is severely impaired. In my view, and I have to say that of my colleagues, we're talking about weeks rather than months, certainly no longer than three months. But you must appreciate that these situations are a matter of subjective judgement and we rarely agree amongst ourselves on the question of timing.'

'But in this case you do,' interrupted Jeff, anticipating the final words.

'Yes. In this case we do, Mr Knight. I'm sorry.'

'There's nothing at all I can do? Jeff was exhausted himself, he'd hardly slept for several weeks.

'Just be there and see that she enjoys these final few weeks. It will be good for you as well. It will help afterwards. If you feel the need for counselling, either now or later, we will be happy to arrange something. It might help you both.'

'Thank you, doctor.'

As Jeff walked slowly back to the room he decided that he would not tell her the truth. He had always said that if he were ever terminally ill he wanted to know because there were things he'd want to do, but there was nothing she could do.

Maybe in herself she already knew, maybe not. Perhaps she was no longer capable of even thinking along those lines. He would stay with her, night and day until the end.

He was just turning the corner towards Sally-Anne's room as he saw the nurse leaving it. Jeff was a very experienced negotiator and high level salesman; the movement of her head and feet as she half saw him out of the corner of her eye, told him everything.

She turned towards him. She saw in his eyes that he knew. 'It might be best just to wait for a few moments so that we can clean her up.'

'But I've only been gone ten minutes and she was sitting watching television and talking to me.'

'I know, I was there when it happened. I'm not a doctor but it was almost certainly a massive brain haemorrhage. She wouldn't have known a thing about it.'

The doctor arrived as the nurse finished speaking.

'I'd like to go in now.'

'Of course,' replied the doctor, and the three of them entered the room together.

'Do you ever get used to death, doctor?' asked Jeff for little more than something to say.

'No, but we are able to shut it out a great deal of the time. To detach ourselves. We have to.'

'Can I stay with her?'

'Of course you can, but I do need to examine her first, for the death certificate. It will only take a few minutes. I suggest that you go with the nurse, have a drink and then come back in, say, fifteen minutes. You can sit with her alone then.'

'Thank you, doctor.'

When Jeff returned Sally-Anne was lying in bed, propped up with her pillows as if she was watching television, her hands folded neatly in front of her. He sat for nearly an hour holding those hands and crying. At last he drew himself away, kissed her forehead and left the room.

The house had never seemed so empty before. It must be knowing for certain that she wasn't coming back, he thought. He'd known it since that day the doctor had told him about the complications, but somewhere deep down in his subconscious had been the faintest of hopes that the doctor was wrong. That alone had given the house life. Now it was gone.

He started to make the funeral arrangements but was unable to concentrate. The undertaker agreed to take care of everything, even to the point of contacting friends and relatives to give them the news. He would call that evening at six for the details.

Jeff tried to sleep but it was impossible, so he called a cab to take him to the park, where he walked and walked. Time meant nothing, and there was an eerie calmness about him that disturbed him. It was a most odd sensation and one that he would never be able to describe. Almost as if *his* body and soul were no longer in physical contact with each other.

The undertaker arrived a few minutes after Jeff returned to the house. A sombre man, but not morbid or morose. They agreed the 21st November as the date for the funeral and, to his great surprise, Jeff felt considerably better after the undertaker had left. It was not to last.

There was just one message on the answerphone. 'Jeff. Brad.' The tone was curt, officious. 'The matter is in hand and will be accomplished. This is just to remind you what will happen to you should anything happen to me.'

'Bastard.' he said consumed with hatred for his former friend. 'Bastard.'

Gary Walton's newspaper article was a triumph in its own right. Suddenly the small town proprietor was big time business. Gary was an old pro and had published the article under Enzo's name, not for the benefit of the White House, but for his own.

I need you to sign a contract, Enzo. Say half a dozen articles a year for three years. I'll write them for you, but now that the buyers are flocking, they mustn't find out that I wrote that article.'

Enzo laughed. 'No problem, I'll sign anything. Tell them what you like and post it to me here in Washington.'

'Really?' It was too easy, thought Gary.

'Really, no problem, Gary. You help me, I help you. It's as simple as that.'

'You'll earn out of it as well because it was your idea and you did the hard bit. You got into the White House.'

'Not that hard,' replied Enzo, thinking, if only people knew just how easy it was the world would be a far more dangerous place.

'I've had TV companies wanting to make a series of half

hour documentaries. They want you to narrate them. Can you do it?'

'What, write them? No way, you know that.'

'No, they'll write the scripts from the articles and the taped notes. They want you to do the talking, most of which will be voice over.'

Shit, thought Enzo, this was great, just great. Here he was, God knows how close to death, planning to assassinate the President and suddenly a spin off from the operation was giving him the greatest legitimate opportunity of his life. 'Yeah, whatever,' he replied.

'Enzo, I don't like it, you agreeing that easily. What the hell are you up to?'

'Gary, don't worry. I promised you your letters and you'll get them when I complete this mission.'

'Mission?' came the anxious response. 'That sounds like a military expression.'

'Well, investigation, mission. What's in a name? Now if you really get your act together and let me have the questions for Clinton and organise those TV boys in the next week, you will have the biggest scoop of all time, I promise you, Gary. Nothing with ever touch it. If you don't get the act together in that time you'll regret like hell not getting that first article out on time in October.'

'Can I fax you at that hotel?'

'Sure, I guess. Do what you have to and then speak to the desk clerk. It's your ball, baby, run with it?'

'It'll all be with you in an hour. When are you going back to White House.

'Miss Culpan was so thrilled with the article she asked me that very question not an hour ago. I said I'd get back to her, I didn't want to seem pushy.

'You get me the questions and I'll ring her first thing tomorrow.'

'In an hour and,' Gary hesitated, his voice was suddenly overcome with emotion, 'thanks, Enzo, you don't know what this will mean to me.'

'A bigger pension, I hope!'

'That's what I'm after, thanks.'

True to his word Gary faxed through the information within an hour and the following morning Enzo spoke to Miss Culpan again. 'The President was most impressed with your article, as I told you yesterday. He would like to discuss the final article with you personally at some stage. He suggests that we meet and that you let me have the draft and then the two of you look it over.'

Enzo was unable to believe this. 'That might be difficult in the near future as my schedule is very tight, but we've got time on our hands for the final article.'

'Okay, but when can we do the preparatory work?'

'I can do that this afternoon, I've just been let down for today.'

'It will mean altering my programme, but that's okay. If you can let me have the draft I'll take it on from there.'

'Okay. Three o'clock.'

'Fine.'

'What about some photographs? There's no hurry — I'm sure there'll be good opportunities in the next couple of months. We can pick out something significant.'

'There's the perfect opportunity this month.'

'Yes?' replied Enzo as calmly as he could.

'The Kennedy Memorial Lunch on 22nd November. If you make sure that I have the draft in the next week, I'll speak to the President and suggest it. It won't give you more than a few days notice, but keep the day clear. There won't be a better opportunity.'

'The 22nd. I *will* do that. It is the perfect opportunity.'

'See you tomorrow, Mr Friggli.'

It took Enzo three hours to work his way through the questions Gary had drafted and, although he felt exhausted at the end of it, he enjoyed it. He had also taken a liking to Miss Culpan, she reminded him of his oldest sister. He hoped that when the shit hit the fan, as it would, not too much landed on her.

The following afternoon Gary was on the phone, delighted with the tapes. 'I'll write it tonight and fax it to you in the morning. I've only listened to the first half hour, but it's great. I'll also give you a list of questions for the President himself for when you meet him.' Gary's enthusiasm was boundless.

'And thanks for the signed contract. I'm about to do a deal, effective after the series end which will push the price up.'

'Don't be greedy, Gary. You've got to write the articles then.'

'No problem. A piece of piss, as my English brother in law would say. It will also mean I can run the big scoop I hope.'

'Now that I can promise you,' said Enzo.

CHAPTER THIRTEEN

'Well then, boys, how goes the plan?' slurred Matt Andrews as he met with Powers and Edwards in the Manhattan Hotel cocktail bar in New York.

Powers had found it increasingly difficult at their weekly meetings to tolerate Andrews' drinking and this time he snapped. 'I see no point in carrying on a conversation with you when you are drunk.'

'And I,' replied Andrews suddenly appearing totally sober, 'see no point in carrying on a conversation with you when you are patronising and offensive. Sure, at times I get a little cheerful, but that's all. You spend your entire life treating all around you like a piece of dog shit, but not me, buddy, not any more.' The force of his words visibly shocked Powers, who was not accustomed to anyone challenging him.

'Now look,' began Edwards in a vain attempt to calm the two men.

'Butt out, John,' said Andrews, 'this is between me and the big shot here. I've had more than enough of his arrogance and unless he apologises and agrees to behave in a civilised manner from here on I'm going to pick him up and put him straight through that plate glass window.' There was now no doubt about it, Matt Andrews was most certainly both sober enough and strong enough to carry out his threat. He had reached the end of his tolerance so far as Powers was concerned.

'Look, Matt,' began Powers in a smooth conciliatory tone.

'Don't come the old soldier reasonable bullshit with me, Harry. Are you going to treat us both like people or do we find out just what the breaking strength of that window is? It won't go first time, I'm pretty damn sure of that.'

Powers knew he was beaten, but what could Andrews actually do long term — nothing. There was nothing for it but to agree and then to arrange an accident for Andrews.

When you had killed once, he thought, they say it gets easier. He was a little over a week away from knowing and it must be easier still when you had only organised the killing rather than actually carried it out.

'Okay, Matt. I apologise. There are reasons, but I accept that I would be bullshitting to make them and that I should treat you differently. You are not staff, you are both partners. We are all in this together.' Powers was rattled. His usual calm authority was missing.

'You'd better believe we are,' said Andrews, 'because if anything happens to me the whole can of worms will be blown wide open. You're not the only one who keeps dossiers and has people tailed.'

Powers was taken seriously aback and hoped it didn't show. If it did, Edwards would not have noticed and Andrews wasn't watching and didn't care anyway, so he worried needlessly.

'Now we've got that straight and understand each other, I need a drink. You can pay, Harry,' continued Andrews. 'My pleasure, I think we all need a drink.' Powers concealed his relief.

Andrews smiled broadly. 'Claret for me, a bottle.'

'A small white wine for me, please,' said Edwards more nervous than ever.

'So are we on schedule?' asked Andrews exchanging his wine glass for a large goblet.

'Yes. I spoke to our man today and he has confirmed to me that he is in a position to complete the transaction on the day in question.'

'Do we know how or where he is going to do it?' asked Edwards.

'No. I did ask but he felt that it did not concern us.'

'He's right, none of our business. In my book the less we know the better,' said Andrews.

'I think we should meet and be together, don't you, Harry?' replied Andrews doing his best not to smirk and barely succeeding.

'If *you* think so, then I am happy to agree to that, are you John?'

'Essential. Where do you suggest?'

'According to the White House Press Office, the President is in Washington all day that day. At lunch time he will be hosting a Memorial Lunch for Kennedy, but that is inside the White House, so I see no possibility of the event happening there.'

'We want to be able to know immediately, which means having constant access to a television. I suggest we book a suite for a small conference in a hotel, organise a television, lunch, supper and just spend a quiet day waiting.'

'Makes sense to me, Harry.'

'And me,' said Andrews, 'but make sure that we have plenty of provisions. I sure hate standing around with nothing to do just waiting for things to happen without a glass in my hand.' He finished the first bottle of claret and rapped it on the table to catch the waiter's eye.

'As you wish.'

'You're doing well, Harry boy, but just remember to keep it up. I'm not just talking about today, and this great country has got large plate glass windows all over it. Sure as hell it wouldn't take me long to find another, wherever I am.'

Powers did not reply.

'I'll book the hotel,' said Edwards quietly as they went into the restaurant for supper.

Enzo had made three trips to New York to see Frank Austen, who was still making totally unnecessary refinements to the gun when Enzo finally went to collect it. He paid the balance of the fifty thousand dollars and returned to Washington eight days before the job was due to be completed.

On that last trip to New York he'd decided to have himself a woman. He'd never been near a woman other than a whore since he had tested positive; as far as he was concerned, whores could take their chance. It was functional but relieved his tension, which was all he needed to do. He'd decided he would have a few more in the next week. It did relieve the enormous tension he was feeling.

Miss Culpan had been ecstatic about Gary's first draft and, in addition to issuing Enzo with his pass for the Memorial Lunch, she had booked an appointment for him to see the President personally on 11th December. She had, however, issued a word of caution. 'I am afraid that if something more important arises the President may have to postpone the meeting. We do have to tell everybody that, just in case there is an emergency.'

'I understand. Don't give it another thought. If, for any reason the President is unable to keep the appointment, believe me I will find it in my heart to forgive him.'

'Thank you, Mr Friggli,' said Miss Culpan. 'A lot of people take offence when they are told.'

'A lot of people would, I am sure, but I'm not a lot of people.'

The town of Mostar had been home to a substantial force of Croat soldiers since their major offensive in May 1993 had trapped as many as twenty thousand Muslims in the old town on the east bank of the Neretva river. That all changed in early July, following a massive offensive by the Muslim forces despite the Croats mobilising all males of military age in the city.

The weather was becoming hotter by the hour, and with both food and water supplies running low, the Muslims had mounted an all-out attack on the Croats and had succeeded in driving the Croat militia from the city. Food was still scarce and the water supply was unpredictable, but there was a feeling of pride in the streets as Hamdi made his way westwards out of the city. It was under Muslim control, but more importantly, it had been regained. That was a far greater morale booster than simply holding a position.

Hamdi felt great sadness as he looked over his shoulder at the city slowly disappearing behind him. He wondered if he would ever return.

The journey was slow but uneventful and, once he was fifteen miles or so from Mostar, he didn't see another soldier. He walked peacefully along the northern bank of the river to Bar, where there was no sign at all of the civil war that raged in the rest of the former Yugoslavia. The journey took him several days and tested his stamina to the full, but his mind was sound, and he could cope with the physical discomfort. From Bar he caught a bus to Ulcinj to wait in the little coffee shop as instructed.

His contact would be there every evening between seven and nine.

It was half past five when he arrived.

Where once the coffee shop would have been alive with tourists, it was now almost deserted. The owner, well past seventy, busied himself behind the counter, but in truth had very little to do and three locals sat playing cards at a pavement table.

The awning was in need of repair. Inside, the coffee shop was seedy. No doubt it had looked better in the days of tourism, but the posters on the wall had become faded and torn and the walls themselves were in need of painting. It was hard for Hamdi to accept that it was not yet two years since the coffee shop had last been alive with people.

The furniture was old and worn, which, when it was clean, had no doubt been part of the rustic appeal. But now it was dirty and offputting. Although he never drank alcohol in them Hamdi appreciated the character of the pubs of Oxford and thought back to them. The Turf, The King's Arms, The Lamb and Flag; the memories all came flooding back. What would they look like stripped of people, of memorabilia, of life? They were old, like the coffee shop, but it was hard to imagine them deserted. His favourite for food had always been the Trout at Wolverton, but it was a close run with the Perch at Binsey. How many people around the world remembered this coffee shop with affection? The comparison was unfair, and he knew it: people such as he lived in Oxford for several years, tourists visited

Yugoslavia for a couple of weeks.

He walked slowly around the town, where life was much as he imagined it would have been before the advent of tourism and the birth of Yugotours. He had found it difficult to settle back into his homeland after his time at Oxford, and wondered how these people were re-adjusting their lives to the tranquillity and, no doubt, poverty that had existed before the tourist boom. Perhaps they were simply thankful not to be caught up in the horrors of the war. How, he wondered, would Albania react to shelling and fighting so close to their borders, if the battle came to Uncinj?

When he returned to the coffee shop it was still not seven o'clock, but he ordered another coffee and took two spoons from the cracked cup on the counter. Having stirred his coffee he put them one on top of the other in the saucer as instructed, sipped the coffee and waited. He sipped it several times and was only thankful that he did not have to drink it all. Clearly the war had destroyed the supply lines to Uncinj as well as the rest of the country: the coffee was "local".

By seven o'clock there were over thirty people milling around, chatting amongst themselves. The transformation was dramatic. They had arrived in twos, threes and fours. He soon lost count of the total.

It was twenty past seven when a man about ten years younger than him approached his table, which had become something of an island outside of the main activity.

'May I please take?' he asked picking up a chair.

'Please do if you wish.'

'That is very kind of you, thank you.'

'It is my pleasure.'

The man scanned the coffee shop with his eyes and spoke again. 'Hamdi?'

'Yes.'

'Good. My name is Tony.'

Hamdi looked surprised. 'Tony?' he said.

'Yes, many people my age have western names.'

Hamdi laughed, 'Why didn't they tell me?'

'We were not sure who would meet you. Sometimes we have people in here that we do not know. We are scared that they might be secret police, so we are very careful. That is why we crowd the shop, in that way no-one is obvious.'

'You have done this before? asked Hamdi, surprised.

'Once, yes,' Tony replied with pride.

'I feel very safe.'

'Good. Have you eaten?'

'No,' replied Hamdi trying not to seem over keen. He didn't want to erode their food supplies.

'Then you must eat. Do you like fish?'

It was over eighteen months since Hamdi had eaten fish. He loved it.

'I love them,' he replied, gratitude etched into every syllable.

'Then let us go and eat.'

Hamdi followed Tony to a small cottage and most of the crowd dispersed, leaving the coffee shop empty again. They were joined for supper by three young men who, Hamdi learnt, were members of the fishing boat crew.

'We will leave early,' said Tony, 'just before dawn.'

'Why do you do this for me?'

'We all have our reasons, they do not matter.' The answer was another conversation stopper. Hamdi thought of Alexi. Had he made it safely back to Travnik? He hoped so.

'How long will it take us?'

'Three to four hours, it depends on the strength of the tides.'

'So it will be a day for you, there and back?'

'Almost, but we will do some fishing but we will land some fish at sea from other boats so all will seem well when we return to port tonight.'

'You are enjoying this, aren't you, Tony?'

'Very much, yes. But we do realise how serious it is. We may not have guns at our heads, but we understand.'

'I am sorry, I did not mean to insult you.'

'You did not, please do not worry. Eat and enjoy and then

we must all sleep for our early start.

Hamdi was not sure what to expect of the fishing boat, but it was very modern and equipped with all the latest technology.

'When the tourists came we were like the fishermen in Cornwall in England. We would fish for the cash crop. In the summer, that was people.

Hamdi smiled. There was so little difference between people the world over, why did they fight each other? Why was territory so important? He was not being critical of others to the exclusion of himself: territory was critical to him, but would be rather be Red than Dead? At the time he had voted no, now he was not so sure. He nearly had been dead. Did his religion mean that much to him? What would his family have said, given the option that split second before the bullet had passed through them, unleashing its deadly load? He would have said, yes. He felt ashamed, deeply ashamed.

The boat made steady progress at about six knots across the Adriatic Sea towards Italy and safety for Hamdi.

'We will land in a village called Vieste where we have friends. They will look after you and see you onto your train to Rome. It will be boring all those hours on the train, not like this at sea,' laughed Tony. The others barely spoke.

'How did you arrange all this?'

'In the days of the tourist we made many friends, but even before that the fishermen were friends. The men of the sea are comrades, not as with communists but as with men in arms, you understand?'

'Yes, I understand,' said Hamdi. 'I am very grateful to you.'

'It is nothing, we are pleased to help.'

The small port of Vieste came into view shortly after nine and within half an hour they had docked. There were only a few fishing boats moored in the harbour, the fleet, such as it was, having left for the day. As they tied up a small, chubby faced man with jet black hair and dark skin walked slowly towards them. 'Signor,' he said conspiratorily and to Hamdi somewhat over- dramatically. 'It is safe, now, please come.'

Hamdi shook hands with Tony and the other crew members who were clearly anxious to put to sea again as soon as possible. It was the only time that Hamdi detected any apprehension amongst them.

'Go,' said Tony. 'Go quickly.'

'Thank you, Tony,' began Hamdi.

'Just go, please.' said Tony as he handed the Italian a small package.

Hamdi needed no further bidding. The last thing he wanted was to endanger the lives of Tony and his friends.

'Come,' said the man on the quay again anxiously as he held a hand towards Hamdi, 'we must hurry.'

Despite being short and overweight, the Italian walked at a brisk pace which Hamdi found difficult to maintain. It would take many months of good food and care to restore him to his former fitness. They reached the road where stood a rusty old Fiat 500 into which Hamdi was ushered. The Italian did not speak but simply opened the door. Hamdi made no attempt this time to engage in conversation.

They had driven for about twenty minutes before the Italian spoke. 'I am Alfonse, hello.'

'Hamdi,' he replied. 'Hello and thank you for helping me.'

'Okay,' was the clipped response.

'Do you speak much English?'

'No.'

'You Italian?'

'No. Music?' Alfonse said turning on the radio.

'Yes,' replied Hamdi who realised then just how long it had been since he had heard music. The cheerfulness of that single speaker mounted crudely in the centre of the dashboard made him want to cry.

'You okay?' asked the Italian nervously.

'Fine, yes. Okay,' replied Hamdi with a smile as he composed himself.

They spoke very little on the journey to Foggia but, as they approached the railway station, the Italian became nervous again.

'You know what to do?'

'I thought you were coming with me?'

'No, it is too risky.'

Hamdi looked concerned.

'Do not worry, you will be safer alone.'

How he would be safer alone Hamdi could not see but he knew he could not argue. 'Okay.'

'Good. You buy a ticket for Roma and switch at Napoli. Here,' he said handing Hamdi an envelope, 'you take.'

'Thank you.'

'At Roma you wait at number one platform. I will ring them.'

'Thank you,' began Hamdi.

'Now go,' said the Italian ushering him quickly from the car.

No sooner was Hamdi out of the car than it was gone, drawing attention to itself by the speed at which it tried to move away. Hamdi was tired and, despite having eaten both before he left Ulcinj and on the fishing boat, he was also hungry. Mental hunger, he told himself. He knew he was back in civilisation and could get a decent meal.

There was twenty minutes to wait before his train, and having bought his ticket with some of the lire in the envelope, he visited the buffet. He was still wearing Zena's son's clothes, and received some very odd looks as he waited patiently in the queue. His taste buds twitched nervously the closer he got to the display cabinet, and he had an overwhelming urge to simply grab plates of food. The hardest part, he knew, would be waiting with the food on his tray in the queue to pay.

He was determined to be orderly and, having paid, sat at a small two seater table in the window box. That first sip of the espresso coffee was a sensation that would remain with him for ever. As he ripped the clingfilm wrapping from the salami sandwiches his control snapped. In two giant bites the sandwich was in his mouth and he was chewing frantically. The inside of his stomach felt like the inside of a hoover bag, powerfully sucking in whatever the head picked up.

The second and third sandwiches followed equally quickly and it was then that it began to hurt. He had known it would, but the pain in his stomach and the tightness in his chest was somehow a most pleasurable experience. Looking at the clock on the wall, he gathered up the other five rounds of sandwiches and drank the coffee as quickly as its temperature allowed. The serious indigestion hit him half an hour later.

In Naples he had almost an hour to wait between trains. He had eaten the rest of the sandwiches, somewhat more slowly, but was still hungry, and despite the chronic indigestion pains he bought a beefburger. It was almost two years since he had tasted beef and, having finished it rapidly, he strolled over to the bar to buy a glass of Coca Cola. Unlike the coffee, he sipped this carefully until he had emptied the glass.

He was now totally exhausted. His eyes felt puffy and his mind was lethargic.

As he boarded the train he wanted nothing more than to sleep. He began to feel sick. He had known he would, but the initial contest between his brain and his yearning stomach had been comprehensively won by his stomach. From now on, however, he told himself, the brain was in command.

He sat alone in a compartment in a window seat, and was asleep before the train had even left the station. It was not a restful sleep, despite the rhythmic movement of the train. By the time he reached Rome, deeper exhaustion had started to get to him. If was an effort to even lift himself from the seat. Every muscle in his body was heavy and utterly reluctant to perform. Slowly, he made his way towards the barrier and thence to platform one.

There was no pre-arranged coding as there had been for the coffee shop in Ulcinj but as he made his way towards the platform, looking forlorn and out of place, he knew there was no need.

They were waiting for him.

'Hamdi?' asked the woman.

'Yes,' he replied surprised by the American accent.

'I am Carole Atkins and this is Jack Philips.'

'I am very pleased to meet you' said Hamdi extending his hand which they both shook. 'I didn't expect you to be Americans.'

'Does it bother you?' Her voice was soft and friendly. A southerner.

'No, no, not at all. It couldn't be better.'

'Come,' she said as Philips put an arm around Hamdi to stop him collapsing. 'You must rest.'

Hamdi remembered nothing of the journey to the American Embassy but the sheer ecstasy of the warm shower and the crisp clean sheets of his bed was, like that first taste of the espresso coffee, something he knew he would never forget.

The next few days were non-existent. He slept and ate, watched some television and showered three or four times a day. The warmth of the gently pulsating water was as therapeutic as the rest. He recalled thinking in the mountains high above Travnik how marvellous was the human body's ability to repair itself.

On the fourth day he rose normally for breakfast and felt able to talk of his experiences.

'But who arranged for you to meet me?' he asked as he neared the end of his story.

'We received a message in Washington from the White House that an Oxford friend of the President would be arriving from Bosnia at platform one in Rome station and that we were to collect him and look after him.'

He smiled at her friendly, warm face. 'And you had no difficulty recognising me.'

'I would today,' she replied brushing back her shoulder length dark hair.

'So would I.' Hamdi laughed realising it was the first time for a very long time that his laugh had come from his heart.

'But who contacted Washington to arrange it?'

'I've no idea.'

'Nor I have,' said Philips, who was probably a year or two younger than him. An average looking man who would melt into the crowd in any modern society anywhere in the world. CIA, thought Hamdi, more than a little pleased with himself that his brain was functioning so efficiently, even if it had not been when he had first met the man at the station. But was she CIA as well? Did it matter?

'Can you tell me anything?' asked Hamdi realising that he was feeling intimidated by his own assumptions.

'Yes. We received a letter in Washington telling us of your plight.'

'Who from? Why did you respond?'

'That I do not know, I have not seen the letter but I know that the order came from the President himself.'

Hamdi was puzzled. It had to be Moncilo. Who was Moncilo really? Drugging him and searching him was fair enough, even sensible, but had he written to Bill Clinton? What had he said? How had he got it there? 'The President must receive thousands of letters every day, why was this one special?'

'Again, I don't know. Part of our job is to find out more about you.'

'And then?'

'That depends.'

'On what?'

The two agents, for Hamdi had now decided that Carole was CIA as well, looked at each other and then it was she who spoke. 'If we are satisfied that you are who you say you are, then you will be flown to Washington to meet the President.'

It had to be Moncilo, there was no other possibility, thought Hamdi. 'Does he know why I want to see him?'

'We have our ideas but we've not seen the letter. But tell us.'

'I want to tell him what it is really like in Bosnia. He has said he would help the Muslims with weapons and even tried to persuade Europe to do so. We need help. The Russians are arming the Serbs and they are slaughtering our people.'

'A personal appeal for him to intervene?'

'Yes.'

'Pretty simple.'

'Tell me more about your time at Oxford,' said Carole who Hamdi had decided was the senior of the two.

'What do you want to know?'

'Whatever you want to tell me. Start with how you got there, your first day, your first impressions, who you met.'

'Okay, but can I have another coffee first?'

'Sure,' said Carole getting up to pour it herself.

It was an hour and three more cups of coffee later when she spoke again. 'Hamdi, you're tired now. Our discussion has taken a lot out of you. Why not have some lunch, a rest, perhaps a walk and then we can talk some more over dinner tonight.

'We're not here to interrogate you in the normal sense, Hamdi. We've just got to be sure about you, that's all.'

'I understand.'

Hamdi slept for three hours after lunch but didn't have a walk, preferring instead to sit and read the newspapers. Something he had not done for almost two years. The world and not only Bosnia had changed.

The next three days followed much the same pattern but on the third evening Jack did not join them for supper. Hamdi noticed that Carole was no longer questioning him in the way that she had been, they were talking to each other.

'Will you be coming with me?'

'Why do you ask?'

'Curiosity, nothing more.'

'Yes, but not coming with you so much as going back home.'

'You're not based here?'

'No, we came specially to meet you. I've no idea what was

in that letter but they sat up at the very top about it. At first I didn't believe that you knew nothing about it, but I do now.'

'I've convinced you?' he asked suspiciously.

'Not by what you have said in direct response, but yes, you've convinced me. I believe your story. We both do.'

'So I will get to see Bill Clinton again?'

'It sure looks that way, Hamdi. But what then, for you?' It did not sound like an official question.

'I haven't thought that far. I suppose it depends on what happens after my meeting.'

'But you surely can't go back home?'

'Why not?'

'Where exactly would you go, for starters?'

'I've no idea, I've really no idea.'

'You sound tired again, Hamdi. Call it a day if you want to.'

'Yes, I think we should, but I'd like to know when we plan to go to Washington.'

'A couple of days probably. Jack and I have got something else to attend to while we're here but that should be out of the way by tomorrow night.'

'What do I do in the meantime?'

'Whatever you like. We're satisfied that you are who you say you are and that you're here for the reasons you say you are.'

'Perhaps I'll do some sightseeing.'

'Why not? Enjoy yourself.'

'Will I be followed?'

'Do you think you should be?'

'No, but that's not to say I won't be, is it?'

'No, it's not,' she smiled.

'So will I be?'

'Hamdi, do you really think I am going to answer that?'

'No, but you have done, haven't you?'

'That's for you to decide and I'll tell you something, I think you should practice law in the States once you've completed your mission!'

'We'll see…. Can I ask you something?' he said suddenly sounding less certain, rather shy.

'That's what you've been doing all evening.'

'Could we have dinner together in Washington, just you and me as friends? Would that be allowed?'

'As long as I advise my control first, yes, no problem.'

'Would you like to?' he hesitated, 'It's just that,' he hesitated again, 'I'm scared.'

'I understand, really I do. Of course I'd like to.'

'Thank you.'

'The President will see you on 21st November,' said Carole as she joined Hamdi for breakfast two days later.

'That's only four days away.'

'Yes, we fly to Washington tomorrow.'

'Your other business is completed?'

'All completed, yes.'

'It will be a long journey, I think I will spend today quietly. I still get tired very easily.'

'A good idea. We will leave here at six fifteen in the morning. I will arrange for you to be woken and breakfast will be ready at half past five.'

'Thank you.'

Hamdi again hesitated nervously, she pretended not to notice. 'Can I keep the things? The tooth brush, razor?'

'Keep whatever you like, Hamdi, but there's no room on the plane for the bed!'

She felt very deeply for him. Her husband had been killed in the Gulf War and she still read and re-read his last letter, which had frightened her the first time she had read it and it continued to do so. Why him she thought? So few lives lost, why him? But she knew that if you worked behind enemy lines you were at risk in the same way that she was at risk when she went undercover. They had both enjoyed the risk. She still did.

CHAPTER FOURTEEN

The journey to Washington tired rather than exhausted Hamdi but he soon adjusted to the time difference, much to his surprise. His first night in Washington was spent in a CIA safe house, but the following day he checked into a small hotel on the outskirts of the city. He had twenty thousand dollars from the bank raid organised by Moncilo in Belgrade and had so far spent none of it. The American Embassy in Rome had paid for his ticket to Washington.

Carole Atkins agreed to have dinner with him on 20th November and he was due at the White House at eleven thirty the following morning to see the President. Both situations unnerved him

They dined in a small bistro and enjoyed each other's company, but were both tense.

'Does it unsettle you to have dinner with someone you have been investigating?'

'Not investigating, Hamdi. Vetting, would be a better word.'

'Okay, vetting. But it seems to trouble you.'

'No,' she replied, releasing tension from her body as she spoke.

'But you seem very uptight. I know I am, but why are you?'

'It is the first time I've had dinner alone with a man since my husband died.'

Hamdi was embarrassed. 'I am sorry. I had no idea. I shouldn't....' 'Don't be silly, Hamdi. It had to happen and I'm glad it has happened, really I am.'

'That's good. Do you want to talk about it?' Hamdi was genuinely sympathetic — his natural manner.

'There's not much to say. He was killed in the Gulf War, working behind enemy lines so I don't know too much about exactly what happened.'

'That must make it harder.'

'I used to think so, but not after listening to your story. To see your family killed and to hear your children screaming out for you as they died, that must be much harder to bear.'

'True, but not to know at all. It could have been anything.'

'Exactly, so I comfort myself with the fact that it was a single bullet or a mine and instant death.'

'Did he not have colleagues with him?'

'Yes, but I don't know who they were and prefer it that way.... Now let's not spoil the evening by talking about me. Are you looking forward to tomorrow?'

'Yes, but I'm very nervous.'

'Why, you know he's only another man.'

'Yes, but he has all the resources at his disposal. I'm scared that he will not help my people and it will be because I have not been able to put the argument across well enough, to convince him of the suffering and the need.'

'He might have all the resources, Hamdi, but believe me he is not as experienced as I am in interviewing people and I can tell you that you will put the situation across very convincingly. Don't worry and don't try too hard. Just tell it the way it is, as you did to me and Jack.'

'You mean that?' he asked, momentarily encouraged.

'I mean it, Hamdi. But if anything or anyone can convince him, you can with your story. The problem is he agrees with people at the time and then does nothing about it.'

'From what I've read in the papers that seems to happen a lot, is that true?'

'What, broken promises and changing his mind?'

'Yes.'

'It does with all politicians, but it seems to be more so with him. He's had endless problems with getting his administration together, which hasn't made it any easier, but there have been several U-turns.'

'What sort of problems?'

'Most of them stem from the backgrounds of the people he's being trying to appoint, including allegations of sexual harassment, non-payment of taxes and employing people without work permits.'

'He's tried to give people like that jobs in Government? I can't believe it.'

'It's true.'

'The press seem to also have a down on his wife.'

'They're afraid of her.'

'What do you mean, afraid?'

'I mean it, afraid and people in the White House now won't even talk to the press in case she finds out.'

'I'm in the dark. She is obviously not behaving like the President's wife normally does.'

'You could say that!' laughed Carole. 'She's got a bigger political staff than the Vice-President and cronies all around her.'

'Can she get away with that?'

'She has. Most of them are feminists and careerist lawyers.'

'You amaze me, Carole. Who are these people, how does this happen in America of all places?

'There are those who say that she really wields the axe and determines whether political careers live or die. There's no doubt that she feels safe with her own people around her, people like Maggie Williams and Melanne Verveer, but what worries some of the staff more is her friends such as Marian Wright Edelman and her unofficial adviser and confidante, Susan Thomases. '

'What do they do?'

'Marian is a black lawyer and activist and Susan is just an unofficial adviser, but some of the crueller gossip columns hint that she may be a lot more than that.'

'That's terrible,' said Hamdi. 'America is a country we look up to, like Britain, not one where we would expect to see nepotism in Government.'

'I don't think the people are very keen on the situation, but there is nothing we can do, not for three years more at least.'

'You don't think he'll be re-elected?'

'I'm not even certain he'll be re-adopted by the

Democrats from what some of them are saying in private.' Hamdi was beginning to tire. 'I think we should be going now. I want to be at my brightest tomorrow. Thank you for sharing your evening with me. I feel as if I am returning to the real world.'

'I've enjoyed it as well. Believe me, Hamdi.'

Hamdi paid the bill and called a cab which dropped Carole off at her flat before taking him on to his hotel. 'Good luck tomorrow,' she said as she left the cab.

'Perhaps he needs it more than me!' Hamdi called back feeling bolder with each minute that passed.

Hamdi slept well for a few hours but woke at three thirty in a sweat having had a nightmare about the massacre in the woods. He could hear the children screaming and he could still hear them as he woke. He sipped water but was unable to return to sleep.

After breakfast he dressed in the suit he had bought the day before and caught a cab into the centre of the city. He intended to walk through the park to the White House, but decided before that to buy a small pocket notepad and a pen.

The explosion was several times larger than the one at the World Trade Centre in New York earlier in the year, and it ripped through the main city centre car park with the same devastation. Hamdi heard the explosion, but despite his experience at home did not recognise it for what it was in the split second before the blast swept him across the concourse into a concrete pillar, before a Ford was embedded in the same pillar.

The blast tore concrete floors apart and the fires raged for over three hours before the fire brigade gained control. In all, over six hundred people were treated for injury, twenty seven of whom were to die. Hamdi was one of the thirty one bodies recovered from the carnage, but he wasn't found for three days.

The FBI and the City police department were inundated with callers claiming responsibility, but as with the World Trade Centre bomb, no culprit was apprehended. The similarity did not stop there. No-one would deny or confirm the story that fifteen minutes before the explosion a warning was given from a man claiming to be from the former Republic of Yugoslavia.

'D'you think the blast had anything to do with Olive Skin, whom I assume we are no closer to tracing?'

'I don't know, sir, I just don't know,' said Steve, sounding as tired as he was feeling after his weeks in the Control Centre. 'We're no closer knowing who he is or if it is even the White House that he wants to breach.'

'I doubt that the bomb is connected,' said Scott. 'If it was it had to be as a diversion but from what? And nothing has happened.'

'Have all the guest lists, press lists, chauffeurs, staff lists been checked and rechecked for tomorrow?'

'Yes, sir. If there's an assassin in there then I think it is somebody who has turned who until now has been clean and is considered respectable.'

'I've been through the list as well, Steve, I can't fault that. Every last one of them is known in some way or other.

'What about the Italian names on the list, there's quite a few?'

'They all check out and Mr Harbuckle doesn't recognise any of them. Short of keeping them all out we can only be thorough tomorrow, sir.'

'I know we'll be that but if, as you suggested some time ago, Steve, it's another death wish assassin, we could still be in trouble.'

'We don't know yet that the Iraqis' is a death wish assassin. We don't know what she plans to do.'

'But you'll pick them up as soon as they pass through the first security check so that they are well away from the action.' 'Yes, sir.'

'Good. And then pick up Mrs Harworth and her keepers afterwards in case there is any radio contact between them.'

'Yes, sir.'

'What about the Tourle sisters?'

'I don't think they're a threat but just to be on the safe side we'll run them through it when they arrive and probably just keep them out of the reception, even if they look clean.'

'Yes, I would. Keep them out of it just in case one of them has decided to use an explosive tampax. I'm very unhappy about Rebecca's mental state, she could be unpredictable.'

'Right, sir, I'll see to it.'

'Then there's little more we can do. I know you're not likely to sleep, either of you, any more than I am but I suggest you do at least try.'

There is no such thing as a welcoming Crematorium, but the one in East Washington's Garden of Remembrance must be the closest to that description. Set in nearly two hundred acres of well kept gardens and woodlands with distant views of the ocean it resembles a national park.

The Chapel itself is of white stone with a red tiled roof and inside it is furnished with light oak throughout. Although it seats three hundred and fifty people with standing room for another hundred, it was inadequate on that fresh early winter's morning of 21st November.

As the hearse drew up to the open double doors, again of light oak, closely followed by the cortege, Jeff could hear the organ playing Sally-Anne's favourite hymn, Rock of Ages.

They had never been churchgoers and had never in their entire married life discussed the question of religion, but Jeff assumed that he was doing what Sally-Anne would have wanted. It was what he would have wanted and he had that very morning written a letter to that effect and placed it with his Will.

Jeff walked alone behind the pallbearers carrying the coffin into the chapel. Once it had been placed on the podium be bowed to it slightly before taking his seat in the front pews.

'Dearly beloved...' the minister began as the organ faded away.

Jeff had arranged a simple service with just three hymns,

a reading and a short address by the minister. As the curtains closed around the coffin during the last hymn Jeff resolved to rebuild his life and not to repeat the foolish and immature mistakes that he and Sally-Anne had made.

The slight whirring of the motorised conveyer belt that took the coffin into the furnace was drowned by the singing of the congregation. As that final hymn finished the organist returned to Rock of Ages and Jeff followed the minister along the aisle to the double doors. He shook every hand as the huge congregation left. 'Thank you for coming,' he said time and again until he though he might go mad.

Most of the congregation attended the wake. The service having started at two thirty it was therefore just after six when Jeff arrived home slightly light headed. He poured a large scotch and paced his study waiting for the undertaker to ring.

'Hello,' said Jeff answering the phone immediately.

'Mr. Knight?'

'Yes.'

'I can confirm that we did indeed invite Mr and Mrs Harworth and we spoke to Mr Harworth personally.'

'Thank you,' said Jeff who replaced the receiver briefly before lifting it again and punching in the cab company's number.

'The bastard,' he shouted.

It took the cab less than ten minutes to arrive and just under a quarter of an hour to reach Brad's house.

'I'm sorry,' said the maid, 'the master is not at home.'

'I don't bloody believe you,' yelled Jeff brushing her aside and storming towards the drawing room which he found empty.

'I did say that the master was not at home, sir,' repeated the maid as Jeff slammed door after door on the ground floor and began to work his way up the house until he reached the attic bedroom. There be found Brad in bed with the Iraqi agent.

'Knight is turning over Harworth's house, Steve. Do you want us to go in?'

'I know, I'm listening. Leave him to it. I think he might save the tax payer some money judging by what happened before he left home.'

'You bastard,' yelled Jeff, 'too busy screwing some tart to come to Sally-Anne's funeral. I suppose Bridget is off somewhere else screwing a toy boy.'

'Now look,' began Brad, but Jeff had no intention of listening. He drew his gun from his inside coat pocket and shot Brad at a range of four feet straight through the heart. The Iraqi agent moved towards her bag and her own gun but was too slow. The second shot went through her heart from the back and she collapsed forwards onto the floor in a pool of blood.

The maid who had followed Jeff through the house had run downstairs screaming at the first shot, but Jeff had ripped every telephone from the wall as he had systematically searched the house.

'D'you want us to go in now, Steve?'

'No, leave it. Let the police go in when they get the call. I don't want us involved.'

'What about the bugs?'

'The police won't think to look for them, we'll send the cleaners in later.'

The cab had waited and he was back home inside fifteen minutes. Hurriedly he wrote a note warning that the President's life was in danger before locking himself in the garage.

'Knight has shut himself in the garage, Steve. Do we leave him?'

'Yes.'

'As soon as the police arrive pull everybody back, but until then stay in place just in case he's twigged it's us and is planning to slip away.'

'D'you think he is?'

'No, I think he's topping himself and again I don't want us to have any involvement but I don't want to run the risk of losing him now either.'

'So they'll all be mystery deaths. No connection with an attempted assassination.'

'That's the way we want it.'

Jeff connected the swimming pool hoover hose pipe to the exhaust pipe of his car, fed it through the slightly open window, sat in the car and started the ignition.

The police found him an hour later and his note was immediately passed to the CIA.

George Gillespi decided to return to Washington with Lech for one last visit to the city.

'Are you sure it's wise?' Lech had asked.

'I feel safe, but at my age so what if I am wrong?'

'There are better ways to die than a bullet.'

'There are also many worse ways, Lech, as you know.'

The giant Boeing took off from Heathrow at four thirty and it was exactly five thirty UK time when, sitting in the movie, Gillespi looked at his watch and remembered that small, sweaty motel room thirty years ago. He remembered exactly the feelings he had then. He began to sweat.

'So, we're still looking for Olive Skin,' said Scott as he and Steve sat drinking coffee on the morning of the twenty second.

'And we're no nearer finding him than when we first started.'

'What are we going to do?'

'We're going to change the security arrangements. I want everybody to have to walk across as large a room as possible one at a time with a line of security men on each side. Make them all walk through a human passage of us and I'm going to stand at the end and eyeball them as they leave the passage.'

'One at a time?'

'Yes, no-one starts down the passage until the previous person has left and then each person knows that all eyes are on them. Sixty or seventy of us is over a hundred eyes.'

'I like it, Steve, but what about the time?'

'I don't give a shit about the time, an assassin won't like it and that's all that concerns me.'

'Suppose,' began Scott timidly.

'Yes.'

'I was just thinking back to all the theories about Kennedy's assassination and in particular the CIA. Suppose....'

'I've thought of nothing else for over a week, Scott. There's nothing you and I could do. It would make a complete mockery of the weeks we've been down here living on processed food and breathing manufactured air.'

'With everyone knowing we've had a tip off about an assassination and are trying to stop it.'

'That's why I'm going to be there. If anyone wants to kill the President, anyone, he's got to get past me first.'

'Get a move on, Angie, or we'll be late.'

'I'm nearly ready, Beccy, but I want to look my best for the President.'

'I doubt he'll even notice you.'

'Won't I be presented?'

'He's not Royalty.'

'But surely he will say hello to everyone.'

'That depends.'

'On what?'

'On whether anyone gets to him before he's said hello to everyone.'

'What do you mean, "gets to him"?'

'Kills him, you silly girl.'

'You don't really think...'

'That man of yours won't have given up the idea just because you and I wouldn't help him.'

'Do you really think...' began Angie again.

'Maybe I will, you never know.'

'Beccy, you're mad, do you know that?'

'Yes, I do,' she replied slowly, 'and so does my doctor so I've got nothing to fear.'

'Do stop teasing, Beccy. I'm ready, come on let's go.'

'Who says I'm teasing?'

Enzo woke early and was in the restaurant for breakfast at seven. He ate well and then returned to him room and, despite the hundreds of times that he had practised it before, he closed his eyes and assembled the gun just one more time.

He completed his letter to Gary Walton and sealed it.

Then he wrote a letter to each of his brothers and sisters and sealed them, putting something personal into each one. His watch, his cuff links, his medallion, his two rings, his gold lighter and his silver cigarette case.

His final letter was to the CIA naming Harry Powers and stating that he had acted alone. John Edwards who had made the introduction and Matt Andrews, whom Powers had tried to suggest to him was running the operation, had no connection with it. This letter he left on the dressing table but the others he posted in the hotel reception before showing for the last time.

He had polished his own shoes but his suit, shirt and tie had been cleaned and pressed by the hotel laundry service the night before. He dressed himself with great care in front of the long mirror on the inside of the wardrobe door. He took particular care with the knot of his tie. He very rarely wore a tie, but when he did, he liked it to be perfect. It was the Italian in him.

The reception began at noon but Miss Culpan had suggested that he should be there a little early as he might be able to get some informal shots of the President. Her words had amused him in a warped sort of way. He was going to strike at exactly twelve thirty.

He tested the camera one last time to make sure that it

flashed and that the shutter clicked open and shut. He could assemble the gun in seventy three seconds so he would be seen clicking away before slipping off to the john to prepare the weapon.

He would arrive early and watch the entrance with a view to going in at about eleven thirty. Miss Culpan had said that the security clearance should take about fifteen minutes at that time, so he would be inside the White House for the reception before mid-day. Plenty of time to spare. At eleven a.m. he left the hotel room for the last time, his room key securely in his pocket, but did not stop to pay the bill.

Once on the pavement outside the hotel, he hailed a cab.

'The White House, please.'

12.22 p.m....Washington

On any other occasion the faulty air conditioning would not have troubled them. The mental anguish they each secretly harboured only served to increase their perspiration. That it would be successfully completed was not in doubt. That the American nation would be saved from humiliation was not in doubt. That the world would be a safer place was not in doubt.

They were silent, motionless, waiting expectantly for the next eight minutes to pass.